half mast

half mast

a novel by Christopher Null

sutro press

Copyright © 2002 by Christopher Null

All rights reserved. No part of this book may be reproduced or transmitted in any form or by any means, electronic or mechanical, including photocopying, recording, or by any information storage and retrieval system, without permission in writing from the publisher.

Published by Sutro Press, San Francisco, California.
www.sutropress.com

Printed in the United States of America

Cover by Julian Quayle

Layout and design by Mike Kobrin

Library of Congress Control Number: 2002092157

ISBN 0-9720981-0-0

10 9 8 7 6 5 4 3 2

For Z

September 20, 1999

I am not crazy.

My shrink doesn't think so, and he should know, right? He went to medical school. I've seen the diploma.

Dr. Carter says I'm just "troubled," and that I should "try to get it all out." On paper, he means. He even gave me the very journal in which I'm writing these words.

"Writing about the past is the only way to rid yourself of it." That's the only thing that seems to help in cases like mine, he says, so I'm going to give it a shot. I don't think it's going to matter in the end. You can't undo what's been done. So as a note of fair warning to the poor loser reading some nobody's memoirs: This story is not a happy one.

Going forward, I suppose if I have any chance at sanity down the line, I should try to do what Dr. Carter says. "Writing it down will help you organize your thoughts," he says. "Once it's down on paper, you'll see there's nothing to get so worked up about. You're not crazy, Alex. You're just stressed out."

Not that he would know. I never told Dr. Carter the truth. How could I? I've kept my promise not to tell for ten long years, and I'm not about to spill it now.

Writing this journal, or this story—whatever it is—already feels like a betrayal. A betrayal of myself and of the friends who helped me out. Travis told me when I got into this, "There's no statute of limitations on murder." He's right. I looked it up last year. Travis was the smartest guy I ever knew.

From what little I've told Dr. Carter, he is of the belief that Travis was a bad influence. Leave it to a shrink to find someone else to blame for my problems. He says my parents messed me up, too. But he's got it all wrong.

After all, it was my idea to kill Steve Williams.

❖ ❖ ❖

September 22, 1999

Dr. Carter said to start out by writing about myself. A more boring topic I can't imagine.

I am not a bully. And I am not a monster. Far from either, though I don't expect you to understand that yet. While I can't explain and don't expect forgiveness for what I did, please try not to think I'm

7

mean or evil.

When you're in high school, you just don't have the life history to put something like murder in perspective. I'm not trying to excuse what I did, but at the time it just didn't seem so wrong. I didn't give much thought to its ongoing impact on my conscience, or the over-powering guilt that would consume me, or even the intrinsic value of human life. All I knew about morality came out of books and movies. In fiction, consequences are immediate and severe. You kill somebody, you go to jail. Or someone avenges the person's death. In the movies, no one ever suffers through a decade of sweaty in-somnia and stomach ulcers after committing a murder.

But I'm not trying to blame Hollywood. That's Dr. Carter's trick. I take responsibility for what happened. It's just that I never really got much exposure to the classic Judeo-Christian ethic—Do Unto Oth-ers, the three wise men, Turn the Other Cheek, and all that business.

Which is not to say that classic religion would have done much for me, anyway. I'm baptized Episcopalian. I remember it, because I was twelve years old. I think my grandmother shamed my parents into it. What kind of people wait twelve years to baptize a kid?

Okay, time out. Like Dr. Carter says, stop and count to ten. This is not about my family. This is my doing, my fault, my cross to bear—so to speak. No one told me to do it.

But what else was I supposed to do?

❖   ❖   ❖

September 23, 1999

I guess I should write about a central character in this story, and that's Travis Pickford. A funny thing: I didn't know his last name was Pickford until three years after I met him, because everyone always called him Travis Bickle, after the character in *Taxi Driver.* Even our teachers called him Travis Bickle. They thought it was hysterical.

But I hadn't ever seen *Taxi Driver,* so I didn't get the joke. It aired on the USA cable network (heavily edited, I think) one night when I couldn't sleep, and after about an hour I made the connection to all the "You talkin' to me?" jokes and, of course, the name. I haven't ever seen the uncut version of the movie. I guess I should rent it. I hear it's pretty good.

Three years before I saw *Taxi Driver* on late-night cable, I met Travis Bickle—I mean, Travis Pickford—in the library at Fall Valley

Middle School, where we were both eighth-graders. Travis had transferred to Fall Valley when we were in sixth, but I never had a class with him until eighth. Travis said his old school, somewhere in Colorado I think, wasn't all that seaworthy when it came to academics. It was a sports school, much like Fall Valley High (a.k.a. "Fall High" by its few detractors; a.k.a. "High Fall" by those who really detest it), although his Colorado school didn't even have an honors program. I'm not sure it even had science classes, though Travis has been quite complimentary in the past about the quality of his old school's hot lunch. You've gotta look for a silver lining, I guess.

It took Travis two years to prove himself in Fall Valley's moron-level classes so he could work his way up to Advanced and Honors, where I was. Then our paths began to cross with some regularity.

Like I said, I met Travis in the school library. Now Fall Valley isn't in the buckle of the Bible Belt, but it's certainly somewhere along its leather. We didn't have the censorship problems that I've heard about at other schools, but we didn't have the country's best selection of alternative fiction, if you catch my meaning. Most of the novels were these pea green, blood red, or tan-and-gray tomes written by authors I'd never heard of then and I sure haven't heard of since. A shockingly large number of westerns. I won't even try to explain that one.

Poring through the library stacks for undiscovered gems became something of a pastime for me. My dad worked and my mom volunteered or was otherwise socially engaged, so there was no real reason to go home after school. And I was horrible at sports (an issue which would create quite a few problems for me later in life), so there was no reason to go outside, either.

As it turned out, Travis was in the same situation. He was as skinny as me—maybe skinnier even—and short. Or maybe it just looked that way, I don't know. We never really measured.

Travis and I were regularly the only after-school patrons of the library, and it was only a matter of time before we got together to compare notes. Travis was also interested in fiction, eschewing, like me, the stacks and stacks of pictorial Jacques Cousteau books.

Our meeting was a pretty simple affair. I'd had *Atlas Shrugged* out for three straight weeks (that is a long-ass book), and he wanted it. Finally he asked the librarian who had the book, and privacy laws in middle schools not being what they should be, she simply pointed my way, toward the carrels near the reference section that I favored.

"You almost done with that?" Travis asked me.

9

"Huh?"

"I want *Atlas Shrugged,* and you've had the only copy for three weeks."

"Oh. Yeah, I'm about done with it. You can have it on Monday."

"Great. You should check out *Stranger in a Strange Land*—if you like sci-fi."

"That's not some L. Ron Hubbard crap, is it?" I asked.

"No man, it's Heinlein. It's classic. You'll like it."

He was right. I liked it a lot.

If you took out the little card in the back of each book that showed who had checked it out—if you took that card out for all the books I'd read, you'd see Travis's name somewhere else on the card for at least nine out of ten of them. By the end of the year, we'd both read all of the same books at least once. Travis turned me on to *Catcher in the Rye.* I turned him on to *Cat's Cradle.* We read all the classics. And we became friends.

I didn't have a lot of friends when I was a kid. I remember that my mother was so excited when she met Travis for the first time.

❖   ❖   ❖

September 25, 1999

Travis and I graduated from middle school in May 1986, full of the apprehension and excitement of moving up to a new class of experiences. It would be packed with new people, a new geography, and the knowledge that would propel us along the path to becoming competent adults.

Yeah, right.

My mother didn't hide the fact that she was excited to have middle school over and done with for me. I'd made no friends, had no achievements to speak of, met no girls. The classic shy loner syndrome. She openly hoped that high school would be different for me, but she didn't realize that the pecking order remains intact. She could have transferred me to a school in Omaha a thousand miles away. It wouldn't have mattered. On day one, I would have been exposed as just another geeky, socially unredeemable kid with an IQ too high for his own good. It would only be a matter of time before the ruthless teasing would begin.

But at Fall Valley High, it would simply pick up where it had left off three months earlier, as if nothing had happened. Some of the faces would be different, and the walls would be a different color, but I didn't think for a second that the situation would be any different. It's really just like anything else: politics, religion, the company where you work. People come and go, but nothing ever changes.

Don't feel bad for me. You get used to it. It could've been worse.

Travis and I hung out that summer, mostly at the video arcade. The arcade got a Gauntlet machine that year, and we sunk hundreds of dollars into it, trying to beat the sucker. We never did. I don't think you can.

Once, toward the end of the summer, we got so far along in Gauntlet that we thought we were going to win it for sure. In Gauntlet, you play one of four medieval heroes, treasure hunting through level after level of monsters and mazes. We were on level 86, and we were sure the end was in sight. But every time we got out of the level, we'd pop back to level 84. The levels kept repeating, suckering more and more quarters out of us. We ran out of money eventually, and those fateful words—GAME OVER—flashed on the screen.

Travis didn't say anything. He simply walked outside, picked up a brick, came back in, and smashed it through the screen. He didn't even smile. Or frown. Sparks flew everywhere—and we ran like hell.

I don't know why we never got caught. The arcade owner had seen us every day for almost three months. Surely he could've tracked us down. But in the end, he was probably too lazy and just had his insurance company pay for it. Some people take advantage of the system whenever they can.

When we got back to my house, we hid in my room, catching our breath, waiting to hear the sirens of the police cars coming to take us way. But they never came. My mother called me down to dinner, and Travis had to go home. And that was it. Before he left, Travis smiled the grin of someone who knows he's gotten away with something. "You see?" he said. "We beat that fucking machine after all." We both laughed.

Travis left, and I went downstairs to eat. I was still scared we'd get caught, but I remember that sense of power I felt, knowing that I had taken action, that I'd done something that carried consequences with it, that no one was going to push me around anymore. Or so I thought.

In retrospect, I suppose I really didn't do anything wrong. Travis threw the brick. I just ran away. It's not a crime to run away if you haven't done anything illegal, is it? I guess I was just doing what

I've done all my life, but it sure felt rebellious at the time.

After the Gauntlet incident, Travis and I mostly just went to the movies, until school started a few weeks later. Even bad movies don't make you mad like video games do.

❖ ❖ ❖

September 28, 1999

It's Tuesday night and I've got nothing to do but watch TV, so I figured I'd write instead. It's starting to get cold out here in Chicago. In another month it'll be below freezing. Makes me miss Texas sometimes, but not enough to go back.

Through some bizarre oversight of bureaucracy, Fall Valley High was the only high school in our area. There were four middle and seven elementary schools, but the kids from all of them go to Fall Valley High when they graduate. Fall Valley had more than 5,000 students when I went there. It had been built for 3,000.

Despite the similar names, Fall Valley Middle and Fall Valley High had very little in common. At Fall Middle (pop.: 650), there weren't enough people to make a lot of trouble. Teachers could keep an eye on things. People who started things got sent to the office, they got suspended. One guy gave this kid a swirly in the bathroom. He got expelled, and even though his parents sued the school, he never came back. Fall Valley Middle, for all its faults, was very good to me.

I was in the highest level of all my classes. They called it Level One, which translated to Honors at Fall High. My grades were almost straight A's in middle school, which pretty much made me a nerd, especially since math and science were my best subjects. History was, and remains, my worst. I just can't bring myself to care about things that happened before I was born. Other events in more recent history have had a much more lasting impression on my life, and it's in understanding (or forgetting) these events where I try to put my energy.

When you think about it, Fall Valley High is bigger than most companies in America. For perspective, the Smucker's jam company has fewer than 2,000 employees. Fall Valley High has cliques and sub-cliques, warring factions of jocks, five strata of coursework, three libraries, two cafeterias, parking for 2,000 cars, a full-color newspaper, and a football stadium that the pro teams have used to practice in.

You'd think that in a school that big, you could lose yourself in the crowd. But FVH isn't *that* big. It's at a critical mass where no teacher will ever know your name, but no surface area is left untouched by some guy or gang laying claim to it. There's no hiding in the library at FVH. That's somebody's turf.

I make it sound bad, but FVH is seen as the jewel of the southwest, which is why there hasn't been a new high school built in this area in over thirty years. The standardized test scores stay high, beyond all expectations to the contrary. The graduation rate is the best in the country for a school of its size. Colleges love FVH. Pro sports teams love FVH. The government loves FVH, and the posh remodeling jobs it got in the summers of 1989 and 1995 are a testament to the kind of funding the school gets.

For everyone else, FVH is a juvenile paradise on earth.

For me, it was hell.

❖ ❖ ❖

October 1, 1999

Steve Williams. Born October 23, 1971. Scorpio—strong-willed with lofty goals. Same birthday as Pelé, Martin Luther King III, and "Weird Al" Yankovic.

Steve was the firstborn of Lee and Bonnie Williams. Maj. Williams was a retired Army officer. Schooled at West Point and a decorated Vietnam vet, he'd reached the rank of Major before being injured during a field exercise and retiring from the service. Maj. Williams moved his family to Houston in the late 1970s, where he took a job as a trainer and coach for the Houston Oilers football team. Maj. Williams was legendary for pushing the Oilers to physical extremes, which was crucial to their success on the football field in the mid-1980s.

Mrs. Bonnie Williams was a homemaker, housewife, and socialite, often seen in photos at parties and fund-raisers with a stiff drink in one hand and her mouth wide open in a cackling smile. A college dropout, Bonnie was a trophy wife married (one must assume) to help Lee's rise through the officers' ranks. Post-Army, she was helping the family climb up the social ladder, as best she should.

Steve was the first of two children. As a boy, he received all the attention from his father, who encouraged his natural athletic ability from an early age.

Steve dominated any sport he played in. From his first games of T-ball and peewee football, it was clear that having young Williams on your team meant you would sweep the season. He scored all the goals, runs, baskets, and points. He knew virtually nothing about teamwork, pursuing the greater glory for himself, always.

By the time he hit middle school, Steve was a budding legend. The inter-school football games were a mockery of the sport, as Steve would regularly pass and run his team to forty- or fifty-point victories. His arm was incredible, and he could throw passes of any distance with deadly accuracy. When his teammates were unable to catch, he would simply crash his way through the defensive line and score the touchdowns himself. He never punted on fourth down, and he never went for field goals.

In his first year of high school at Fall Valley High, Steve concentrated on two sports: football and baseball, both of which could be played without interfering with each other, and which ranked as the then No. 1 and No. 2 most socially important games in Texas.

He made varsity in both without having to try out. Not only did he immediately displace the would-be quarterback as the starter, a veteran senior, he also took the guy's girlfriend, who was three years older than Steve. Legend had it that *he* dumped *her* when she went to college the next fall. He led the football team to a Texas championship that year, and our baseball team finished sixth in the state. He was nothing less than a hero for FVH and the community. I heard about it all the time on the news, and since Steve was one year ahead of me, I knew I'd be seeing plenty more of him in the years to come.

Academically, Steve was in Advanced-level classes, above the rank and file of Academic but below the geeks like me in Honors. Pushed on by his father, Steve made good grades—good enough to play sports without fear of reprisal from "No pass, no play." Maybe his teachers were helping him out. Who knows?

To the outside world, Steve was a prince among men. If he wasn't so damn good on the gridiron, people would say, he'd be the next CEO of Exxon. Or Coca-Cola. Or wherever they happened to work. He was just such a damned good guy.

Let me tell you the truth. Steve Williams was a very bad man. No, he was a very bad boy. A really rotten kid with no redeeming qualities. This is not to say that I don't feel remorse over his death, but I would understand if others didn't feel any.

This was the point when our lives crossed.

October 4, 1999

It's Monday morning. It's freezing cold. I tried turning the heater on last night, but no dice. The furnace is busted; it happens every year when it's been off all summer. Thinking about Steve kept me awake. I guess by writing about all his suburban heroism I've developed a little soft spot for the guy. That's bad. Gotta push through it. I did the right thing. I'm sure of it.

This could have happened to anyone, in any school, in any city. The setting isn't important. It could have been a university of 30,000 people. Or not a school at all. It could have been a big conglomerate. Or the post office. All it takes is a popular bully and a target for his aggression. Here, the bully was Steve Williams. The target was me. The thing is, most places where this kind of thing happens, the target never does anything about it, and everyone around turns a blind eye. At Fall High, people ignored our situation just the same, and no one ever thought the target would strike back. It just never happens.

My first day at FVH was, as they say, one for the books. (Some irony that this is the book into which it's going to be written.)

After filling out paperwork in homeroom we got to hear what would be the first of an endless series of loudspeaker admonishments from Mr. Patterson, our principal. Then it was off to first period, and my first real taste of high school academics.

For me, that was Honors trig. I took algebra in middle school, so I got to place out of it at FVH. But most of the people in our class hadn't. They were sophomores, already jaded by the drudgery of high school and the apathy of the teachers. They were looking for alternative amusements. And Steve Williams was part of their little group.

You have to understand that I knew none of this. Like I said, I was a bit of a math nerd, and I figured everyone else in the class was too. If I'd known then what I know now (that Steve was "testing out the Honors waters" to boost his GPA), I would have kept my eyes down and my mouth shut. But I had to go and show off.

I guess I thought I could change my image—if you can call it that—by proving myself as a worthy intellect, despite my skinny physique and funny hairdo that never looked the same from one day to the next.

Our teacher, Mrs. Anderson, issued textbooks and had us read from Chapter One. It was something about the fundamental operations of geometry. Since Steve was already the school stud (though I didn't know him from Adam), he was picked to do the reading.

Of course, the man-child was an idiot. He stumbled through the book, unfamiliar with jargon that wasn't used in the locker room, and when he hit the word "sine" he pronounced it "seen."

So I spoke up.

"Sign," I half-muttered.

"I'm sorry?" asked Mrs. Anderson. She checked her roll sheet, then added, "Alex?"

"It's pronounced 'sign.'"

"Um, that's right. Steve, can you continue?"

When he didn't start reading immediately, I looked over at him. He was glaring at me like I'd raped his sister. So were his friends, who were packed around him in concentric circles of importance: critical henchmen one seat away, peripheral acquaintances further out. I was clear across the room.

Obviously I'd crossed some line that I didn't even know existed. I may as well have shot him. It took him ten seconds before he looked back down at his book to pick up where he left off. He pronounced "cosine" properly.

I'd signed my death warrant on the first day of school.

❖ ❖ ❖

October 7, 1999

That was my only class with Steve, but it was enough. Math is the only subject where you can place higher or lower depending on test scores and prior coursework. Everything else was categorized by grade. That was fine by me.

It wasn't until lunch that I ran into Travis for the first time that day. He didn't have much to say. They stuck him in Academic-level classes because he didn't have enough of a track record in higher-level coursework, and his parents didn't care enough to make a fuss. He whiled away the day listening to his moron classmates crack each other up by asking to go to the bathroom every five minutes. He said on more than one occasion, "It's going to be a long year."

We got our usual lunch—French fries, candy bar, pair of Twinkies, and a Coke—and sat down at the very end of the last table along the far wall of the cafeteria. I didn't even notice when Steve and his buddies approached.

A shadow fell across the table, and Travis slowly stopped chewing a fry, ketchup still clinging to his lip. He looked up as I felt an oversized hand clutch my shoulder—just hard enough to know this would not be a friendly visit.

The hand belonged to a guy named Brett Vogon, a hair- and tooth-bleached jock who always got beaten out by Steve in the race for quarterback, girls, and homecoming honors. Rather than compete, Vogon had adopted an "If you can't beat him, join him" attitude, and it appeared to be paying off. Vogon got to do all of Steve's dirty work.

He spoke before I turned around. "We've got a problem, kid." His voice cracked. Puberty had still not finished with him, but he fancied himself an apprentice Mafioso.

"What's that?" I asked, genuinely confused.

"Mr. Williams doesn't like to be corrected."

"Mr. Williams? Who the hell is that?" A moment of silence passed as I realized I was digging myself deeper. Only then did I turn far enough to see Steve glowering at me through a fence of steroid-enhanced, chest-puffing bozos. Vogon pointed out my error.

"Oh," I muttered. "Sorry."

"You'd better be," Vogon quickly retorted. I have since learned: Never let a bully get the upper hand in an argument. Never admit you're wrong. Never say you're sorry. Any sign of weakness against an opponent like this will be exploited to its fullest extreme.

"Who the fuck are *you?*" Travis's voice grated my ears from across the table. I spun around, knowing that this line of questioning could end only in tragedy.

"I'm Brett Vogon. Who the fuck are *you?*"

"I'm the guy that's gonna kick your ass," replied Travis.

Unless Travis was a black belt and I didn't know it, there was little chance that any ass-kicking would occur, at least not in Vogon's direction. With a half-dozen flunkies, Vogon and his crew were about to beat the shit out of Travis. They'd probably tear me apart as well, just for associating with the guy.

"Trav!" I shouted, desperate for him to shut up. It was a gut instinct.

"Bring it on, ass-wipe," taunted Vogon.

But as Travis slowly stood up, almost a full foot shorter than Vogon, we were saved by a wandering teacher on lunch detail suspicious of the raised voices, and who wanted nothing more than to avoid an incident on her first day back to work after a three-month vacation and too long without a cigarette. "What's going on here?" she said.

Vogon replied, "Nothin'."

"Good," said the teacher. "Sit down or go outside."

I don't think she saw Steve in the pack, or she never would have been so curt.

"This ain't over, dude," said Vogon, as he strolled through the double doors to the courtyard.

"Yes it is!" yelled that teacher in return. She was sure the voice of her authority carried the weight of lead.

Steve shot one last look at me before the doors shut behind him. This was all *far* from over.

❖ ❖ ❖

October 13, 1999

The furnace is fixed, but the smell belching out of it is so foul I have to cover my face to breathe. Sleep is out of the question, leaving me awake and alone with the demons of the past.

You may think that someone who could kill a person in cold blood was cut from special cloth—like some special mindset is required to do the deed. That's just not true. Anyone can kill. All it takes is enough provocation. I use this knowledge every day. I never provoke anyone on the sidewalk or the bus. I avoid conflict whenever possible. I even avoid eye contact. Like it or not, we've all got murderers hidden somewhere, deep inside. I too am mortal, like anyone else.

In freshman English, our first assignment was to read *Beowulf,* the classic Nordic adventure saga that every high school student in America reads, for some reason or another. I'd read it two years earlier, but I'd already forgotten the story. Recently I read it again just to refresh my memory. It's good.

In ancient Denmark, the ogre Grendel was destroying the kingdom. Even the Hall of its mighty King Hrothgar was not safe. No one could stop Grendel, as no weapon could damage his leathery hide. Nothing could stop Grendel from feasting upon Danish royalty for twelve long years.

The Geats, who occupied the area of southern Sweden, sent Beowulf, an invincible warrior, to help out the Danes. King Hrothgar was very grateful, offering the warrior anything he wished if he could stop the beast. Most of the other Danes were green with envy over the favoritism being shown this outsider, but Beowulf was such a stud, what were they going to do? Beowulf put down all challengers.

Grendel came to the hall that very night. In the fight between Beowulf and Grendel, Beowulf ripped off Grendel's arm completely, and Grendel ran away in fear and in a bit of pain, presumably to die.

Alas, Grendel had a mother, a demoness as it turned out, and she was none too happy with her son's death. She burst into the hall the next night, killed Hrothgar's best friend, and absconded with her son's dismembered arm. She fled, and Beowulf gave chase.

The chase ended in the demoness's underwater lair, where Beowulf found even his amazing sword useless against her. However, he discovered another sword, the Sword of the Giants, in her cave. And with it, he killed Grendel's mother. He also found the body of Grendel, and cut off his head for good measure.

Beowulf returned to Sweden and ruled as king for fifty years. Then, new trouble arose after a man stole some treasure from a dragon's lair. This pissed the dragon off, and it began ravaging the land.

Beowulf, despite being old and slow now, figured he could take on the dragon, mano a mano. He went to the dragon's lair, and sure enough, the dragon breathed fire on Beowulf. And although the dragon kept melting Beowulf's swords, eventually Beowulf's much younger friend Wiglaf came to the rescue, and Beowulf was able to kill the dragon with a well-placed thrust of his dagger.

But the beast had poisoned Beowulf, and he was about to die. He gave Wiglaf the throne of the Geats, and died a hero.

That's the story. And we when we analyzed it in class, it was funny how little I agreed with the teacher's interpretation. I didn't voice my dissenting opinion, so I got an A on the *Beowulf* exam.

Consider the depth of meaning in *Beowulf*: Grendel and his mother were obviously up to no good, and Beowulf earned his keep by killing them. No problem so far. Cutting off Grendel's head to show off might have been a bit much, but I can let that slide.

So then fifty years go by, and Beowulf becomes the subject of songs and poems. He's a hero. And it's obviously gone to his head. Here we have a seventy-year-old man going to kill a dragon by himself—a dragon that was just angry because people have been stealing from him. Who wouldn't be? When Beowulf realizes he can't kill the dragon after all, his buddy has to save his ass. And in so doing, Wiglaf gets the throne, and he becomes yet another egomaniacal ruler of the land.

When I first starting thinking about the story, I fancied myself as Beowulf. Steve was Grendel. He had ravaged the countryside for years, but only I was clever enough to stop him. I was the hero for saving the world from his menacing rampage.

But looking back, now I think that I was like the dragon, and Steve was Beowulf. I had been wronged, and I was seeking revenge. And in the end, I killed the proud and arrogant Beowulf. Thing is, another jerk would inevitably take his place. And of course, in some way, Beowulf and his ilk would kill a part of me too. Either way, everybody but Wiglaf bites it, so I guess it doesn't really matter.

I try not to think about it too much. Most people think it's boring, and that it has no relevance to their lives. But I love that book.

❖ ❖ ❖

October 10, 1999

Alison O'Malley was the prettiest girl in the school.

At least to me she was. She had pale skin and long, insanely curly red hair. I guess most people thought she was a little intense looking, but I always thought she was radiant. Alison and I had the same freshman English class, and she really loved poetry, especially the poems that I could never make any sense of. Although she hated *Beowulf,* as I recall.

Looking at my old freshman yearbook, Alison looks a little gawky and misshapen, like her head was too big for her body at the time. She would grow and fill out a lot in the next year or so, but she never had a lot of boyfriends. The few she did have—well, I was not one of them.

I doubt Alison ever knew that I existed, despite the fact that we regularly had classes together, and I always tried to sit near her in each one of them. I never found out what she was really like as a person, except that she was pretty quiet and not prone to the giggling hysteria that plagues most late-teen girls. That's worth a lot in my book.

Steve Williams took an interest in Alison at the end of my sophomore year, his junior year. Why? Because Alison, in turn, had attracted the attention of a senior named Mac Wilson, who was going to take her to the prom—unheard of for a sophomore. Steve had to step in and show Mac up, whisking Alison away on prom night, leaving poor Mac up the creek, with a hundred-dollar rented tux, a thirty-dollar corsage, and a six hundred-dollar limousine out front. All dressed up and nowhere to go, as they say.

It's said that Steve deflowered Alison that night in the field behind Fall Valley Stadium, where guys generally took girls for pre- or post-prom nookie. They went to the prom afterward, and that's how the rumor got started, as Alison was in a daze the entire night, her outfit rumpled and torn. For the few weeks left in school that year, the rumors were flying that she was a total slut. (You could pretty much guarantee that by the time a rumor reached my ears, everyone else had heard it first.)

During finals, Alison sat weeping softly at her desk. I would glance over at her Scan-Tron forms to see how she was doing. None of the little rectangles were filled in.

On the last day of school, the nurse carted Alison off for a meeting with her mother. Her mom must have known what had happened to her, but no one ever questioned Steve about it. He never apologized to Alison. In fact, he never spoke to her again after prom night.

I never figured out why she went with Steve in the first place. Mac Wilson seemed like a nice guy. He would have treated her well. But, you see, Steve was like a movie star. When he was around, people couldn't be held responsible for their actions. Normally sane individuals would do insane things to win his attention. Or do even more extreme things to avoid his attention. I can attest to that.

Alison killed herself that summer. Valium overdose. Her mother had a prescription.

❖   ❖   ❖

October 14, 1999

Dr. Carter wanted to know today how the journal was going. I sort of shrugged and said, "Okay." He said to keep at it. That I should try to write every day. Flipping back through the pages, it looks like I've already covered a lot of ground. A lot more than I thought I'd have to write about, anyway. But there's so much more of the story to tell.

It had been a week since the incident with Steve and Vogon, and I thought he might have decided to take pity on a weakling like me and let the issue slide. Or maybe, I thought, he was just too fucking stupid to remember what had happened.

Turns out Steve knew how to bear a grudge. He held one against me for over two and a half years.

Travis and I were walking home. Even though it was at least three miles to our neighborhood, we hated the bus so much we often chose to walk. There was nothing to do at home anyway, and this way we could pick up some chips or Cokes at the Stop N Go en route.

We were maybe 100 yards from school when I tripped and fell on my face. Or rather, I was tripped and fell on my face, sending my books skittering away, coming to rest in a puddle.

Steve and his crew were tailing us. Vogon had immobilized Travis in some kind of arm lock, and he wasn't struggling. "You've fucked with us twice now," said Steve. I guess it was the royal "us" he meant. "And no one fucks with us twice."

"Especially not a freshman," piped up Dewie, a chunky linebacker who was always bringing up the rear in these little altercations, owing to his copious girth.

"You see, kids," Steve continued, "the problem is one of respect. A lot of people heard you make your little comment in trig. A lot of people saw your buddy try to show off and stand up to us at lunch. What do you think that does to my rep?"

I didn't say anything, though by now I'd climbed to my feet.

"Answer him, doofus!" yelled Dewie.

When I didn't speak up immediately, he stormed up to me, curled a fist, and punched me in the stomach. Man, it hurt. I curled up into a ball and fell on the ground again, holding my belly in agony.

"Get him up," Steve ordered his goons.

Dewie and this other guy named Lou, who never said much, pulled me to my feet, each holding an arm out straight, like Jesus on the cross.

"This isn't over, you understand," said Steve, standing right under my nose—or rather, I was right under his nose, since he was a good deal taller than me. "I'm going to make an example of you. I have to. I can't have a couple of freshmen punks screw with my rep, you know. So you'll do what I say, when I say, or things are going to get really messy for you two." He took a breath. "What's your names, anyway?"

"Alex."

"Travis." That was the first (and last) thing Trav said to them that day, or ever. He was already learning: Avoidance is the best strategy when it comes to enemies bigger and more powerful than you. I never got that through my thick skull.

"Okay, girls. We'll be seeing you again real soon."

They let us go and walked back toward school. Steve and his gang didn't walk home or take the bus. They drove, of course.

I gathered up my books, and Travis and I walked home in silence. It was going to be a long school year.

❖   ❖   ❖

October 18, 1999

I don't have any musical talent, so band and choir were out as far as electives went. I could have taken art, but my father always said that art was for sissies, so rather than get into a pointless debate, I figured I'd take my "mandatory creative arts elective" in theater. I don't know why dad didn't think theater was for sissies. I think he'd seen *Death of a Salesman* off-Broadway a few years back, so he figured it was noble enough for his kid.

Well, I don't have to tell you that FVH was not a *Death of a Salesman*–type school. It was a *South Pacific*–type school, at least it was my freshman year.

In case you're not familiar with the play *South Pacific,* I'll summarize. The play is a sappy love story (and a musical, mind you) that takes place on an island in the South Pacific. A war is brewing, and while the hero and heroine get closer, so does the threat of battle, which would call away the sailors on the island. There's lots of comedy, and lots of singing and dancing, too, including the classic, "Some Enchanted Evening."

That's what I remember anyway.

When you're a freshman, you don't just go get a big role in a play like this. Mainly, you work on constructing sets. Sets are built out of wood and canvas, like paintings, in order to be as light and mobile as possible. Our job—in between studying issues like the practice of voice projection, the difference between stage left and stage right, and the ancient Greek origins of the theater—was essentially to paint.

We painted canvas walls, canvas sunsets, even canvas huts covered with straw that we glued on with an industrial-size tub of paste from Wal-Mart. There was a lot of canvas that needed a lot of paint.

So I was taking art after all.

I was also given a role as a member of the chorus, a sailor who sung and danced in a couple of numbers during the show. I didn't really have to audition. These types of roles are not glamorous. It's mostly just jumping around and making a fool of yourself for three minutes, then hightailing it offstage. You didn't even have to sing very well (which I couldn't do anyway), since the tape-recorded music and the other vocalists could drown out even the most tone-deaf extra.

It was November when FVH put on its first public show of the season. I remember my mother was very excited, and she got dad to come home early from work so he could see my stage debut. They paid six bucks at the box office like everyone else. I saw them sit near the back, at my dad's behest, before the show started.

Just like we'd done in practice, we shuffled across the stage, swung our arms crazily, climbed on each other's shoulders (well, I climbed on other guys' shoulders, not the other way around . . . but that's another story), and belted out the tunes. At the end, the audience applauded with gusto, as if Laurence Olivier had done *Hamlet* in their very presence. That's what happens when it's all parents in the crowd. Fall Valley High's *South Pacific* was probably no better than Fall Valley Middle's *South Pacific* would have been.

We didn't care. We had worked for three months to put the show together, and it had been fun. Now that I think about it, it was one of the few times I can remember enjoying myself in school. Never mind that, in subsequent viewings of the videotaped performance, I realized it was worse than a Pauly Shore movie. At the time, we were on top of the world.

I went out to the parking lot after the show to catch a ride home with my folks. I remember I was still beaming from the thrill of the play. In fact, I was still wearing my sailor costume and stage makeup.

My mom hugged me and said she was proud. She loved it.

My dad said I looked like a fag.

Come Monday morning, I found myself with a trumpet in hand, sitting last chair in the FVH marching band.

❖ ❖ ❖

October 25, 1999

Speaking of my father, he came up at today's meeting with Dr. Carter. I'm surprised it took this long. Carter wants to blame my problems on everyone—everyone but me. It makes sense, I guess. Coming to terms with something you've brought upon yourself is tough. I haven't been able to do it. "Blame your parents" and you've got a convenient target for your anger, like those little dolls they make you punch and scream at. Hitting and screaming at yourself doesn't do any good.

So why not humor the doctor?

My father is an attorney for a relatively large practice in the city. His office has over 250 employees, and visiting was always a bit intimidating, with its highly shined wooden desks and walls. I always wondered how they polished the corners of the ceilings, where the ornate trim was flung twenty feet up in the air.

As a busy lawyer, my dad wasn't home much. But he always made time to coach neighborhood little league and peewee football. Since my dad was a coach, I was "encouraged" to play these sports.

I learned at an early age that I had no talent for any of them. While I had good hand–eye coordination (from playing video games, I guess), I couldn't persuade a baseball bat to connect with the ball to save my life. While I was slightly taller than most of the kids my age, I couldn't make a jump shot or block a basketball. As for football and soccer, well, I had zero talent there. During my very first game of peewee football, I managed to fracture my wrist, ending my football career some thirty years prematurely. I learned to swim, but not very well, and I was bad at the more genteel sports of tennis and golf. Fortunately, my mother intervened before my dad signed me up for rugby.

So I'm not an athlete, and I don't particularly enjoy watching sports on television, either. He never really understood that I'd rather play a game of computer basketball on the Atari than watch it on TV. Pretty much every avenue I had for relating with my father was completely eliminated at an early age.

Like I said, we didn't see my dad much. After I washed out of sports, my father began putting in longer and longer hours at the office. My mom would hold dinner until nine, sometimes ten o'clock. Sometimes he made it home. Sometimes we ate without him. Even if he was there, he just turned on whatever pro sports game was on TV. Between football, basketball, and baseball, there was always something on for him to watch and analyze.

My dad kept intricately detailed notes about team rosters, scores, disabled lists, stadium conditions, and more. Once, to better relate to his son or somehow impress me, I guess, he wrote up a new batting lineup for the Texas Rangers, which he said would be much, much better for them. He said he was going to send the list to the manager, it was that good. I think it ended up in his pile of sports minutiae with everything else. I guess by working over those lists and charts, he could occupy his free time and still be in the same room with Mom and me.

25

Of course there were weekends. Usually, Saturday morning began with an order from my mother to mow the yard. Sometimes I would pretend to be asleep to get out of it, but then I'd hear the mower running, and I'd know my dad was doing it without me. I was expected to mow the lawn, and in the hot, humid summers of Texas, it was the most horrible of jobs. I'd sheepishly put some pants on and mow what sections he hadn't done yet. The more he mowed, the worse I'd be chewed out later.

Even after six years of mowing that lawn, I could never do it right, according to my dad. I wasn't overlapping the mower wheels enough with the previous row. I was overlapping the mower wheels too much with the previous row. The blades were coming up off the turf when I made U-turns, and the grass wasn't getting cut there. I was sloppy around the trees. I took too many breaks. I was going too slowly. I was going too fast. It was never right. He always had to fix it after I was done.

If any memory about my father is more vivid than any other, it's how he looked—and smelled—after a Saturday morning working in the yard. The man would be covered in sweat, cut grass, and mud, no matter what the weather was like (and yes, we mowed the lawn rain or shine). It was inhuman how much that man could sweat. It was absolutely primal.

Invariably, after a grass-cutting session, he'd come in, breathing through his mouth, take his shirt off, turn on a sporting event, sit down on the couch, and drink a can of Miller Lite in ten seconds flat. Then he'd tell mom to get him another one. Eventually he'd fall asleep, reeking of fertilizer and gasoline and covered in a sheen of sweat. Much of his reek would be imparted to the couch, which Mom had steam-cleaned on a biweekly basis.

I would go take a shower and, usually, go back to bed.

The postscript to this story is that some strange rot has been slowly eating that lawn for the last twenty years. It started up by the flowerbeds, near the house, and slowly, the grass died at the rate of about a foot each year. My father would fertilize and water like it was nobody's business, but nothing could stop that rot. Every four or five years, we'd dig up the dead grass, then go to the nursery and pick up big pallets of sod, which we'd plant in its stead. The next year, the rot would just begin again.

Eventually, he gave up on the grass and just extended the flowerbeds toward the street. Our front yard is about half flowerbed now. I find this incredibly amusing.

October 28, 1999

In my good old golden school days, it's fair to say I was something of an easy target. Just like on *Wild Kingdom,* the strong prey upon the weak. That's the way it is in nature. That's the way it is in high school.

The fact that I was in theater (at least for a while) was bad enough. My scrawny build and soft-spoken demeanor made things worse. I was relatively smart, so I represented yet another part of society that the teeming masses would have rather seen eliminated. And once Steve and his gang established that I was not some secret karate master and was not going to fight back, well, that pretty much cemented my place as one of FVH's token whipping boys.

It took a few weeks for the word to spread. After that, the parking lot, the courtyard, the bathrooms, and anyplace near the gym or the locker rooms became my personal no man's land. I got the occasional wedgie, that's for sure. Hell, I even gave the occasional wedgie to friends of mine. No big deal.

The swirlies were a little harder to deal with. That's where they stick your head in a toilet and flush. The swirling water is supposed to make your hair twist up into a cone. I don't think it works that way in reality. My hair—and clothes—typically just got soaked. I spent many a fleeting moment, after the tardy bell had rung, frantically trying to dry myself beneath the hand dryer. It works better than you might think. You just have to keep punching the button because the air stops every thirty seconds.

While classmates snickered at my late arrival, the teachers were oddly understanding and rarely, if ever, said anything. I don't know if they were trying not to embarrass me by forcing me to describe the circumstances of my delay in front of the class, or if they were simply unwilling to place themselves in the middle of intra-student conflicts, which they all knew were raging, all the time.

In retrospect, I believe neither of these is fully true. Teachers expected bullying (if you want to call it that). It wasn't sanctioned or condoned, but teachers cast a blind eye on the swirlies, the tripping in the halls, and the locker graffiti. It wouldn't have been a regular high school without it.

Steve and his crew were behind a good part of my torture, but after they'd staked their claim on me, it opened up the gates for lesser bullies to prey on me too.

In high school, there's a pecking order for everything. Jocks have a pecking order: Varsity football beats varsity baseball, for example. Geeks even have a pecking order: class rank. Band has an enforced pecking order where you actually sit in a row from best player to worst player. And the tough guys have a pecking order too. This rule isn't written anywhere, but it's probably the best understood of the lot.

For a lesser bully to cross a greater bully is like starting a gang war. Since most bullies are themselves not very comfortable with abuse, these territorial lines are never crossed. To do so would bring down the whole system, and there was plenty of fresh meat for all the grinders to share.

So I took my abuse from various factions, though Steve Williams and his crew were my prime tormentors. While the Williams gang preferred the swirly, the Ryder gang preferred the old knock-your-books-out-of-your-hands trick, and a well-timed rampage against dozens of victims could leave an entire hallway littered with mixed-up papers and splayed-open texts. This was great fun—for observers.

The Taylor gang was into old-fashioned violence. They supplied the after-school beatings to anyone different than them: too short, too fat, too tall, too skinny, red hair, black hair, bad dresser, good dresser, homosexual tendencies . . . you get the idea. I took a couple of beatings myself from Taylor, though I believe Steve might have actually put a stop to them. It just wouldn't do for Steve Williams' chosen manservant to get the crap beat out of him by a rival. That luxury was reserved for Steve himself.

Another group was into shoving. Apparently that was as clever as they could get. Another group, which I secretly admired, were masters of verbal abuse. They could make freshmen cry inside of thirty seconds. Ironically, it was this little clique, headed by the notorious James "Jimmy" Brantley, that took the most heat from the administration, as they plied their trade on just about anyone, and too many girls developed eating disorders on account of Jimmy's vicious cow- and pig-calls.

Jimmy got expelled during my sophomore year. School wasn't the same without him.

❖   ❖   ❖

November 6, 1999

Travis and I saw each other at lunchtime, and from time to time we'd get together after school in the library to scour the place for new books that had slipped past the censors. FVH had a huge magazine archive, and it was fun to look through the old trade journals of electronics manufacturers, cement companies, and monasteries.

In the evenings, though, we parted ways to work on our homework. Or rather, I'd work on my homework, and then I'd do Steve's. Or to be completely and perfectly accurate, first I'd do Steve's, and then I'd do mine. *Sometimes* I'd get to mine, that is. Homework was the first task Steve put me on, and it was only the first in a never-ending pile of Steve's dirty work for which I was not cut out.

Normally after I gave Steve his homework in the morning, he'd let me know how he'd done on the previous day's assignments. If it wasn't an A, he'd rip up the homework I'd done for my own classes. Since I hadn't even taken any of Steve's sophomore-level classes, except for trig, which we were in together, I rarely did very well. As a result, I did not turn in much of my own homework, and I quickly became a B student.

I later took to hiding my homework so Steve couldn't find it. This did not deter him. Once he got a D on a history assignment I did for him (I told you it was my worst subject), and he and his friends searched my backpack for a good ten minutes before they gave up. They were about to let me go, but Steve then suggested that maybe I'd stuffed my assignment down my pants. Dewie was the one who found it there. The wedgie he gave me was so thorough the elastic of my underpants completely tore off. I later tossed them out in the bathroom and went commando for the rest of the day.

When my work for Steve began to regularly slip into B's and C's, he gave up in disgust and found some weakling sophomore to do his work. Apparently I hadn't lived up to his expectations. This was not the last time I have failed to meet someone's inflated expectations of what I can do. Just because you're "smart" doesn't mean you know about subjects you've never studied!

When Steve found a new sucker to take over his homework, he let up on me for a while. But before my "break," they left me with a final blow to ponder, completely removing the door from my locker and absconding with all of its contents. Then they smeared excrement—whether dog, human, or other, I never found out—throughout the entire inside of it. It took a week for the administration to figure out what to do about the situation, and I sat in meeting after meeting with counselors and principals who actually thought I had done it myself. I told them it wasn't me, and that I didn't know who could possibly have done such a thing. Eventually they figured I must be telling the truth and simply replaced the locker entirely.

The smell of shit lingered there for a month.

Travis was of no help in any of this. While he would help me clean myself up after a beating or help my pick up my books and papers after they'd been ransacked, he was never around during the actual incident, lingering in the voyeuristic crowds that would gather to watch what was effectively the only entertainment in the school. I don't blame him. Had he shown his face he would have gotten the same treatment. I would have done the same thing.

I still wonder why it wasn't Travis instead of me who got the brunt of Steve's wrath. All I had done was correct Steve in math class. Travis had openly threatened him in the cafeteria. On second thought, maybe it was actually *because* Travis openly threatened Steve that he escaped in one piece. Steve could respect aggressive behavior and a foul mouth. The meek and timid were the ones he hated. And while Trav certainly bore his share of punishment at the hand of Steve Williams, it just goes to show that a little swagger really can go a long way.

So in the end, they mainly left Travis alone. And since I proved myself worthless at doing his homework, Steve had to find some new way for me to "help him out" and pay off my debts to him.

This was a task that would take him several weeks.

❖ ❖ ❖

November 7, 1999

In the meantime, Travis and I filled our weekends and holidays with various games of skill and chance.

First we learned how to play poker from a couple of books on the subject (which, ironically, we discovered in the school library). Eventually, we rounded up a couple of guys to play with us, though no one was willing to play for anything higher-stakes than nickels.

One of our recruits was James Johnston, the school's resident history buff and the tallest guy in the student body. He was one of the three people who actually took Latin instead of Spanish, German, or French as his mandatory language course. James had a bad habit of pronouncing English words with a Latin flair. Thus, "corporate" would be pronounced "corpor-*eight*" and "objective" would sound like "objec-*thive*." But worst of all, James would pronounce "Caesar" as "Kaiser." And for some reason, he was always trying to start discussions about ancient Rome or the Kaiser salad. Needless to say, this was an extremely annoying habit.

However, James had an incredible knack for calculating probabilities in his head, and he was a very formidable poker player. Great at dice, too. But James was terminally broke, so he would never wager any money on the games. It's probably just as well.

On the other hand we had Tommy Steuart. Tommy was a short and portly kid who fancied himself a rock musician. He was always practicing electric guitar in his garage, and every three months or so he'd announce he was forming a band with a name like "Crimson Tears" or "Spastic Colon." Invariably, these plans would fall through and the band would never play together in public. We never even saw or heard any of them practice, and I'm not sure any of these bands ever existed.

Tommy certainly pretended as if they did, making up T-shirts and business cards for every one of them. To this day, I still have a stack of Tommy-band shirts somewhere in a never-unpacked moving box, all unworn.

A motley crew the four of us made, and our mothers often pointed this out. I'm sure these weren't the role models my mom had envisioned for me when I was growing up, but I am also sure she thought my spending time with them was better than sitting home alone, watching TV or playing on my Apple IIe computer.

Which is probably not the case. Our hobbies were not altogether productive. Aside from playing cards and dice, we'd wander through the neighborhood at night, taking the one-mile walk to the Stop N Go to pick up potato chips, ice cream, or Twinkies. Giant bottles of Coca-Cola and Dr Pepper were mandatory, of course. We'd go to the movies when something good was playing.

Oftentimes, James would tell us to punch him in the stomach or kick him in the nuts, just to see "if he could take it." (At the time, James was really into *Soldier of Fortune* magazine and was carrying a little knife on his belt to show off as a mercenary-in-training, I guess.) I frequently took James up on his challenges, and invariably, he could take it. Whenever he got a cut or scrape (which was often), he'd rub salt into the wound so it would leave a scar. He thought it made him look intimidating. It really just made him look bizarre and freakish. I guess there's a market for that sort of thing, though.

While we spent a lot of time playing card games and taking these nighttime Stop N Go excursions, mostly we did what I mostly still do now: nothing. We sat around Travis's living room and watched TV. We shot the bull. We stayed up late and slept well into the next day.

We listened to a lot of music. Not the pop crap that was common in the late 1980s. Classic rock: The Who. Steve Miller. The Police. The Stones. Cheap Trick. Yes. A little Asia from time to time. And a lot of Pink Floyd. Travis, Tommy, and I would go to concerts when we could catch a ride and when he had the money (James always stayed behind). And a couple of times we went to the Floyd laser show at the planetarium.

I have to say, the show was lame. The music was awesome.

Many a Saturday night/Sunday morning would end with a playing of *Dark Side of the Moon*. By our junior year, the cassette was so worn out we had to buy a new one. *Dark Side* remains one of my favorite albums of all time, and the last two songs, "Brain Damage" and "Eclipse," are the best of the best. "Brain Damage" is a song about a "lunatic" the singer sees getting closer and closer; at the end of the song, he realizes, "The lunatic is in my head," and they lock him up in the nut house.

Then the music shifts keys and segues straight into "Eclipse," a poetic chant about, well, everything. All is well, the song says—all you can touch or see, love or hate, create or destroy—it's all all right. Or so we are led to believe as the song concludes:

> All that is now
> All that is gone
> All that's to come
> And everything under the sun is in tune
> But the sun is eclipsed by the moon.

How true.

❖ ❖ ❖

November 14, 1999

Thanksgiving is coming. We are supposed to remember things that we're thankful for.

I can't really think of anything.

Back at Fall Valley, computer math was my favorite class. Computers got me a job, so there's that to be thankful for.

With computers there is only a right and a wrong, an on and an off, a one and a zero. There is very little room for interpretation or subjectivity: Your program either works or it doesn't. I never did figure out why they called it computer math. We did next to no math in the class, the whole year. Instead, we learned how to program Apple computers to print our names, sort a list or two, and do cheesy, ultra-low-res graphics.

Laurel Townsend had no ability at any of this, and why she was even in computer math is still a mystery to me. Drop-dead gorgeous, Laurel could have had any guy in the school. Rumor was, she had, on many occasions. Laurel was obviously destined for an MRS degree, but I have to give her credit for giving legitimate education a shot in the meantime.

Laurel was not your typical high school slut, though. She was genuinely very nice, or at least she pretended to be, and did an awfully good job of it. She was even nice to me, and that I had to appreciate.

Our final project of the semester was to write a program to generate some kind of picture. It didn't matter what the picture was. But you got bonus points if you made the picture move and even more if you included music.

One guy made a giant eyeball that winked and cried. Another guy did an overhead view of an auto race. At least three people made static "VH" logos for the band Van Halen. I made the skyline of Paris, with the sun going down and the French national anthem playing in the background.

Laurel was trying to make a simple horse, but try as she might she could never get the program to run. Even the teacher, Mrs. Anderson, couldn't help her, so one day, the due date fast approaching, she enlisted my aid. I spent about ten minutes debugging the program, which looked okay for the most part, only to find that she had substituted a lowercase "L" for the number one in a critical line. An "l" for a "1"—they look almost exactly the same, and only through sheer luck did I discover the mistake.

After class, Mrs. Anderson asked me what I thought I was doing.

"Helping out Laurel. She was never going to finish otherwise."

"You can't help other people on their assignments, Alex. And no one can help you. It's in your student handbook."

"I was only checking over her work to find the bug. It was an L where a one was supposed to be, that's all."

"It doesn't matter. Technically, it's considered cheating."

Mrs. Anderson wrote me up and sent me to the office. I got five days of lunch detention hall, which means you have to eat your lunch in silence in a little room with all the other lunch D-hall people, and I got ten points off my assignment. (But I still got an A in the class.)

Laurel didn't get written up at all. I'm happy she didn't. Helping her out was one of the few noble things I did at FVH, and it gave me a bit of a swelled head to do it. I think I imagined myself a Knight of the Round Table, helping the damsel in distress against over-whelming adversity. Laurel got a B on her horsie project, which was better than she had hoped for—or deserved.

The only downside to lunch D-hall, aside from missing my regu-lar meetings with Travis, was that Steve knew I was missing, and by Monday, his two little brain cells had rubbed together long enough for him to come up with a new form of torment. And although he could not possibly have suspected it, ultimately, it was this new ha-rassment that would lead to his demise.

❖ ❖ ❖

November 16, 1999

On Monday I was back in the cafeteria as usual, and I had practi-cally forgotten about Steve, since the last we'd encountered each other was during my final, lackluster homework ghostwriting as-signment nearly a month earlier (well, that is, if you don't count the locker incident).

Steve and his crew approached our table from behind me, and I didn't realize anything was amiss until Travis stopped chewing, went silent, and flicked his eyes up over my shoulder at the guys casting long shadows across our lunches.

"It's been a while, Alice." It was Vogon's grating voice.

I turned around. "It's Alex, asshole."

Vogon raised a fist as if to knock my head off, but Steve stopped him. "Calm down," Steve said. "There's plenty of time for that later."

Steve pointed to his usual table in the center of the cafeteria— the logical place for the center of attention to sit. "You know our table?"

"Yeah."

"Go get us our lunch and bring it to us there."

"What?"

Steve sighed at my failure to understand his brilliant plan. "Go get our lunch. We'll give you a few bucks —"

The chubby Dewie piped in, "Yeah, your dad's so poor he proba-

34

bly can't even give you milk money!"

After the group's ridiculous tittering subsided, Vogon stuffed a few crumpled bills in my hand.

Steve continued, "We expect our lunch within five minutes. The period's half-over. Is that a problem for you?"

I said nothing.

"Is that a problem, Alice?"

"No." I felt the lump in my throat drop back into my stomach to fester.

"Well get going, then."

Each of them gave their orders, which were easy to remember, because they all wanted to same thing: pizza and a cheeseburger, double order of fries, and a Coke. They started to walk away, and I called out, "How am I supposed to carry all of that!?" That was six trays.

Vogon turned to reply, "Why don't you get your little friend to help you?" They laughed all the way back to their table.

I turned and looked at Travis, who quickly said, "Don't look at me, dude." I didn't expect him to help out. He would have only opened himself up for more abuse at their hands.

The cashier at the checkout line looked at me funny when I placed the order, but she was kind enough to let me make two trips to deliver the trays to Steve and Co. Steve and his crew didn't say a word when I dropped off their lunches. Nor did they ask for the change, which amounted to about 35 cents.

These lunch deliveries continued for the next two and half years. During that time, I would amass over $150 in change, which I put in an enormous, empty pickle jar in my bedroom.

My parents would at one point tell me how proud they were I was saving money.

❖ ❖ ❖

November 21, 1999

My mother called today. As usual, she had *nothing* to say, but she mentioned that my father and she had just returned from a road trip. Which reminded me of something.

Twice a year or so, our family would drive the hundred and fifty miles or so to Austin for a weekend by the lake or, more likely, a college football game.

Invariably, I'd beg to go to my favorite restaurant in the world, the Magic Time Machine. And invariably, I was so annoying about it that they'd take me.

Magic Time Machine was an intricately designed restaurant-cum-playground. The gimmick was that all the staff dressed as characters from history or popular TV shows and movies. An Elvis Presley (or two) was always in attendance. Marilyn Monroe was commonly impersonated. Various *Star Trek* characters, gangsters, rock stars, and veiled women also made regular appearances. In the worst case, they'd just put a guy in an ape suit if he didn't resemble someone or couldn't do an accent. A lot of the busboys were ape men.

The décor was designed to match the eclectic staff. One table would be a post-modern sheet of aluminum. Another would be a giant mushroom from *Alice in Wonderland*. The best thing was that every time you went to Magic Time Machine, you didn't know what kind of table or waiter you were going to get. A kid could get lost in the experience, and dinner regularly took two hours or more.

Eventually, though, we'd have to leave the Time Machine, and we'd usually make the long drive back home that night, because dad didn't want to spring for a hotel. I'd sleep in the back of the car. Monday morning would eventually roll around, and it would be back to the grindstone of school and slavery.

I last went to the Magic Time Machine in 1989. By then, the place had lost most of its charm, and just about any costume qualified for representation by the waitstaff, including Lucky the Leprechaun, from the Lucky Charms cereal box, who served us during our last meal there. The restaurant closed down a few months after that. A large seafood chain bought the building and remodeled it with big bay windows.

Nothing is permanent in this world. I'm surely not the only one who knows that.

❖ ❖ ❖

November 30, 1999

Fall was well underway, and the leaves were falling like hail from the big oak and pecan trees in the neighborhood. Instead of mowing the lawn, my Saturday-morning job became raking the leaves, which took twice as long to do but was only half as miserable because it had finally begun to cool off.

One Saturday night, James showed up at Travis's place with a new acquisition he had obtained through the classifieds in the back of *Soldier of Fortune*. He had it wrapped up in a blanket, and by the shape of it we knew it was a huge gun of some kind. Slowly he unrolled layer after layer of the blanket to reveal what appeared to be an enormous automatic weapon.

"Jesus!" Travis shouted at him. "What are you going to do with a machine gun!?"

James looked down at his feet, "Well, it's not really a machine gun, it only looks like one."

"What is it, then?" I asked.

"It's a pellet gun."

There was a moment of silence then we all started laughing. James turned red in the face, embarrassed.

"That is so lame," said Tommy.

Travis finally said, "You know, if a cop sees you with that thing, he's going to shoot first. You aren't going to have time to tell him it's a BB gun."

"It's not a BB gun, it's a pellet gun."

"It's the same fucking thing, you big dork," said Travis.

After a twenty-minute lecture from James about how BBs and pellets were *completely* different, we went outside to do some shooting. We were fourteen-year-old boys after all.

Shooting at empty soda cans was fun for a while. But eventually, we got tired of that and started shooting at full soda cans. We'd shake them up until they were about ready to explode on their own, then put them on a fence post, aim from across the backyard, and blast them into oblivion. It was practically better than fireworks.

James wouldn't let Tommy shoot the gun because he had said it was lame. Tommy kept apologizing and saying he was sorry, but James wouldn't give in. Finally, we ran out of pellets and went back in the house. Travis wouldn't let James keep the pellet gun inside, so he left it wrapped in the blanket on the back porch.

It got late after a few games of Trivial Pursuit (during which none of us impressed the others with his knowledge of trivia), and we all slept on Travis's floor.

In the morning, James went out back to polish his new weapon, only to discover someone had stolen it. They left the blanket. To this day, I'm sure that Tommy was the one who took it. He probably just got up in the middle of the night, took the thing back to his house a few blocks away, and sneaked back to Travis's undetected. Tommy was kind of a jerk that way.

Whatever the truth, the gun was never recovered, and James never bought a new one. Fifty bucks or so was a lot for him to save, borrow, or steal. After his initial anger the next morning, we never spoke of the incident again.

Honestly, I have never cared too much for shooting. When you get nervous or rushed, it's hard to aim straight.

And you'll never kill anything that way.

❖　❖　❖

December 3, 1999

December is here, and until April or May rolls around it's going to be miserable in Chicago. Not that it matters where you live. Christmas is always misery.

Back at Fall Valley, the holidays meant that football season was over. The by-product of this was that Steve had more free time in which to torment me, but the holiday season had made him quite festive in his choice of punishments.

I don't remember what I did. I was probably late with lunch, or maybe I ordered the wrong thing. Whatever it was, it was worthy of a new form of torture.

This time, I had to clean out Steve's gym locker, along with those of his pals. After four months of acting as a haven for bacteria and mildew, this was a rubber glove job. Going through the piles of nasty jock straps and mold-crusted towels was something I'll never forget. But it was the smell of industrial deodorizer, ammonia, and stale sweat and urine that made me want to heave every evening. I still can't go into a locker room to this day.

I did one each afternoon Monday through Thursday and two on Friday to finish up the job. I got home late on Friday evening. Doing two lockers that night took longer, but I knew it would be worth it not to have to go back to the job on Monday after school.

When I came through the door, I knew something was amiss. It took me a couple of minutes to figure out what it was: My dad was home, and we were going to eat a family dinner at a normal hour. My dad was *never* home before seven, so it never occurred to me to call and say I wasn't going to be home until late.

They were sitting around the dinner table, meals in front of them, untouched, just waiting for me to join. I quickly sat down and started eating. I must have smelled awful, but no one said anything.

My dad finished about half his plate before anything was said. "So, how come you're so late getting home?" he asked. He wasn't angry, just curious, really.

"Steve made me clean out a bunch of gym lockers." Now I had never said anything about Steve and his crew to my parents, so to them, Steve could have been Coach Steve or even Principal Steve. I don't think my dad heard anything but "gym."

"Really? That's great. It's good to see you taking an interest in sports again."

My mother choked on her food over that statement, and started coughing so badly she had to excuse herself from the table. We could hear her gagging in the kitchen, but she sounded like she would be all right.

I didn't really know how to respond to my dad's comment. Obviously he was so deluded that he selectively heard what he wanted. Finally, I said simply, "Yeah."

"Well, that's great, Alex. That's great."

He returned to eating his meal in silence, and my mom came back to the table, and no one said anything else that night. A football game was on TV.

Monday afternoon, Steve inspected my work and was impressed. He said so.

"I'm impressed, Alex. This is a fine job."

"What's that smell," asked Dewie. "Is that lilac?" The overgrown moron stuck his head deep into his locker.

"Yes it is. It's a new air freshener," I said.

"That's great. It smells like a flower garden in here!"

"Yeah, that's great, Dewie. Now shut up!" Steve snapped at him. He turned back to me. "You've done such a great job here, Alice, that we're going to let you clean the rest of the lockers. I'm sure Dewie would like the entire locker room to smell of lilacs. You can finish the job over Christmas break, and we'll inspect your work when we get back."

I was speechless for a moment. I'd come close enough to vomiting once too often on this one-week job. I wasn't about to do it for another month. No way. I put my foot down.

"No way."

"What's that?" Steve couldn't believe his ears.

"I'm not going to do it."

"Yes you are, or else I'm going to beat the shit out of you."

39

"I'm not going to do it."

Vogon was first to punch me, and it landed in the stomach. The unexpected fist knocked the wind out of me and doubled me over in pain. I went down on one knee.

"You gonna change your mind, Alice?" asked Vogon.

I shook my head no, and someone, Steve, I think, kicked me in the jaw, which knocked me down on my belly on the cement floor.

They took turns kicking me, size 11 through 13 shoes sending me careening around the locker room like an oversized hockey puck. After a few minutes I lay curled up in the corner in a fetal position, begging for my life.

"You're not gonna cry, are you?" asked Steve.

Too late. Cry I did, mixing the tears with the blood running from my mouth and nose, which was staining the ground. At first they just stood over me and laughed, but finally they left, their laughter and taunts of "fag," "wuss," and "pussy" echoing through the air to reach my ringing ears. I guess they were afraid they'd get caught. Or maybe it was just the spirit of Christmas.

I remember cracking a slight smile there on the floor. Christmas was coming, and there would be no Steve for a month.

I had gotten out of locker detail after all, and the price had been well worth it.

❖   ❖   ❖

December 6, 1999

I avoided my parents for a few days, and eventually the bruises and swelling subsided. This was not particularly difficult to do, as my dad was always at work and my mom was out shopping or visiting her lady friends during the day. I could sleep late in the mornings and stay out with Travis and the gang at night, thus avoiding Mom and Dad altogether.

Christmas came and went. My mom gave me twenty bucks to get something for my dad. I bought an eight-dollar belt and pocketed the rest. By New Year's Day, the house was completely stripped of all its holiday decorations, and the yearlong buildup to Christmas began anew.

Of course, I spent the bulk of my vacation time with my friends. Christmas break was just an extended weekend for us, and every night we'd stay up late, listening to tapes, playing games, and shaping our philosophies of life based on the latest books we'd read. (Remarkably, we all quickly found ourselves drawn to Sartre and Kierkegaard: existential doomsayers with little or no expectation of redemption.)

But one of our favorite activities during downtime like this, when we had week after week with nothing to do, was to venture into the woods behind our subdivision. Protected only by a low and rusted barbed-wire fence, it was a constant source of amusement and inspiration to venture into the unkempt forest, because none of us knew what was on the other side.

These day trips eventually stretched into many hours. We would trek deeper and deeper into the woods with each excursion, leaving just enough time to make it back out before it got completely dark. And with each trip, we'd pack more and more gear to the point where we looked like a team of survivalists.

Our amateur survivalism never paid off, though. All we ever found were trees, trees, and more trees, with no end in sight. When you're a kid and on foot, hacking your way through dense foliage, things seem enormous. While we never made it through to the other side of the woods, I'll always remember the feeling that we were venturing into uncharted wilderness territory, and every time we made it back alive to tell the tale.

Two or three years later, those woods suddenly disappeared. By then, we had a car and had simply driven around the area to discover that the forest was really just a smallish grove of trees, a rough circle maybe fifteen miles across, that ended at the interstate. But our suburb was thriving, and explosive growth eventually made that land very valuable, and the owner of the trees and the rusting fence finally sold out. The woods were torn down completely over the course of six months. In their stead now sit row after row of nearly identical, affordable designer homes, perfect for first-time home buyers.

I still like to remember the times we spent in those woods, sitting on a fallen, decaying log in a clearing, the winter sun filtering through the latticework of leaf-bare twigs above. Eating from a sack of trail mix, or even lighting a campfire and cooking hot dogs on sticks and burying potatoes to bake in the coals. Climbing a grand oak's low-hanging branches with a pair of binoculars, just to see if we could get a sense of where we were, and to make a futile attempt to see through to the other side of the forest.

But like I said, we didn't know it then: There was nothing on the other side.

December 7, 1999

When late January rolled around, it was time to put such idle thoughts to rest. School was beginning again.

One of the first things that happened when I returned was the introduction of a new student to our mix, a guy named Berge whose family had moved from Sweden or Denmark or one of those icy places.

I was one of the first people to meet Berge because he was in the band and he played trumpet, and the rule for new students who join in the middle of the year is that they start in C Band, at last chair. This meant that I would now be second-to-last chair in C Band, my first move out of the cellar.

Now I hadn't learned squat about playing the trumpet in the last three months, so it was probably a relief to the director Mr. Dugan when Berge challenged me on his second day at Fall Valley High.

I've already written that the way band works is that people are ranked by their ability to play their instrument, and you sit in order based on that rank. The best is called first chair. The worst is called last chair—ninth chair in my case, with Berge in a new tenth chair. You are not stuck in these chairs. If you want to move up, you can issue a challenge to the chair immediately above you. I could challenge Rhonda Bezier in eighth chair, and she could challenge the guy in seventh chair. First chair could even get out of C Band by challenging last chair in B Band, and so on up the line. The inter-band challenges were only allowed during the summer before school started, because otherwise your class schedule could get all out of whack due to moving between the bands, which had class during different periods.

Berge was a good musician, and last chair in C Band was certainly not the place for him. He obviously wanted to move up to A Band during tryouts in the spring, but he wasn't going to sit in last chair for the entire semester and play the crummy parts that I played. So he challenged his way up, starting with me.

Had I any sense at all, I would have simply conceded the challenge without going through with it. But that most human of flaws—pride—reared its head, and in my two days of being ninth chair out of ten, it was just too nice to *not* be last that I couldn't just forfeit. The challenger picks the music you'll play when he issues the challenge, and you have three days to practice.

And practice I did. In my room, three hours each evening, working on twenty measures from "Pomp & Circumstance" over and

42

over again until my mother finally had to tell me to stop. (Not because of the monotony of the song, but because I still couldn't play worth a damn.)

The challenge came around on Friday afternoon. How it worked was, the two students would go sit in a big closet with the door mostly shut, and Mr. Dugan would sit outside it and listen. The students decide who plays first, and when you come out after both have played, Mr. Dugan anoints a winner.

Berge offered to go first, and his rendition of P&C was flawless. He probably hadn't even needed to practice. He was a really good trumpet player.

I, however, was so nervous and untalented that I screwed up on the first note. And the second, and most of the rest along the way. Finally, I put down my trumpet in obvious defeat and we went outside to hear Mr. D's decision.

To his credit, he acted as though was a tough choice before telling us that the first player was the champion. He also acted surprised to hear that it was Berge, and not me, who had gone first. So I was back to last chair on Monday.

Berge made first chair in C Band before the end of that six weeks, challenging as often as he could. Our sophomore year, he earned third chair in A Band during tryouts—unheard of for a sophomore—and eventually he worked his way up to top of the top. He was drum major senior year, though I doubt he'll be remembered for it.

Still, Berge was quite a musician. There was no shame in losing the challenge to him.

❖ ❖ ❖

December 10, 1999

My lunch duties for Steve and his friends picked up right where they had left off. The first day back from vacation, Steve sent me to fetch a slice of chocolate pie for each of them for dessert, celebratory sweets for making it back to school after all of four weeks away.

Word spread to Steve and his minions quickly, though, when Berge beat me out for ninth chair in band, and it was only a day later that I found my locker inscribed with a new bit of graffiti: "Worst Band, Last Chair, Big Loser."

The upside of this was that Steve stopped calling me Alice for a week and instead called me Big Loser, which, at least, was something different, even if it was no better. What really bothered me, though, was not that Steve and his gang called me Big Loser, but that they thought it was a clever jab and would snicker uncontrollably anytime somebody said it. You'd think it was the wittiest thing on earth, like calling a fat kid Fatso. The world is not missing a great humorist now that Steve is off its surface.

I complained to custodial about the graffiti, and within a week they had put a fresh coat of paint on my locker. This made the locker easy to find, as the new paint contrasted slightly with the faded lockers on either side. So I guess Steve did me some good after all. The principal made an announcement, too, saying that anyone vandalizing school property would promptly be suspended for a week. This ended the graffiti for several months.

Which reminds me of another funny locker story from later that year. When the overcrowding problem at FVH got really bad, we had to share lockers. James, my pellet gun–buying friend, was assigned to share a locker with me, which worked out well because James didn't really care to use it at all, leaving me with most of the space.

James had the top shelf, and he used it to create a little diorama of debauchery. He put an empty, well-scrubbed Wild Turkey bottle up there along with a little shot glass. He had some other stuff, like some poker chips and a pair of headphones, too. Of course, the whiskey bottle got us in trouble after some do-gooder freshman spotted it and turned us in.

We found ourselves hauled down to the principal's office for questioning about the bottle and the shot glass, which had been confiscated during third period.

The principal had gathered four or five assistant principals and counselors in his little office, everyone whispering in concerned tones over what to do about this empty whiskey bottle. Kids had been busted with alcohol on campus, but no one knew what to do about an empty bottle, and referring to the student handbook had come up with nothing much.

When James and I showed up they immediately asked whose it was. James, of course, took the fall—after all, it was his bottle—even though he had checked with me before he put it there. I had said, "Sure, fine with me," and the stuff was there the next day.

The best part happened next, when, in a bizarre twist, they brought in the soccer coach, Coach Lipinki, a.k.a. Coach Pinky, as some kind of expert witness on Wild Turkey. You see, the bottle

44

had a tiny amount of clear liquid at the bottom of it, and the administration was completely puzzled as to what it could be.

"Well, it ain't Wild Turkey. Wild Turkey's a *deep, dark brown,*" said Coach Pinky, a look in his eyes obviously wishing it really was Wild Turkey, so he could taste-test it right then. I didn't know what gin blossoms were at the time, but Pinky had the worst case of them I've ever seen, his nose covered with the red highways that only the most serious lushes get.

The administrators passed around the bottle, each trying to smell for some hint of what the liquid could be. They passed it around a second time. No ideas.

"It's water," confessed James. "I cleaned out the bottle several times, and there's just a little water left over."

"Who gave you the bottle?" asked the principal, obviously looking for a deep conspiracy to break up and make the case for a promotion to superintendent.

"My dad, of course."

Eventually, they realized there wasn't going to be a drug ring or a liquor sales operation to bust here, so the principal dismissed the rest of his staff and turned his full attention to us. We were busted on a "paraphernalia" rule in the handbook. James was suspended for three days. I was sent back to class. The bottle and shot glass were confiscated.

The end result of this experience was actually to ratchet up my esteem, just a tad, in the minds of my fellow students. I was now a potential troublemaker, and the Wild Turkey story followed me around until graduation, when I taped a Wild Turkey label to the top of my mortarboard.

It didn't make me popular or anything, but at least no one ever called me Big Loser again.

❖ ❖ ❖

December 15, 1999

Sometimes I was called The Prisoner, but not by anyone who had ever met me. The Prisoner was my handle, a nickname I went by on computer bulletin board systems (basically the precursor to the Internet).

I certainly wasn't the only Prisoner. Lots of people had been enchanted with the 1960s television show over the years, and I was just the first one to take the name in our area code. After the Internet became a big thing, I soon ran into a dozen other Prisoners, and eventually I abandoned the name altogether.

But back in the late 1980s, The Prisoner was unique, and bulletin boards were thriving. Bulletin board systems, or BBSes, were largely run by high school kids like me in their rooms or college guys in their dorms. All you needed was a computer, a dedicated phone line or two, and a modem, and you too could run a system whereby anyone in the city—or the world, if they wanted to pay the long distance fees—could call in. Once on a BBS, you could leave messages for other people via e-mail or through public forums, download or upload software (usually pirated video games), read text files on any subject you could imagine, or play crude online, text-based games.

Bulletin boards had fanciful names like Dragon's Lair, Crystal Palace, or even Zen Wedgie, derived from the avowed focus of the board or the mental condition of its creator. (Dragon's Lair was for Dungeons & Dragons aficionados; Zen Wedgie was for extreme, random goofballs and nutjobs—I frequented both boards.)

Most of the BBSes are gone now, except for really, really underground stuff like child porn rings and crime syndicates, both of which would probably love to be connected to the entire world through the net were it not for the security risks. But back then, if you wanted the latest version of the game Ultima, you had to either get it from a friend and copy the disks, or download it off a BBS. Or buy it at a store. (Yeah, right!)

Life on the BBSes was a third existence for me, something apart from the horrors of school, and a needed break from Travis and the guys, none of whom were into computers. Meeting people and communicating on the boards also carried the added benefit of anonymity. It's something that people who chat on America OnLine have also discovered, for good or bad. A fat slob can say he looks like Brad Pitt. One-legged Nancy can say she's told she looks like Gwyneth. They're made for each other, and when one decides to fly halfway across the country to meet the other, both of them are disgusted and they never speak again.

As The Prisoner I could be the cross between Lenny Bruce and Cary Grant that I've always wanted to be. All communication on the boards was done through typed messages, and never in real-time unless the board had multiple lines (a rarity), so you could craft your words carefully, spending as long as you wanted. I was very good at this, and within six months or so, I'd finally worked my way into the inner circles of the local BBS scene. The thing that put me over the top was winning a flame war with a guy who went by the name of Ant. A flame war is basically an argument of insults, and thanks to a book called *1,001 Insults and Comebacks* that I'd unearthed in my dad's home office library, I could win any such battle of wits. All you had to do was spend enough time flipping through the book for the right verbal slam, and you'd leave him with nothing left to say except, "Fuck you!" or, "Man, you suck!!!" At that point, the war was over, and everyone watching the back-and-forth on the message boards knew who the winner was.

Soon enough, I found myself with full access to the latest games and other programs. I invariably downloaded those games and kept careful indexes of what I had on the hundreds of floppy disks in my room. I've always been a stickler for keeping good records, and given fifteen seconds, I could tell you where in the stacks my eight disks of Ultima V were, or what disk had Microwave on it. Not that anyone ever asked me to locate these disks so I could show off the system.

I also had access to the vast archives of secret files on the boards, which ran the gamut from "Beer is better than women" joke files to directions for making free phone calls to bomb-building plans. Files like these would later help me craft the plan set into motion in two years' time, with devastating accuracy and impact. But at the time, it was comforting simply to know where that information could be obtained.

❖   ❖   ❖

December 21, 1999

This is the one good thing about the holidays: There is no one around to bother you. The week before Christmas, everything just shuts down, stuck in time. Nothing gets done, and no one cares that it didn't get done. I love it. Gives you a second to think. Or not to think. Whatever.

When pressed, or even asked nicely, I am always happy to spell out my three rules to live by. Everybody has rules like these—don't drink caffeine, go to church every Sunday, and so on. You probably have rules of your own.

My rules are pretty simple. First, I never trust vegetarians. Everyone needs protein to live, and it's unnatural not to eat meat, since we are really designed as carnivores. So if you're a vegetarian, I may

47

give you the time of day, but I'm not going to take your mutual fund advice.

Second, I never trust a man who doesn't drink. I can understand if you've made a lifestyle choice or if you're a recovering alcoholic, but people who don't drink have no way to chemically loosen themselves up. It took a lot of alcohol to loosen me up, so I speak from experience. I try not to apply this rule to women because you never know when they're going to be pregnant and not drinking because of that, and I have gotten myself in trouble by asking that question before, so I exempt females from this rule.

Finally, another rule that only applies to men, and that is never, *ever* trust a man with a hyphenated last name. If your given name was hyphenated, you need to drop half of it, as soon as is legally possible. Even though it's not your fault, you look like you're part of the second group of men with hyphenated last names: You got married and you and your wife created a hyphenated last name. This is a totally pantywaist thing to do. If your girlfriend has that much control over you that she can make you change your name, you should just go ahead and castrate yourself right now. You should be the woman, and she can be the man.

So those are my Big Three rules, but of course I have some others, which I'll write down here for posterity:

I never drink milk. Humans are the only species that consumes milk after infancy, and it isn't normal to do so. Plus, milk has a lot of pus in it from the bovine growth hormones, and that can't be good for you. So stay away from the stuff. (Though I do enjoy ice cream, sadly.)

Do not ride a bicycle, anywhere, ever. If you are riding a bicycle on the street and I am driving, I will not pay any attention to you. If you are on the sidewalk, I will push you off or throw something in your spokes. You are too slow for traffic, and you probably don't obey traffic signals. Bicycles do not exist in my eyes.

Finish everything you start, even if it's no fun. This applies especially to bad movies. If you pay to see *Citizen Kane,* you're going to watch the whole thing, right? Well, even if you pay to see *Weekend at Bernie's,* you should watch the whole movie, because you never know when it's going to redeem itself and become brilliant. Sure, with a movie like *Bernie's,* this is not likely, but you'd be surprised how many low-grade movies, TV shows, and books have one shining moment (even if it's the fact that it's finally over). So never walk out of a movie, and never quit watching a video in the middle. You owe it to yourself.

Private schools do not teach you anything useful about life. Never send your kid to a private college, especially. You are flushing your money down the commode if you do that. Lots of people from FVH went to private colleges, and they are all now bartenders, waiters, or public school teachers. You don't need a degree from Harvard to do those jobs. I went to public schools all my life, and some of it was rough, but public school hardened me, and my outlook on life is very balanced now.

There's nothing wrong with holding a grudge. This is simply the same thing as having a good memory, but people often misinterpret it as being malicious. If you can remember that some girl slapped you ten years ago, that will save you the embarrassment of talking to her at a bar tomorrow. She just may slap you again! If you have been wronged, it's important to constantly remind yourself through a mental checklist of names, dates, and wrongful activities. If you find this list too difficult to keep in your head, there's no shame in keeping it written down on paper or in a computer database. (As you can imagine, my Steve Williams file is quite extensive.)

Oh yeah: Eating eggs is eating unborn animals. That's just sick.

Cleanliness is next to godliness. It is important to know where all your things are. I don't move my stuff around the apartment, ever. Everything has a place where it fits and should stay. This way, you don't have to expend energy looking for stuff that is lost. What a waste! If someone messes up your stuff, they are making you waste your energy, and you should put them on your grudge list.

Paranoia is natural and healthy. If you believe that you don't have enemies, you are being naïve. Steve Williams thought he had no enemies, and look what happened to him. Enemies are all around you. Someday you'll get called into your boss's office and you'll be sanctioned or fired, all because you pissed off some peon who complained to Human Resources about you. If you can't be nice, at least watch your back.

Just because you like things done in a certain way, don't let anyone tell you you're a control freak. If you know the best way to get something done, you should do it that way, and you should help other people see that your way is best. There's no shame in that, although you may create some enemies (see the section on paranoia, above) in people who resist your suggestions. Hold your ground, and remember that you are right. But watch your back!

Die well. I have always imagined that my death will be some bizarre occurrence you'd see reenacted on *Unsolved Mysteries* or *Dateline NBC*. Maybe I'll be slain by my wife or by a hit man she hired in some kind of insurance scam. Or maybe my car will just blow up one day when I turn the key in the ignition—victim of an IRA terrorist bomb. Or a plane crash. Unfortunately, you don't have a lot of control over this, so try to stay healthy and live as long as possible. You don't want to die of cancer or a heart attack. That is not dying well. Steve Williams died extremely well. It was a little bit disgusting there at the end, but I think his death was quite sexy.

That turned into a much longer list than I thought it would be.

❖ ❖ ❖

December 22, 1999

With or without lists, that freshman year seemed like it would never end. Winter came and went, but the cold weather seemed to make Steve averse to causing trouble, so aside from my regular lunch duties, he mostly left me alone. For a while.

This gave me some much-needed time to focus on my schoolwork, as my grades had been slipping all year. By spring break, I was ready for a vacation.

My family has a tradition of taking short vacations that aren't too far away, mainly because my dad can't stand being away from work for more than a weekend. Four days is really pushing it. A week is out of the question.

Typically this meant a trip to the beach at Padre Island, an eight-hour drive or a one-hour plane ride from home.

Don't get me wrong. I appreciated any chance to get away from Fall Valley, but going to the beach has never held much appeal for me. First, it's hot, and it was hot at home. Why go someplace just as hot? Second, the water is disgusting. The Gulf of Mexico is filthy with the oil of a thousand spills over the last two decades. It burns when you go in it. The last time I ever went in, I got stung by a jellyfish. Why would you want to swim in the ocean?

Third, sunburns hurt. A lot. Because I have never been much of an outdoor type, I am fairly pale, skin-wise. This means I get sunburned fast. There is no stopping at "tan" for me. It's straight from ghostly white to beet red. This means a week of peeling, a month of applying aloe, and a year of worrying about skin cancer. Where on earth is the fun in that? (As a side note, I keep hearing that pale skin is "in." Will someone tell that to the people who keep telling me to go outside?)

I also do not enjoy being covered in sand all the time.

Plus, there's nothing to do at the beach except sit there and, maybe, read a book.

We did have a few traditions on these little trips. We'd play miniature golf at the local, wacky mini-golf place. My father never ceases to delight in regurgitating the tale of how I threatened to run away after losing a game once (no, I can't even play miniature golf). Apparently during this little fit, I also threw my putter into a neighboring, weed-covered field, and it was never recovered. It cost my dad $15. However, I do not remember any of these events and cannot vouch for their accuracy.

A couple of times we chartered boats to go deep-sea fishing, parasailing, or some other activity that whiles away the daytime hours. On the deep-sea fishing trip, the sea was rough enough that I spent three hours throwing up and five hours asleep in the cabin. They didn't catch any fish, and that was the end of those excursions.

And of course, we always had to eat seafood at some tourist trap. While Mom and I generally got the heaping mounds of fried catfish and sickeningly large hush puppies, my dad always ordered raw oysters by the dozen. Sometimes he ate three or four trays of the things, which have always disgusted me. But on our last trip to the beach, my dad got so violently sick from the oysters that we had to stay there an extra day for him to recover.

I should add that to my list of rules of to live by: Never eat raw oysters.

❖ ❖ ❖

December 23, 1999

Mom just called and wanted to know if I was coming home for Christmas. I told her we were too busy at the office. Funny, I tell her that every year, but this is the first time I don't actually feel bad about it.

As a kid, I was a constant source of distraction and disappointment for my parents, and for that, I often feel regret. Over time this has passed, and now I'm able to write about the antics that, under different circumstances long ago, did not seem as funny.

When I was eleven years old, I found myself obsessed with a subject that most eleven-year-old boys are taken with: fire. In fact, to this day, I'm still obsessed with fire. I'm convinced that it's the thrill of lighting matches and burning things that drives the vast majority of smokers into the habit.

When you're eleven, fire is a big deal because you don't have the easy access to its creation that adults do. That year, I met a ten-year-old neighbor with the unfortunate name of Clifton who was also consumed by the magic of burning things. He and I spent many hours in the woods, vacant lots, golf courses, garages, or even the street, setting fire to leaves, papers, or twigs, whenever we could find unattended matches (which had usually been abandoned in the woods, vacant lots, golf courses, garages, or the street).

Firecrackers were another common diversion during the Fourth of July and New Year's Eve holidays, and the lax policies of the stands that set up right on county lines to avoid local laws prohibiting their sale made obtaining illicit fireworks relatively simple. All we had to do was scrape together a few dollars from our allowance and convince somebody's older brother to drive us out there.

But fireworks were a seasonal vice. Mainly we just wanted to burn stuff, and we threw ourselves seriously into accomplishing that goal.

At the close of a long, hot, dry summer, Clifton and I became determined to realize one final and grand masterwork of flammability by building a small bonfire. For days we collected newspaper for kindling, twigs of varying size to build up the base, and a pile of dead leaves to create plenty of smoke.

Our choice of locations for the big event was probably foolish, and it would ultimately be our downfall. At age eleven, it had not readily occurred to us that our little experiment could get us into trouble, and Clifton's wisenheimer of a brother, Roy (an equally unfortunate name, but for far different reasons), spotted us building the bonfire behind a tree on the golf course behind Clifton's house.

Roy, fourteen years old at the time, politely inquired as to what we thought we were doing. Stupidly, we told him, and I figure it was less than ten minutes until Roy had blabbed the entire plan to his mom.

We proceeded undaunted, and we lit the bonfire with a lighter Clifton had found in a gutter. The blaze was a huge success. In fact, it was such a great success that the flames were reaching six or seven feet high, and we realized, in true Dr. Frankenstein style, that we had created something beyond our control. Even worse, the dry grass of the golf course looked like it could easily go next, starting a chain reaction that could take out the whole block.

Being desperate yet relatively clever young lads, we high-tailed it back to Clifton's house to obtain the obvious solution to our woes.

We opened the sliding-glass back door and strolled into the kitchen, where Clifton's mother was cooking dinner.

"Boy, I sure am thirsty," I feigned. "I could use some ice water." Sure, I thought, a simple glass of water would be all that was required to put out the fire.

While I'm sure an eleven-year-old kid asking for ice water is very continental, Clifton's mom was onto us from the start.

"You started a fire, didn't you?" she said, disappointment in her eyes, resigned to the obvious truth.

Clifton and I looked at each other and then down at our feet. "Yes," we said, almost in unison.

Clifton's mom just shook her head, quickly retrieved a large bucket and, while it was filling with water in the sink, pulled on a pair of rubber galoshes.

Calmly, she took the full bucket out to the golf course and dumped it on the now-raging wall of flames. It went out nearly instantly, and she quickly stamped out the glowing embers within a minute. Soon there was nothing left but a black, charred circle in the grass to remind us of the crime.

Clifton's mom took me home immediately, and she calmly explained to my mother what had happened. In all fairness to Clifton's mom, she was extremely fair and good-natured about the incident, and she downplayed the fire's disaster potential, even though it was her house that would have gone first. But Clifton's mom promised a stern punishment for Clifton, and she suggested the same for me.

I was sent to my room until my dad got home so "he could figure out what to do about this." The sentence was handed down that evening: My birthday party, three weeks away, would be canceled. Plus grounding and a belt spanking.

I never found out what happened to Clifton. We kind of blamed each other for that incident and drifted apart after that. A year later, Clifton's dad, a geologist for an oil company, was transferred someplace else where they still had oil, and I never saw or heard from Clifton again.

But I'm still obsessed with fire, despite the trouble it's caused me. I even made my own napalm from scratch during my freshman year of high school, which is what reminded me of this story in the first place.

All you have to do is dissolve Styrofoam in gasoline and you get a jelly that will ignite with a spark and will not burn out until it runs out of fuel. Put a can or a bucket over the fire, and it'll burn right through it.

I recommend you work in small batches, only ignite your creation over a cement surface, and stand as far back as you can while it burns (though close enough to enjoy the show).

❖ ❖ ❖

December 26, 1999

Christmas is over. My mother sent me three ties. I have told her repeatedly I never wear a tie, but she's convinced it's good to have them "just in case."

Somehow, and I don't remember the exact circumstances, near the end of my freshman year, Steve drafted me to help him out on the baseball field after class "shagging balls." Out of fear of being beaten, I'm sure I complied readily. After all, the school year was ending, and I could take a little abuse now to reach the three months of sanctuary coming up.

Shagging balls meant that one guy lobbed easy pitches to Steve and his teammates, who hit them as far into the outfield as possible. I then had to fetch all the balls and bring them back to the pitcher.

In theory, I was supposed to throw them back, but there was no way I could throw a ball 200 feet or more with any kind of accuracy, so I'd typically have to run up until I was within seventy-five feet of the pitcher's mound and throw it back from there, then run back to the outfield to get the next ball.

Of course, each time I did this took about a minute and a half, and they didn't wait for me to get the first ball before proceeding to the next. So, soon, the outfield was littered with baseballs, and within fifteen minutes, they had completely run out of balls at the pitcher's mound.

The catcalls started then, for me to "hurry up my pansy ass," to "get my sorry ass in gear," and to "move my ass before they kick it so hard they lost a shoe." Try as I might, there was no way I could keep up with all the balls. Before an hour was up, I was too exhausted to continue.

For some reason, Steve let me rest. When I saw him and his crew huddling up near the dugout, I should have known that something was up. But I was too grateful for the chance to lie down in the overgrown grass of the baseball field to care.

Finally, Steve called me back to home plate. I went.

"You wanna take some hits?" he asked.

"Huh?" I figured he was asking me if I wanted to get beat up.

"You wanna hit some balls?"

Now this was certainly a strange turn of events. Why would Steve want me to hit some balls? A fleeting thought went through my mind that he just wanted to watch me miss them all and laugh, but that was quickly replaced by the foolish notion that he was genuinely grateful for all my hard work. In other words, this was a reward. Quickly I persuaded myself that Steve, in his own perverse fashion, wanted to make amends and be friends.

Don't laugh. At the time, it seemed possible.

I figured out the truth soon enough. I selected a bat and stood at the plate, while Steve and his cronies all hung out in the infield. As I've said, I'm no sportsman, so when the pitches came in at seventy, eighty miles per hour, I just kind of stood there and tried not to get killed. The balls whizzed right by, loudly clattering into the chain-link backstop each time.

With every pitch, Steve and Co. laughed their asses off like it was the funniest thing they'd ever seen: a guy who didn't swing a bat.

So I steeled myself to take at least one swing at one of the slower pitches. I had no illusions of hitting a home run, but I just wanted to hit *something*, to show Steve I wasn't a complete wimp.

They gasped when I swung the bat. And when the aluminum bat collided with the pitched ball with a dull clunk, they held their collective breath.

The ball dribbled out toward the pitcher's mound, and I dropped the bat in severe pain. Apparently I hadn't held on tight enough or, more likely, just had no clue what I was doing, and the vibrations down the length of the shaft hurt so badly I could do nothing but let go.

They howled louder than ever.

Finally, they got over the humor of the situation, and Steve came over to talk to me.

"That was really good, Alice. You hit the ball. Now see if you can't hit it a little farther."

Again, I was suckered in by his not-unkind words, so I rubbed my hands on my jeans, picked up the bat, and strode back to home plate for another swing. If nothing else, I was going to show him that I would beat him at his own game—that he couldn't knock me down by laughing at me.

The next pitch, however, would knock me down otherwise. The ball beaned me right in the head with no warning. I wasn't wearing a helmet, and I crumpled up like a crushed sheet of newspaper, going fetal on the ground.

I don't remember a lot after that, but no one was laughing. I remember looking up at the circle of people around me. "Walk it off," they chanted. "Walk it off." In the mind of the jock, walking cures any malady.

But walk I would not do. I could barely even see. They talked amongst themselves, probably trying to figure out how to make this situation even more hilarious, but in the end, of course, they could come up with nothing.

Steve started kicking first. I can only be grateful that none of them was bright enough to think to pick up the bat.

A beating is never fun, but Steve had to get one last thrashing out of his system (and into mine) before summer came along. By this time I had learned: Keep your head protected, and you'll come out okay.

When it was over, I crawled to the dugout to rest. When it started to get dark, I picked myself up and shambled home, skipping dinner and sleeping straight through until morning.

The last week of freshman year was a time for studying for finals, signing yearbooks, and cleaning out lockers. Steve found himself occupied with activities like this, too, and he left me alone most of the time, comfortable that my last good beating would hold me over until the fall. Our teachers said their goodbyes, and I left Fall High for the last time that year. I was one-quarter of the way through my high school career, and no end appeared to be in sight.

By the time my final grades showed up in the mail, two weeks into summer vacation, I knew that I had become a B– student, plummeting from an A– average in eighth grade the year before.

My parents asked the usual questions, but deflecting them was easy. Just say you're overwhelmed by the new environment or the size of the school, and they'll let you off the hook. A good excuse for my dad was that I had been preoccupied with some girl. That always cheered him up, giving him the chance to regale me with tales of his high school days as a young Casanova, and how girls were so much trouble, but what could you do about it? And on and on. By the time he finished one of those stories, he had forgotten the entire reason for the conversation. He just slapped me on the back and headed to the kitchen for another beer.

On the last day of school, Travis and I had emptied our lockers and were walking home along the sidewalk when we heard Steve's enormous Jeep come thundering down the road behind us. You always knew when his truck was coming because something about the engine—either a flaw or an intentional modification—made it sound so loud, almost like a Harley-Davidson motorcycle. The sound of a half-dozen jocks screaming, "Fall Valley *rules!*" was another dead giveaway.

I figured we were in for trouble, since it was the last day of school and all, but Steve just barreled on by, going 45 in a 25 mph zone, his buddies yelling all the way. We stopped to look as they passed, but they never even slowed down. Steve simply laid on the horn, blaring it nonstop as he zoomed through the suburban streets. He disappeared around a corner, and that was the last I saw of him for three months.

Steve had made it through another year of high school, and he was too preoccupied with his own achievement to give me a second glance. His accomplishment—getting through sophomore year—was clearly something that he was very proud of.

❖   ❖   ❖

December 30, 1999

Dr. Carter and I met again today—kind of a "let's wrap up the millennium" chat to see where things stand.

He's pretty happy, I think. He said, "Alex, I'm really happy about the progress we've made over the last year. Your sessions lately have been cathartic and cleansing, I think, and I believe we're getting to the root of your problems."

Keeping this diary seems to have made me more talkative in my sessions with Dr. Carter, but he's a fool to think we'll ever get to the root of my problems. Like I said, I'll never tell him my secret.

You might wonder why I go to a therapist at all, if I'm not going to tell him the truth about what I did and why I feel the way I do. I wonder that myself sometimes, but like the good doctor says, I do seem to be making some progress. So maybe he can help me, even if I don't tell him everything.

A little truth can go a long way toward sanity.

❖ ❖ ❖

January 1, 2000

What a disappointment. What happened to all this millennium panic stuff? No power outages, no riots, nothing! What am I going to do with thirty gallons of bottled water?

On New Year's Eve, I stayed home, watched MTV, and drank. Just like old times, I guess. It reminded me of the summer after my freshman year, which Travis and I spent engaged in a singular pastime that we had stumbled upon quite by accident: drinking. I am not proud of this.

Travis's older brother Rick was a freshman in college at The University of Texas, and typical of college students, he returned home for a summer of laziness. Rick had quickly found his way into the lush life at college, and when he came back to Fall Valley that May, he brought a present for Trav.

It was a half-empty bottle of gin from some local, no-name producer that probably cost less than five bucks. "Here," he told Travis as we sat in the living room playing dice, "this shit makes me sick, so you can have it."

Such generosity should never be questioned, and immediately we were struck with what to do with the gift. We stashed the bottle away deep in the recesses of Travis's closet and headed, quite naturally in our minds, to the bookstore, to buy a bartender's manual. At fourteen we fancied ourselves already too mature to drink liquor by the shot, and we quickly became taken by the idea of learning everything there was to know about mixed drinks. While the jocks got wasted on light beer and wine coolers, we would outdo them and woo the ladies by whipping up something cool that had a cherry or an olive in it. You know, classy.

The guide we bought was a thick, blue tome that I still own, called *The Complete Guide to Cocktails and Libations*. Six hundred and seventy-four pages of drink recipes, most of which sound disgusting and—I would soon find out—taste disgusting, too. The bookstore clerk looked askance at us when we shoved our money over the counter, but there's no law that says a kid can't buy a book about alcohol.

We ran back to Travis's, shut the door to his room, and began studying, underlining drinks that we'd heard about on TV or in the movies, like the Manhattan, the Bloody Mary, and the Sloe Gin Fizz, or that we just liked the sound of, like the Blue Lou. We were going to become the youngest sophisticates Fall Valley had ever seen.

Our hopes were quickly dashed when we realized that a half-bottle of gin and a six-pack of Coke was not going to get us very far toward our goal of become teenage Gary Coopers. But thanks to what must have been a decades-old bottle of dry vermouth stashed deep in the bowels of the Pickford family refrigerator, we decided to make the famous Martini our first experiment.

We stashed the bottle of gin in the meat locker in the garage, and Travis invited James and Tommy over to join in the fun. Late that night, when Travis's parents had gone to bed and Rick had left to visit his friends, we set up shop in the Pickfords' kitchen and prepared to open the bar.

James was jumping off the walls with anticipation. "Extra dry," he kept telling us, "extra dry!"

"Do you even know what extra dry means, James?" asked Travis.

"No, but that's the way they always order it."

Tommy piped in, "I want mine shaken, not stirred." He then laughed himself silly.

"All of you shut up, okay," I ordered, the appointed mixmaster for some reason. "Trav, do you have any olives? We can't make martinis without olives."

After a hasty search came up empty, we put the gin back in the cooler and headed out to Stop N Go for the usual weekend supply of chips, Cokes, Twinkies . . . and olives.

We assembled the martinis in paper cups, partly so we could destroy the evidence later, but mainly because Travis couldn't find any martini glasses. When we finally cracked open the ice-cold bottle, I'll never forget the smell of rancid rubbing alcohol that wafted out. I don't know what possessed us to think we were going to like it.

The bottle of gin was almost empty after we measured out four servings, each with a lone olive swimming at the bottom of the cup. "Here's to the best martini you're ever going to have, gentlemen," said Travis, as he lifted his cup in a toast. Cautiously, we sipped, each pulling priceless grimaces as we tasted our concoction.

"I can't drink that," said Tommy, pushing his cup aside.

"Well I shook yours *special*," I pointed out. "You better drink it."

"Here, you can have it," he offered.

59

"I can't drink mine either," said James. He made a sour face, adding like a baby, "It burns my throat."

"That's the point, you idiots," said Travis. "I can't believe you guys are such fucking wusses. Especially you," he said to James, "Mister *Soldier of Fortune* tough guy."

"A real mercenary can drink a martini," I added.

Appropriately shamed, James pretended to sip at the drink some more, but I figure he just dumped it in a plant later when no one was looking.

In the end, Travis and I were the only two who could finish our drinks. We silently acknowledged each other's prowess with a nod, even though the liquor was the vilest thing we had ever put down our throats.

"The next ones will be better," Travis said.

"We just need better ingredients," I added.

"Exactly."

"And we need more stuff."

"A lot more. A full bar."

I'll never forget that cocktail. It was really disgusting, and the taste hung around in my mouth for hours, but Travis was right. It was the best martini I've ever had.

❖ ❖ ❖

January 3, 2000

Even though summer meant mowing the lawn in 100-degree heat, it was great. Sleep in, stay up late, no classes, no Steve Williams. We had our martinis, and there was plenty more alcohol to follow. And we owed it all to James.

James was the bearer of myriad strange qualities, but none was so readily apparent as his aforementioned freakish height: almost 6-feet-7. Six feet, 6 ⅞ inches to be exact, and James was rarely inexact. James also had the patchy beard and moustache that made him look both older and even stranger, and when he was wearing some of his trashier attire and had neglected to wash, which was more common than I care to think about, he had the very appearance of a weathered homeless guy—the kind you go out of your way to avoid.

In other words, he was perfect for buying alcohol for us. At face value, he appeared old enough, and any cashier in his right mind would want nothing more than to complete the transaction as quickly as possible to get him out of the store. The Safeway down the street was notoriously lax in its ID checking as well, so obtaining beer and wine from there was almost always an in-and-out affair, no hassles. Travis, Tommy, and I put up the money, James took the risk of making the buy, and he got to share in the haul. Everyone was happy, and we never got in trouble.

The problem was that Texas prohibits the sale of hard liquor in grocery stores, so you had to go to a real liquor store to get vodka and bourbon, which we were desperate for. Beer and cheap wine were fine, but we really wanted to work through *The Complete Guide to Cocktails and Libations,* and that would require exotic mixers like Drambuie and Chambord.

Our local liquor store was tricky, though. It was called Fred's Liquor, and it looked like Fred was the only employee, because I never saw anyone else manning the register whenever I peered through the barred windows.

Fred looked like he was about eighty-five years old, and he was the meanest son of a bitch you can imagine. The first time we sent James in, armed with seventy bucks to get a bottle each of vodka, whisky, tequila, gin, and rum, he was summarily booted out inside of thirty seconds. In Texas, a minor can't even go inside a liquor store legally. With grocery-store beer buys, you could buy a bunch of household stuff and slip a six-pack or two in with the other merchandise to avoid getting hassled. Fred would have none of that.

We tried sending James in to Fred's on three or four occasions, with decreasing levels of success each time. The last time he went in, Fred actually whacked James on the ass with his cane as he shooed him out, yelling that he'd call the cops next time he brought his sorry, underage ass in the store, and that he'd beat James silly, too. I could hear Fred yelling at him from around the corner, where we were hiding out. James told us he wasn't going back in, ever.

There weren't any other liquor stores within walking distance, so until somebody turned sixteen and got a car, we were stuck with the low-alcohol-by-volume beverages you could get at Safeway. Beer, wine, and wine coolers. That was it.

None of us cared much for the taste of beer at first—pretty typical, I guess. We tried to make it fun, experimenting with the designer beers they put on the shelf above the Budweiser, Miller Lite, and Michelob, although we drank plenty of those brands, too. For each new beer we tried, we'd save one bottle, stashed in a glorious collection in the back of Trav's closet. The rest of the empties we tossed into the gutter outside Travis's house to hide the evidence.

Not that Travis's parents would have cared, I figure. They probably knew all along what we were doing in their living room, and they were probably glad we were doing it there instead of behind the school or, even worse, behind the Stop N Go. In their house, we were safe.

None of us could drink more than one or two beers a night, so we cut it with wine coolers and occasionally jug wine. A personal favorite was the wine they sold in carafes—you just popped the metal lid and glug-glug-glugged it right down, often spilling it all over yourself.

As you might expect, all of this drinking and no tolerance for it made for a summer of rapid drunkenness and goofy conversations and gaming sessions. Once we played poker, and Tommy got so upset after we took all his money that he ripped up all the cards. They were Travis's cards though, and Trav got so pissed that he made Tommy eat at least a handful of them.

Another time, James fell asleep and was later found sleep-wrestling with a stepladder in the Pickfords' kitchen.

I had my share of drunken experiences, too, including one time where I drank a whole bottle of Pinot Noir and proceeded to run around in circles through the Pickfords' house, starting at the front door, then heading through the den, cutting through the kitchen, back through the living room, and around to the front door again—over and over and over until I finally fell down and puked all over the living room floor. Travis groused as he cleaned it up, asking why I couldn't have done that in the kitchen where there was tile instead of carpet.

You just don't think about that kind of thing when you're wasted.

❖   ❖   ❖

January 6, 2000

This is not to say that the summer of 1987 was all play and no work. I did have a job, working the concession stand at the little league baseball field, for minimum wage.

As you may expect, this was the brainstorm of my sports-freak father, who had been reluctant to give up his pastime of watching little league baseball games, even though he didn't have a child playing on the field. As I've said, my dad loves sports of any kind, from the World Series right on down to T-ball. If there wasn't a pro or college game he could watch on TV or in person, he'd head down to the neighborhood ball park to watch, well, whatever was going on there.

This habit must have earned him the stares and/or jeers of the entire community. If his passion (or fetish) for baseball hadn't been so well-known, I figure most everyone would have pegged him as some kind of pervert.

So my dad struck upon the plan that if I worked at the field, he could come by under the guise of paying me a visit. If he happened to hang around afterward and catch a game or two, well, that was just a bonus.

This worked out well for me, because on the weekends, if I was up early enough, I could duck out of lawn duty by saying I had to head to the field for work. Usually this meant I'd get there at least an hour early with nothing to do and nowhere to go, but it was better than sweating behind the mower in the backyard.

Another kid named Tully worked with me that summer. He was a really fat kid with a pimply face who everyone called Tubby. I just hung around in the background whenever any tough jock types came around, and Tully would take the worst of their abuse. He didn't seem to mind. He never said anything about it. In fact, he never said much at all. But he was really good at cooking fries and making change.

When Tully got there (he was two years older than me and had the keys) we'd start by getting the soda machine ready for business, starting the popcorn popping, putting the hot dogs on the roller machine, and preparing for the onslaught of hungry and thirsty sports fans. Or to be more accurate: the trickle of hungry and thirsty parents.

During the lunch rush, we cooked hamburgers and fries to order. Chicken sandwiches were a specialty. Tully even made his own garlic mayonnaise for them. I think he went on to be a chef in New Orleans.

I got by doing as little work as possible. Tully seemed thrilled to have the chance to play gourmet, and I was all too inclined to let him spread his ample wings by getting out of the way. Tully usually only enlisted my services when people wanted prepackaged stuff like candy bars and Gummi bears, or when it got too busy. The rest of the time, I sat in the back near the air-conditioning vent and read books or magazines. When I was really bored, I'd actually watch one of the games.

By one or two in the afternoon my dad would come by, say "Hey," order a popcorn and a Coke, and go sit in the bleachers to cheer on whomever was playing. Hours later, he'd say "Bye," and go home. And that was it.

Tully and I would close the stand at six and clean up for a half-hour or so, and then part ways. We got paid every Friday, in cash, because the whole operation was a little shady—not to mention the fact that I was under age. My dad thought it was great for me to have a job at only fourteen, and he made me promise to save all the money toward my college education. A separate allowance would be provided for pocket money.

Little did he know that all of it went straight to booze.

❖ ❖ ❖

January 8, 2000

By the time August rolled around, there wasn't much we wouldn't do for alcohol of some kind, even beer. It's amazing how quickly your tastes can change.

I turned fifteen on August 1, and we celebrated by buying a Party Ball, a mini-keg of beer that Coors or somebody used to put out. I don't see Party Balls any more. I guess they weren't selling.

We drank the whole thing and then some, and most of us passed out in Travis's backyard that night, where cleaning up vomit was as simple as turning on a hose in the morning.

James was especially into our newfound beer habit. On our quest to drink every type of beer on sale at the Safeway, we finally ventured into Guinness stout, which had intrigued us for months. With the first sip, Travis and I swallowed and grimaced.

"This tastes like mud," I said.

"It tastes like shit," said Travis.

"No, it tastes gooooood," said James, looking for a little respect for once.

"You're so full of crap, James," taunted Travis. "If you drink that whole bottle, we'll call you Stud from now on."

I don't think James got the hidden joke in his would-be moniker, but he was apparently willing to do anything for a cool nickname.

James said, in all seriousness, "How about you call me Caesar instead?" (Pronounced "Kaiser," of course.)

"I'm not calling you Kaiser, you fool," I told him. "How about we call you Gunther, because you're so tough?"

I meant it as a joke, because there was an over-muscled guy on cable access by the same name that we often made fun of, but James was into it. "Yeah, cool!"

Travis made him drink the stout outside and sit out there for fifteen minutes in case he puked. Trav was cleaning up an awful lot of barf in those days, and he'd obviously had enough. James made it through just fine, and when he came back in, we greeted him as Gunther.

Years later, we still called him Gunther, and we laughed every time we said it. James eventually came to hate the name, but he'd asked for it, and it had stuck.

But "Gunther" wasn't the only thing any of us would do for a drink. To get hard liquor, we ended up raiding our parents' liquor cabinets for dusty old bottles and duplicates that would go unnoticed when pilfered. My dad drank a ton of Jack Daniel's, and people would always bring him bottles of it as gifts. Our liquor cabinet was packed to the gills with JD—more than even he could possibly drink—and it was always easy to take a bottle or two a month.

No one ever noticed. All you have to do is take them from the back of the cabinet, leaving the wall of bottles in the front intact. This way, when you open it up, it still looks full. When a new bottle arrived, my mom or dad would struggle to fit it into the cabinet, but they'd always be excited to see there was just a little more room after all. See, I was doing them a favor.

We got a ton of bourbon that way, plus assorted vodkas and scotches that my dad wouldn't touch (and wouldn't miss). The other guys did the same, but their parents never had the quantity my dad did. When we got really desperate, we'd pour a little off somebody's full liquor bottles into mason jars. Not as elegant, but it did the trick.

Of course, the empties all went down the gutter outside Travis's house.

But by the end of the summer, there was no room left in the gutter. So we started taking our spent bottles to the next gutter down the street.

January 9, 2000

Before we knew it the summer had gone, wasted away in a pool of liquor. By the final weekend before school started, the stash had run dry, and we were reduced to drinking the homemade strawberry wine that James's cousin had made and sent out to all his relatives as a Christmas gift. It was extremely unsavory, but potent.

Within a few hours on Saturday night, we were all well toasted. Travis's brother Rick had just finished packing his stuff to head back to college when he came downstairs from his room.

It only took one look at us for him to reach the obvious conclusion. "You guys are wasted, aren't you?"

Trav took a serious look at him and replied, "No."

Rick said, "Well, I'm going to get something to eat. You guys want to come?"

It would be over a year before any of us would be old enough to drive, and we never, ever turned down an offer of free transportation out of the Valley. We had piled into Rick's backseat within seconds.

Dinner that night meant an evening at Denny's, which is even better drunk. We ordered big breakfast platters—I think I had the Belgian waffle—except for Travis, who got some kind of fish plate, which could very well be the last thing I'd ever order at a Denny's, except eggs of course.

Denny's, like most restaurants of its ilk, offers unlimited coffee refills, so we naturally ordered bottomless coffees all around. This combined with the homemade wine to enhance our drunken bravado with ridiculous energy, and it even sent Tommy up onto the table to do a little impromptu air guitar for the whole restaurant, while he hummed some Kiss song. I was sure we were going to be invited to leave, but it wasn't very crowded that evening, and everyone seemed to get a kick out of the performance, even applauding when he was finished, guitar solo and everything.

When we got back to Trav's place, we stayed outside. It was a typically warm Texas summer night, but exposure to the Arctic air-conditioning in Denny's made the hot breeze feel good on our faces.

We sat on the back of the Pickfords' cars and looked at the stars. James and Tommy wrestled in the yard until Tommy got hurt and limped back to the driveway. Travis didn't look like he was feeling too hot, and soon enough, he hurled his dinner into the driveway. Travis thought of himself as something of a stoic, and to him, throwing up was a sign of weakness, so this turn of events was particularly troublesome for him. James came to the rescue, though, retrieving a garden hose from the side of the house and washing the puke down toward the street.

In the middle of his labor, he stopped, bent down, and picked up a chunk of something from the driveway. My brain refused to accept it: James was picking up a chunk of vomit.

"Did you have shrimp for dinner, Trav?" he asked, closely examining the little chunk.

Trav, lying down on the hood of Rick's car, replied, "Actually, it was fish."

"Oh."

The story diverges at this point. Tommy maintains that James then consumed the vomited fish chunk, grossing out everyone in the yard. The truth, though, is that James simply dropped the chunk back onto the driveway and finished hosing it into the street with the rest of the upchuck.

Some stories just aren't that sensational, and I have no reason to exaggerate the truth.

That was how we spent our last weekend before school started. Sunday I worked at the concession stand, and Monday I was back in class at 8:10 a.m.

❖ ❖ ❖

January 11, 2000

Despite his short attention span for lots of other things, Steve Williams had not forgotten me in the three months we had been apart. On day one, he had me acting as his lunch boy. Apparently that was the only job he felt I could do with any degree of skill, and the lunch lady knew me so well that she let me cut to the front of the line every day. It wasn't all that bad. Travis, James, and Tommy all had different lunch periods than me that year, so I didn't have anyone to eat with anyway.

Steve was now a junior, and the prowess he displayed on the athletic field the previous two years had earned him an extremely revered place in the minds of the student body, the faculty, and the administration. This year, Steve was the starting quarterback for our football team, which only lost one game the whole year—the one game Steve didn't play in because of a twisted ankle. We won our third straight state championship that year. In Texas, you just don't sniff at sporting ability like that.

Steve also got cleverer about his tortures, and he spread the wrath among other kids at school. That year Steve went on a rampage against gay and/or effeminate guys, and some of them lived in sheer terror during the school day. One kid named Tino never used the bathroom at school, because every time he went into a men's room he got the crap beat out of him. He pissed his pants more than once and ran home in tears every time. This thrilled Steve to no end: He had finally succeeded at punishing somebody using the mere threat of violence.

His other pranks got worse, too. He and his pals still smeared shit or dropped fish in people's lockers (though mine was spared), but this year they would superglue the locker doors shut afterward. This made cleanup impossible and often meant the replacement of whole rows of lockers.

Steve developed a real passion for superglue that fall. Once, this senior named Arnold bumped into him in the hall. Steve superglued Arnold's bicycle brakes *open,* and on the way home he ran straight into a truck, breaking a leg and two ribs.

Steve and his friends also started a nuisance campaign against another suspected homosexual, sending in a few hundred subscription and business reply cards for every magazine and product he could get hold of, all delivered to "Pat Landers' Fag Palace." Pat got blamed for the stunt by his redneck dad and was kicked out of his house after a few months of overstuffed mailboxes and telemarketer harassment. (In fairness, even I have to give Steve credit for this extremely clever prank, though I doubt he came up with the idea.)

There was plenty more, which I'll write about later. I knew Steve did all of this stuff because I heard him and his buddies gloating about it at lunch every day. But despite their obvious guilt, people looked the other way, and they never got caught.

What I did was not just for myself.

❖   ❖   ❖

January 12, 2000

That fall, James decided to join the ROTC, against Travis and my stern advice. If you don't know what ROTC is, consider yourself lucky. ROTC stands for Reserve Officer Training Corps. It's basically a light version of the military, and its predominant membership is made up of the sons and daughters of people already in or retired from the military who want their kids to be just like them.

In Fall Valley, this meant the teenage kids of Air Force retirees, ex-marines, and politicos, all of whom had been brainwashed into believing that military service built character. With James, a borderline white trash gun nut, thrown into the mix.

ROTC (pronounced ROT-see) is common at most larger universities, but I don't believe many high schools have the program. Fall High was an exception, of course, and every year, fifteen or so fools signed up for the course.

And it was, indeed, a class, just like Pre-Calculus or Home Economics. Five hours a week, the cadets (there are no "students" in ROTC) learned important lessons about leadership, management, goal setting, ethics, terrain analysis, orientation, the history of American warfare, field medicine, flag-folding, and physical education. Just like in the real military, there was a lot of pushing-up and sitting-up, running in lockstep while chanting, "Sound off!" as well as hoisting and twirling of fake, wooden machine guns. The women of ROTC were exceptionally frightening, and I know there were special ROTC dances—an extremely disturbing scene, I'm sure. James never spoke of them, but he always attended.

ROTC kids wore their uniforms once a week, usually on Friday, to coincide with the day the sports jocks wore their uniforms. It's no surprise that ROTC kids were subject to more derision than any other group in the school. Hell, even Travis and I looked down on them. (It probably goes without saying that I feel the military is a crock of shit. I guess that makes ROTC a miniature, pretend version of a crock of shit.)

Of course, this argument did not sway James. He was really in to the whole history-of-war angle of ROTC, and since he was also really interested in guns and firearms, he figured that was a bonus.

Travis and I enjoyed picking on James after he joined ROTC, and we later dubbed him "Private Gunther," adding a rank to his hard-earned moniker.

James was in full uniform one day when we took a rare class field trip to the Natural History Museum in the city. Some old lady confused him for a tour guide, and James, always the altruist, led her to the exhibit she was looking for.

I had Chemistry as my science elective that year, and I guess we were going to the Museum to study volcanic rock or something. Mostly my inane classmates just gawked and snickered at the mannequins of semi-naked Cro-Magnon men and women.

I found myself drawn to the Earth Science wing, which had an exhibit entitled "Metals of the Earth." Looking at all the shiny nuggets that went in color from silvery white to deep orange to bright yellow to pure black makes you realize that we are all destined to become hunks of coal or iron, blackened chunks of rock buried under centuries of dust, trash, and feces. Every one of us is a walking fossil.

Though we were supposed to move on to look at some moon rocks and asteroid chips, I stayed in the metals exhibit the entire time we were at the museum. I bought a postcard photo of it when it was time to leave.

Chemistry would change my life that year.

❖ ❖ ❖

January 15, 2000

Contrary to the story my mother will tell you, I *did* attend a football game as an ordinary spectator while I was in high school. (This does not count marching band events my freshman year.) It was just the one game, but I did go. No matter how often I point this out, Mom persists in telling her friends that I was totally antisocial and never went to any sporting events. Can you blame me?

It was homecoming, early October my sophomore year. We were playing a fairly weak rival—they always pick a crappy team to play against for homecoming so we'll have an easy win. It makes the players feel good and builds student morale.

I went to the game alone. Travis would have nothing to do with the idea, Tommy claimed to have band practice, and James was AWOL, so to speak. So I double-timed it alone down to the stadium, where the conversion of electricity into hundreds of bright lights had attracted the attention of millions of June bugs and mosquitoes. Seasoned Texas football fanatics know to bring a can of Off! bug repellent to all night games.

I took a seat in the last row, where a few people would go to smoke and escape the rowdiness below. In the pit of students it was like a scene from Dante's *Inferno*. Teens with their faces painted in our school colors (green and yellow), screaming at the top of their lungs, "GO RAIDERS!" obviously laboring under the assumption that more noise would somehow translate into more points on the scoreboard. I find it comforting to think of this simply as the way they practiced for becoming idiots later in life.

Our mostly anorexic cheerleaders jumped around and did half-assed back flips on the track that circled the football field. One, a blonde girl named Veronica, always stuck out from the rest. She was a little bit chubby, especially in the thighs, and she had enormous breasts. She couldn't do flips or anything. She just jumped up and down and kicked her legs, her giant frontal region bouncing like a Michelin tire. Word around school was that she was a slut. Not that I'd know.

We had a drill team, which did choreographed mime while the band played tunes that were popular ten years earlier, mainly surfer music. So why wasn't I up there in their ranks? After I begged him to release me from band hell, my dad probably weighed the options carefully in his mind. Eventually he relented. I figure he decided that he was more embarrassed that I was last chair in the band than that I had sang in a school musical. So I was back in theater that year.

Under the bleachers it was like a Saigon brothel: Make-out sessions lined up along the entire length of the stadium, kids looking for cheap thrills with their girlfriends but with nowhere else to go. Under the pretense of taking them out on a legitimate date, guys would present their tickets, lead the girls into the stadium, and proceed with the smooching and groping, right there in the sticky thick of the spilled Coke, stale popcorn kernels, and sundry other discarded foodstuffs. And the girls were into it, too.

I had a half-rancid hot dog at the little stand. Tully and I always made hot dogs better, I thought. I couldn't eat more than a few bites of it, and I ended up tossing the rest of it under the bleachers, next to the feet of a guy and girl delicately attempting to neck despite mouths full of orthodontic braces.

Eventually we won the game by a margin of 40 points, and the student body rushed the field in celebration. Someone dumped the Igloo of Gatorade on Coach Horseley. The guys with the painted faces picked Steve up on their shoulders and carried him around the field, where he gestured to the crowd like an Egyptian pharaoh throwing out platitudes to the slaves.

From my vantage point high in the bleachers, they all looked like ants, swarming around a fallen berry for a chance at getting a morsel to taste. But soon, the ant pile emptied out, a file of people rushing from the stadium to congratulate one another on winning the game. Steve, the revered quarterback, had his pick of girls for a one-night stand, I'm sure. Meanwhile, his goon friends got the left-overs, got drunk, and passed out in a weedy field somewhere.

I stayed in the bleachers until they turned out the lights, then felt my way in the dark back to the main thoroughfare and walked home. No one was going to claim that I didn't go to any football games in high school.

❖ ❖ ❖

January 17, 2000

Like I said, my dad had relented on the band thing, and I was back in theater my sophomore year. This time, I was sure I would prove myself to the school and my parents as a capable dramatist. After all, acting is little more than sanctioned lying. And I can lie extremely well, having proven it on many occasions.

Unfortunately, the fall show this year was Noël Coward's *Blithe Spirit,* a really long and not terribly entertaining play about a recently remarried man who is haunted by the ghost of his jealous ex-wife. In 1941, this may have been innovative, wryly funny, and clever, but in 1987 it was more droll and obtuse than anything else, especially for a bunch of high school kids who had never been married, much less widowed. I never did figure out how the plays were selected each year. Mr. Davenport, the balding theater teacher who wore a fedora to try to look younger, must have pretty much had free rein.

I was cast in a minor role. As *Blithe Spirit* is not a musical and involves no gaudy costumes, I was certain my father couldn't raise a fuss.

Blithe Spirit takes place largely within the confines of one house, and of course I helped with the set design, painstakingly working on the details of the English country home complete with a fireplace that blew faux flames, windows that looked out onto a miniature garden, a working grandfather clock, and doors that appeared to be made of carved oak (actually Styrofoam).

The set was fabulous. Even if the melodramatic stars of the play weren't all that great, people were going to look at the set and know that a lot of work had gone into the production.

A month went by, and Steve was strangely dismissive of me, even pleasant—almost. I really only saw him at lunchtime, when I served his crew and took my leave, almost universally without a word spoken between us. It was certainly a nice change of pace, but Steve was busy torturing the new freshmen, so he probably just didn't have time to beat me up or put dead animals in my locker.

When late November rolled around, it was almost time for the big performance of *Blithe Spirit,* and Steve and his goons snickered quietly at their table the entire week before. Steve is no master of subtlety, and it was obvious that they were up to something. Whenever I was around, they would try to control themselves and stop giggling, making it even more apparent that they were up to something.

But I didn't think much of it. I always figured Steve had an agenda, but each day he didn't act on it was another day of peace for me. I knew it would come sooner or later. I just tried not to worry about it in the meantime.

Opening night came soon enough. It was a packed house. The performers paced around nervously backstage, rehearsing their lines, clearing their throats, and telling one another to "Break a leg!"

"You're going to do great!" one would say to another, and then they'd hug. I even got a couple of hugs myself.

The play was going well. And people seemed genuinely thrilled during the séance scene, when the lights dimmed and candles flickered across the set.

One of the clever things we'd done was to design a second backdrop for the set to use in the latter half of the play, when the ghost was causing trouble. The second backdrop was similar to the first, but the actors could no longer use the doors, as they were rigged with wire to let the stagehands open them and slam them shut, as if the ghost was acting up. The backdrop had other neat props built-in, like light fixtures that could be remotely triggered to drop off and break on the floor, and a bookshelf that would catapult all of its books across the room. It was extremely clever.

When the séance was at its darkest, we silently switched the backdrops, hoisting the original up into the rafters, and lowering the trick backdrop into place.

When the lights came back up, everyone saw our masterpiece—crudely scarred with bright red spray paint dripping down the canvas to spell out the words: "FAG SHOW."

Since they usually face the audience, the actors didn't notice at first. And the crowd's shocked silence was offset by the immediate and boorish sound of laughter from the way, way back—laughter that I instantly recognized as Steve Williams, Brett Vogon, Dewie, Lou, and the rest of the Williams clan. This continued for several minutes, and soon many other audience members chimed in along with them.

Of course, in the theater, the understood motto is that no matter what happens the show must go on, and on it indeed went, for another hour, at least. All the while, the "Fag Show" marquee graced center stage.

When the curtain closed, the actors bowed as usual but did not return for any curtain calls. Rather, we all went backstage for an impromptu debriefing from Mr. Davenport, his balding head and neck red, wringing his fedora in his sweaty, nervous fists.

Everyone looked really shaken.

"I'm not going to assign blame, but from now on I want all sets and props checked five minutes before showtime," he began.

A ham-shaped girl named Molly spoke up. "I checked everything at six. It wasn't there then."

Mr. Davenport continued, "That left two hours before the show went on for whoever did this to sneak in and get out. Did anyone see *any*thing?" He looked like he was on the verge of tears. Never trust a problem to a professional dramatist. They're too close to their emotions to be of any use.

No one spoke up.

Davenport went on, "Come on, people. Half of you were here at six o'clock. Didn't anybody see anything?"

Now I knew perfectly well who had done this. I'm sure everyone knew. It was completely obvious that Steve was the guilty party. But everyone also knew what Steve did to people who crossed him. I was walking evidence of that.

Davenport covered his eyes as they welled up with tears.

I sighed. I still don't know why I said anything, but I did. It was probably the combination of seeing a grown man crying, my own anger over the work I'd done being destroyed, and my hope that turning in Steve for this would finally get him in real trouble: expelled, or even criminally prosecuted. I muttered something to the effect that it was Steve Williams.

Davenport looked up from his hands. "What? Alex? What did you say?"

I looked around the room at all the eyes on me and repeated, "It was Steve Williams."

Davenport stood up and said simply, "Let's go."

Things moved pretty quickly after that. Mr. Davenport led me by the arm to see Principal Patterson, who had been in the audience and was waiting in the wings. I repeated my accusation to Mr. Patterson, and he in turn dispatched a group of teachers and parents to round up the Williams gang. I talked briefly to my parents and told them to go home.

Fifteen minutes later, I was standing outside the principal's office while he interrogated Steve and his friends behind closed doors.

Another fifteen minutes went by.

Then another fifteen minutes.

I was about to pee in my pants from nervousness when I was called into the room. It was now past eleven o'clock. As I entered, I felt the cold stares of Steve, Vogon, and the rest of them. It was grueling, and time passed in slow motion.

The principal spoke up. "Alex, I've spoken to these gentlemen about the spray paint incident and they deny the accusations. We don't have any evidence except for you. Did you actually see one of these men painting on the backdrop?"

"No," I stuttered.

"Then how exactly did you reach the conclusion that they were guilty of the crime?"

"I heard them laughing about it over lunch."

"You heard a confession?"

"Not exactly, but I knew they were planning something. You heard them laughing in the audience tonight, didn't you?"

"That's not the point, Alex. The issue here is that we have six men who could be severely hurt academically by an accusation such as this, and we have no hard evidence to go on. No spray can, no paint on any of their clothes, no eyewitness account. And you bring me this story that you didn't actually see them do anything, you just heard them laughing about something over lunch. Did you even see any of them with a can of paint?"

Steve was starting to smirk at me, just barely. He knew I was going to lose this round.

"No."

"Then this is all a waste of time. Gentlemen, you can leave. Alex, please have a seat."

Dewie nearly knocked me out of my chair "by accident" on his way out. Steve said, "See ya soon," as he passed. I knew I was in deep shit. Really deep.

The principal looked at me sternly. "You wasted about an hour of my evening, Alex. Bearing false witness is something I take very seriously. I don't know what you have against our football star Mr.

Williams, but this kind of accusation without substantiation is unacceptable. Completely. I'm going to have to put this in your permanent file, you know."

I said nothing, knowing I was beat.

Principal Patterson scribbled some notes on a piece of paper and didn't even look up to say, "Go home, Alex."

I knew full well what would be waiting for me outside. I resigned myself to a brutal beating, which was completed largely with fallen tree branches, shed early by a pecan tree in anticipation of winter.

When they were done, I lay bloodied and crying in the grass. Steve kneeled down to speak to me, putting his mouth close to my ear, which was ringing so loudly I could barely hear him.

He spoke quietly. It was hard to make out the words, but I could hear him well enough — and I remember exactly what he said: "This is going to be the beginning of a new era of pain for you, Alice. I don't know what kind of shit you think you can pull, but your word against mine? That's always going to be a losing battle for you. Hell, you could have caught me on top of a ladder with the paint can in my hand, and I still would've gotten off. But I'm not finished with you. From now on, you're on the top of my list, Alice, and believe me, it's no fun being at the top of the list."

Dewie and Lou piped in, "Yeah, it's no fun."

"No fun at all."

Steve left me with one last kick to the stomach before they walked back to his Jeep and tore out of the school's parking lot, tires burning rubber.

I lay there on the ground for a few hours before getting up gingerly and walking home. I stayed home from school the next day and the day after that, leaving someone else with the task of fixing the set and cleaning up the "Fag Show" scrawl for the following night's show.

❖ ❖ ❖

January 19, 2000

It was at this time that I decided to confess what was happening to my mother. Dr. C. asks me so many ridiculous questions about her, I figure I ought to say something about Mom in this journal.

My mom doesn't work. Not anymore, that is. She and my father used to work together at the same law office. She was a paralegal there, and eventually she became my dad's first personal assistant.

Soon they began to have an affair, and when their romance became public, one of them was forced to resign. My mother left, and she took a job at another law firm.

A year later, they were married. Eighteen months after that, I was born following thirty-seven hours of labor. My dad was making a very good living for them, so Mom quit her job and became a full-time mother and housewife. She hasn't worked since, but when I started going to school, she started doing volunteer and charity work, which seemed to keep her quite busy.

My mother has always been very loving and supportive, but I don't think she knew much about raising kids. She was an only child and didn't have any experience with younger siblings. I am also an only child due to some unfortunate complications during my birth. My father, of course, was never around to give his advice, and my grandmother on my mom's side had passed away by the time I was born. As a result, there was no one to teach my mother how to be, well, a mother. She read a lot of books on the subject, but that's really not the same thing.

And she got a lot of conflicting advice. One day, my mother would let me suck my thumb. The next day she wouldn't. One week I'd get a lot of spankings. Next week I'd get none, even for the same misbehavior. I never got a good sense of what to do to avoid punishment, which led to a lot of trial and error on my part.

An example: When I was about eight, my mother took me to the grocery store. She left me with the cart and went further down the aisle to pick up some honey. I took it upon myself to push the cart, which was already quite full, in order to catch up with her. Of course, I was too small to steer properly—when I get behind a full shopping cart today, I still have trouble driving it, in fact—and in a few seconds I had crashed the cart into a shelf of jelly.

Five or six giant jars crashed to the floor, spilling sticky red jelly everywhere. My mother heard the clatter, spun around, and shrieked. She didn't know what to do, so she just started crying. A manager quickly arrived on the scene, promised her it would be okay, and since she was such a loyal customer there would be no charge for the broken items. This seemed to cheer her up a bit, but she was still a little weepy on the way home.

She didn't speak to me the entire ride back to the house, but she explained my punishment when we pulled into the driveway. Until I learned to keep my hands off things that aren't my business, I was going to have to eat jelly sandwiches every day as a reminder of what I'd done. I don't know how she expected me to prove that I'd learned my lesson—a lesson of *not* doing something—but I ate those sandwiches for two months solid. Eventually we ran out of jelly, and she pretty much forgot about it. The only real result of this punishment was an intense hatred for jelly, which I carry to this day, rivaled only by my hatred for eggs.

In later years, when I was in middle school, we didn't spend much time together. Four days a week she attended some kind of function—a ladies' club meeting, a homeowners association, an anti-drug rally, a beautify our highways get-together, etc.—and she didn't get home until it was time to cook dinner.

I typically occupied those afternoons with a strict regimen of television, and I had a full three hours planned out daily, including reruns of *The Brady Bunch* and *Gilligan's Island.* There was a cartoon in there, and a half-hour of some Richard Simmons workout show, during which I usually went to the kitchen for a snack or actually did my homework.

It's amazing I didn't become one of those porky little shut-in kids, considering my lack of exercise and poor diet. Most people chalk it up to a fast metabolism.

Anyway, the point is that I didn't have a whole lot of adult guidance during my formative years, and neither of my parents were exactly the type you'd want to confide in about "trouble at school." Which is why telling Mom about Steve probably wasn't such a good idea.

❖   ❖   ❖

January 20, 2000

After taking the beating from Steve and Co. in the aftermath of what would become known around school as the "*Blithe Spirit* Fag Show," I returned home to find my mother waiting up for me. Mud-caked, bloody, and limping, I'm sure I was quite a sight. Mom immediately went into panic mode, retrieving an armload of towels, wet rags, Bactine, Neosporin, Band-Aids, gauze, medical tape, and Mercurochrome. My dad was asleep, and she did not wake him.

We sat in the downstairs half-bath while she silently patched me up. My clothes were thrown away, and soon I was a patchwork of bandages and bruises, bundled up in a fluffy robe. She led me into the living room and plopped me on the couch, returning soon after with a cup of hot chocolate.

She sat beside me with her own mug of cocoa and began the questioning.

"You want to tell me what happened?" she began.

I waited a long time before speaking. "What do you think happened? I got beat up."

"I know that. I mean, by who? Was it someone at school?"

"Well there aren't a lot of muggers in the suburb of Fall Valley, Mom. Of course it was someone at school."

My sarcasm wasn't shutting her up as I'd hoped. The interrogation continued. "Do you want to tell me who it was?"

I'd already ratted out Steve once tonight. I figured a second time wouldn't hurt anything. "It was Steve Williams and his friends."

"Steve Williams?" She was incredulous, bewildered. "The football star?"

"Yeah." Why did everyone call him that!?

"Why would he want to hurt anyone? I thought he was a really nice guy!"

"Well, he's not. He's a real jerk."

"Well I'm going to have to call his mother and tell her what her son is up to." She stood up as if to call her right then.

"NO!" I screamed, grabbing her arm.

"Why not?" she asked, puzzled.

"Because it will only make things worse for me. The reason I got beat up tonight is because I told on him to the principal. He was the one that messed up the set."

"Really?"

"Yes."

My mother was silent for a long while. This is why I never confided these things in her.

"Have you thought about fighting back?" she finally asked, desperate to help with some advice.

"Mom, they're twice my size, and there are six of them. They would laugh at me if I tried to fight them."

"I see."

She thought about it again. "What if you paid somebody to protect you? I mean, we'd pay for it."

"What, like in that stupid movie? Mom, come on!" (I later found out she had recently seen the film *My Bodyguard* on cable and decided to pitch its very plot as a solution for me.)

79

"We could transfer you to another school."

"Like where, Mom? The nearest private school is over forty miles away." I knew; I had checked. "Who's going to take me? And Dad wouldn't pay for it. He'd just tell me to suck it up."

"I don't know then, honey. What can I do for you?"

"Nothing. You can't do anything. I hate to say it, but Dad's right. All I can do about this is suck it up. There're only a couple more years to go before Steve graduates."

"Well, that's a good attitude," she said, and she was serious. My mom was always ready to look on the bright side of things.

Mom got up and went to the kitchen for more hot chocolate. When she came back, there were a few minutes of hugging, followed by some more Mom brainstorming, resulting in her idea to sign me up for karate classes, for self-defense. Fortunately, she quickly forgot all about that. In fact, she forgot about my problem altogether.

Soon after we both went to bed, and she let me stay home on Thursday and Friday to recuperate, giving me a welcome four-day weekend. Travis came by on Saturday to see how I was doing, and he slipped me a couple of those little bottles of vodka. "You know, to raise your spirits," he said. They did.

I returned to school on Monday, and Steve was too preoccupied with his upcoming vacation plans to give me much notice, despite my being at "the top of the list." Thanksgiving vacation was later that week, so we only had three days of school. Steve was headed down to Padre Island to do a little amateur surfing in the Gulf of Mexico's 18-inch swells.

On Wednesday, however, Steve did dump an entire tray of spaghetti on me, just for kicks, and because he couldn't come up with something better on the fly. But it was a lot better than getting beaten up. I'll take food torture any day.

❖   ❖   ❖

January 22, 2000

Thanksgiving in our family always meant an hour-and-a-half drive down to the home of my grandparents (my father's folks) for turkey and football-watching on TV. They live in a once-thriving industrial town on the Texas coast. But thanks to pollution, lack of urban development, a horrible climate, and the slow disintegration of the oil market that had built the town long ago, it had become a ghost of a city. It's still rumbling on. Natural gas flares, miles and miles of pipe, and fields of enormous squat cylinders holding endless gallons of crude oil dominate the landscape. Downtown is almost completely boarded up—you have to go to the docks if you want to buy much of anything. The only exceptions are the thriving Wal-Mart and K-Mart superstores, situated across the street from one another, right off the city's main square.

My grandfather worked for one of the oil companies his entire life, retiring at the age of seventy-three. They had lived forever in the same house midway between downtown and the oil refineries. My dad's boyhood room was still the same as he'd left it when he went away to college, some forty years ago. Virtually everything else in the house was stuck in the same time capsule, with the exception of a very few modern conveniences, which I'll get to soon enough.

Traveling to visit my grandparents was a journey repeated twice each year: once at Thanksgiving and once at Christmas. And of the forty or so times I made these holiday trips, the experience was the same. Thanksgiving of 1987 was absolutely no different.

One typically thinks of lunch being served around noon. Sure enough, my grandmother was a cook with recipes under her apron that hadn't changed since World War 1, and every Thanksgiving and Christmas the food was ready to eat promptly at noon.

We never arrived at their house by twelve o'clock, though. At that time, we'd still be at ours, waiting for my dad to get ready to leave. Typically, he'd do some work at the dining room table from seven to eleven, despite encouragement from my mother to get dressed.

Then he'd disappear into the bedroom under the guise of preparing to leave, only to re-emerge five minutes later in a T-shirt and shorts, heading out for "a quick run" before we left. Thirty minutes after that, he'd return home hot and sweaty, just like he did after mowing the yard, and insist that I let him drink half of my Coke or whatever else I was consuming to tide me over until lunchtime.

By noon, he would be in the shower. By 12:45, my mother and I would be sitting in the car, waiting for him to exit the house and join us. It was normally a little after two o'clock when we arrived at my grandparents' for lunch, invariably to the disapproving stares of my Aunt Patrice and Uncle Paul (her second husband—I don't remember the first), who lived near my grandparents and had no such problems with tardiness. Aunt Patrice works at the Wal-Mart and Uncle Paul works at the K-Mart across the street. They can get you great deals on just about anything.

81

The real problem with our lateness was its effect on the food. A turkey was always cooked in the special, 1940s-era poultry roaster. Giblet gravy, one of the more disgusting substances on the planet. Green bean casserole on the stove. Yam casserole with marshmallows melted on top. Cornbread stuffing. Homemade rolls. A can of cranberry sauce emptied into a dish, and left in the unblemished form of cylinder so as not to spoil the presentation. A bowl of pickles and olives. Fruit salad with that white gelatinous substance clinging to the fruit—I guess that was marshmallow cream. Several pies: pumpkin, cherry, and lemon meringue, usually.

And all of this was stone cold by two o'clock.

Everyone was starving by the time we arrived, so we typically headed straight through the house to the kitchen, where my relatives had already lined up to fill their plates. When they heard our car arrive, they started digging in.

None of my relatives seemed to have a problem with cold food. They'd fill their plates then sit down and eat, no questions asked and no grimaces. But I learned early on that a cold Thanksgiving dinner is worse than no dinner at all, so my dining experience became a game to see how I could get a hot meal. First, I'd hide the metal-rimmed china somewhere and exchange it for another, microwave-safe plate from the cupboard. Next, fill the plate up and quietly slide it in the microwave oven—the sole modern convenience in the kitchen—for at least a minute. Last, add items that are supposed to be cold, like the fruit salad, then go to the kids' table to eat.

I ate all my holiday meals with my cousin Jamie. He was the son of Aunt Patrice and her first husband, and he was about six months younger than I. Jamie had grown up in this rural, economically void region, and I don't even think he'd ever been to a city with a population of more than 5,000 people. Jamie was deathly silent and moody, with a square jaw and eyes that pointed regularly toward the ground. We had nothing in common—nothing—and we ate our meals in awkward silence.

After lunch and a slice of lukewarm pie, the grown-ups retired to the living room to watch college football on the big-screen TV my father had so graciously given to my grandparents, expressly for this purpose (and to make Aunt Patrice's deadbeat husband look bad). Within five or ten minutes of flopping on the couch, my dad was asleep, meaning we couldn't go home for hours.

Options at this point were pretty scarce. Either Jamie and I went to one of the Marts, Wal or K, or wandered around the hauntingly vacant streets of the town in search of something, anything, to do. Usually, we did the latter, and Jamie eventually started telling stories about the local houses and their residents. He knew who had lived and, when relevant, who currently lived in every house on every street we passed. He knew where they had worked, when they had lost their jobs, and where they moved. He knew who was in prison and what they'd done to end up there. He knew who was having an affair with whom. He knew everything.

Most of the stories were as boring as the rest of the town, but on that particular day we passed a house and stopped in front of it. It was a smallish, white house with two stories, boarded up long ago but obviously suffering under the hands of vandals.

The windows were covered with only a few tattered scraps of wood. There was no glass in the panes beneath—only wire screens that had been ripped to shreds over the years. The front door stood cracked open a few inches. The boards over it had disappeared long ago. Inside it was pitch black.

Jamie paused and told me about this house. According to his story, in the '60s and '70s it had been the home of a woman and her son. The woman's husband died in a chemical explosion on the docks when the boy was only six, and she was left to raise him alone. Horribly affected by her husband's death, the woman lost touch with reality, ignoring the boy completely. If he had been any younger, the kid would have died from neglect, but he managed to survive, taking care of himself. He never went to school. He just stayed at home, playing with unlikely toys, alone. He also befriended the stray cats in the town, and soon over thirty of them resided in the house or on the weedy, overgrown lawn.

Years later, the police showed up at the house, having been called to investigate an overwhelming stench that you could smell a block away. The boy, it turned out, had killed his mother along with all the cats, and had piled all the animal carcasses on top of her, in her recliner in front of the black-and-white television where she sat all day and slept every night. The boy, then about eighteen, killed himself in the attic. He performed all of these acts with a big kitchen knife, and had finally killed himself by stabbing himself in the head, directly through his right eye.

Jamie said that wounds like those leave a lot of blood, and when he'd gone into the house, on a dare, a few years ago, you could still see the blood stains near where the TV used to be. Splatters of

83

blood led up the stairs to the second floor/attic, where a huge pool had stained the wall near where the boy had done himself in.

But it wasn't the blood stains that were so scary, Jamie said. Blood you expect. It's the other things in the house that give you the creeps. Downstairs it was like a regular home. Living room, bedroom, kitchen. Furniture where it should be, everything relatively tidy. He said there were even lace doilies still on the back of the sofa.

But upstairs was the boy's sanctuary. Newspapers had been meticulously piled up—not as entire issues, though. They had been carefully disassembled, and all the front pages were stacked with the other front pages, all the page threes were in a pile, the page fives in a pile, and so on—all neatly lined up with amazing attention to detail, right up to the day of the murder/suicide.

Along one wall of the room, inexplicably, were rows and rows of mayonnaise jars, with the labels carefully removed. Hundreds of them, stacked carefully to make as efficient use of the space as possible.

Jamie dared me to go up to the attic and have a look, but I demurred. He didn't push it. He said he had nightmares all the time about those mayonnaise jars. It just freaked him out to think about what the boy had intended to do with them, and that they were still there, still standing at attention, waiting for someone, more than ten years later. It freaked me out, too.

Anyway, Jamie said, stray cats wouldn't go near the place anymore.

January 26, 2000

After Thanksgiving, I returned to school as normal, and Steve began to give me near-daily beatings. Well, not exactly beatings. He started by punching me in the arm, once a day, in exactly the same place. I guess he didn't want me out of school anymore, since he couldn't torture me if I wasn't around.

At first this wasn't a problem, but after two days my arm had developed an enormous, tender bruise, and each subsequent punch hurt more and more. At home after school, I'd examine the spot and find black concentric circles spreading farther and farther. It soon became painful to even the lightest of touches, and I started wearing three or four shirts to cushion the blows. It helped a little.

After about three weeks of that, it was almost Christmas vacation. Steve could see me wince every time he came near me, and he offered me a deal.

"I'll stop punching you for a week if you do an errand for me," he said.

"What errand?" I was intrigued, and the pain was so bad I'd do just about anything.

"I need you to take a girl somewhere for me."

"I don't have a car."

"That's okay, you can borrow hers."

"I mean, I don't have a license. I haven't even taken Driver's Ed yet."

"Look, do you want to do the errand, or not?"

It didn't take long to decide. I said, "Yeah, I guess so."

Steve explained the details of the errand. I was to drive a junior named Marisa to a place called the Women's Center, wait there for four hours, then drive her back home. Steve didn't have to tell me she was going in for an abortion. Everybody knew what went on at the Women's Center. I wondered who was paying, but I was surprised that Steve cared enough to arrange for her transportation.

"Why aren't *you* going?" I asked him.

"Dude, I don't go for that kind of thing." Steve's friends broke out in wild laughter.

Steve gave me her address and said to be at her house at 7:30 a.m. Saturday morning. And as promised, he let up on the punching.

The last Saturday before Christmas vacation, I walked over to Marisa's house, about ten minutes on foot. Her house was average for Fall Valley, moderately contemporary with a minimum of character.

I rang the doorbell, and soon a gruff man, obviously Marisa's father, came to the door.

"You must be Steve," he said. Before I could correct him, he added, "Hang on, and I'll get Marisa."

He called for the girl and she soon came downstairs. Marisa was a pretty blonde, but she slouched too much and her hair fell in her face.

Marisa's father said as she reached the entry, "You kids have fun on that hiking trip. Are you going to go climbing in those shoes, Marisa?"

"Shut up, Dad," she muttered, and quickly ushered us out the door and to her car in the driveway.

When we got into her Honda Civic, she turned to me and glared. "Who are you? Where's Steve?"

"He didn't tell you I was coming?"

"No. Where is that asshole?"

"I don't know. He sent me to take you to the clinic. My name's Alex."

"What the hell? He told *you* to take me? I guess he told you I'm pregnant."

"Not in so many words, but all his friends knew about it."

"You're not one of his friends?"

That one got me laughing, but soon I could see that Marisa was not amused, so I shut up. "No. He hates me."

"Great. That must be what he thinks of me, then." Marisa was silent for a few moments, then she started crying softly into her sweater.

I tried to comfort her. "Hey, he does this to everyone. Steve Williams doesn't care about anybody except himself. We're both disposable pieces in his little games."

"Just shut up and let's go. Now I'm glad I'm getting the abortion. I would never want to have that asshole's baby."

Fortunately, Marisa's car had an automatic transmission. I had driven a few times with my dad, the clinic was only a few miles away, and there wasn't any traffic, so getting there wasn't much trouble. We soon arrived at the Women's Clinic, fully intact.

By this time, Marisa had started crying again. Obviously she was experiencing severe guilt over the abortion, which is perfectly understandable. Steve had probably been through this once or twice before and knew what would happen, which is why he sent me.

Marisa didn't get out of the car. We just sat there for a while, in silence. I didn't really know what to do. I tried not to look at her for fear of making things worse. Finally, she spoke, "I have to be in there by eight. So I better go in."

"Okay, let's go."

We got out of the car, and I locked the doors. We walked up the path to the clinic and went inside.

At the reception counter, a middle-aged woman greeted us. "You must be Marisa," she said.

"Yeah," muttered Marisa.

"We just have some paperwork for you to fill out. Is this the father?"

Marisa looked over at me and smirked. "No. There is no father."

"I understand."

Marisa hastily filled in the forms and handed them back to the receptionist.

"It's $350, payable now."

Marisa looked down at me. "I don't suppose Steve gave you any money for this?"

I shook my head no.

Marisa sighed and took out her pocketbook, counting out tens and twenties until she'd amassed the fee on the countertop.

"Okay, come right this way, Marisa," the receptionist said, leading her beyond a thick, electronically locked door that you had to be buzzed through, obviously a countermeasure against anti-abortion militants. Then she said to me, "You can have a seat in the waiting area."

Marisa vanished into the back of the clinic and I sat on an overstuffed couch in the well-appointed waiting room. There was one other guy there, a twenty-something man who kept his head in his hands almost the entire time, stricken with either grief or fatigue or both. The waiting room had a selection of popular magazines, and a television ran the same infomercial over and over again—some cream product that promised to strengthen your fingernails like diamonds.

Hours went by, and after finishing *People, Us,* and *Vanity Fair,* I turned to *Glamour* and then to *Marie Claire,* then to *Modern Bride.* I was about to pick up *Women's Day* when Marisa finally emerged through the same door she'd entered. It had been almost four hours, and I realized I was starving.

Marisa didn't say anything, she just glanced at me and walked straight outside. She was waiting at the car by the time I got out the door.

We drove home slowly and in silence. When we arrived at her house, I carefully parked the car against the curb, driving back and forth, back and forth, trying to ease the car nearer to the edge of the road with little success. (For a first-timer, parallel parking can be a bitch even if the spot's wide open.)

I killed the engine and gave Marisa her keys back. She clutched them like a security blanket then finally looked at me, her eyes red from crying all morning, and probably the night before, too. "Thanks a lot, Alex. You didn't have to do this."

"Sure I did," I laughed. "I pretty much have to do whatever Steve tells me to do."

She looked genuinely puzzled, asking, "Why?"

I laughed again. "Because he'll beat the crap out of me if I don't."

Marisa looked at me askance, genuinely confused. "Steve Williams? He may be a jerk, but he's not someone that would beat somebody up . . . is he?"

"Of course he is. Why doesn't anyone believe Steve is a monster?"

"I don't know, I mean, you know, he's just a nice guy most of the time."

"Well, I don't hang around those circles. Besides, Marisa, I'm sure you can see for yourself now that Steve isn't the great guy people say he is."

Marisa got really quiet again and finally got out of the car. As she walked up to her front door I yelled after her that I was sorry, and that I didn't mean to upset her.

Marisa just disappeared into the house without a sound. I didn't go after her, opting instead to put it out of my mind. After all, what had happened to Marisa certainly wasn't my doing. So I headed back home, anxious to get something to eat.

❖   ❖   ❖

January 27, 2000

That afternoon, the phone rang at our house. Normally, the phone ringing on Saturday evening was not a cause for celebration or alarm—it was usually just a solicitor or a wrong number, or maybe even Travis telling me to get my ass over to his place. But this time was different.

From my room, I heard my mother answer the phone. After a brief and muffled conversation with the party on the other end, she called up to me, "Alex, it's for you!"

Followed by a pause, and then: "It's a girl!"

My first instinct was that it was a joke of some kind. Either my mother was kidding with me or someone was prank-calling. Either way, I'd get on the line and clear up the hoax pretty quickly.

I picked up the phone. "Hello?"

After a second, an oddly familiar voice said in a whimper, "Alex?"

"Marisa?"

"Yeah."

I could hear my mother breathing on the other extension, so I yelled, "Mom, I got it!" With a clatter, she hung up the receiver.

I didn't quite know what to make of Marisa's call, and I quickly got really nervous. Finally I said, "I think she's gone."

"That's good," Marisa replied.

"What's up? How'd you get my number?"

"Well, I looked you up in the yearbook to find out your last name, then I looked in the phone book for people with your last name that lived within walking distance of my house."

"That's pretty resourceful of you."

"It wasn't that hard. I don't have anything else to do."

"Is that why you called?"

A pause. "No. I just needed to talk to somebody."

"Why would you want to talk to me?" I asked, truly perplexed.

"Because nobody else listens like you do. And because I'm sorry for being so mean to you this morning."

"That's okay. You weren't mean. I think I can understand your situation."

"Well, I don't think you really understand my situation, Alex, but I think maybe you can relate on some level."

"Yeah, on some level."

I didn't think I was much of a listener, either. Marisa, like most people, simply confused awkward silence, nervousness, and boredom with paying attention. That's one thing I really like about most women: They will always spin your faults into a plus whenever it helps them out. I didn't like to talk, and that gave Marisa freedom to gab away without fear of interruption.

And gab she did, about Steve Williams, about how she'd been obsessed with him for six years, about how she didn't think he knew who she was but then he wooed her after a football game, about how they'd been on two dates before he threw himself on her in his Jeep, about how she'd gone along with it, about how he never called her again, and about the agony of having to call him when she found out she was pregnant. Totaling up their time together, I figured they'd had roughly a six-hour relationship, which had resulted in months of grief that wasn't anywhere close to being over.

Marisa went on for hours. There was some laughter; there was some crying. I heard her whole life story, from growing up in Eugene, Oregon, to moving to Fall Valley when she was ten to what she ate for a snack five minutes before she called me. But mostly she talked about Steve. I think she wanted me to advise her to forgive him, to forget about him, and to get on with her life. Unfortunately, she called the wrong guy for that. I said nothing, and her grudge festered.

Finally, night fell and Marisa's father called her down for dinner. She thanked me again for being such a great listener and hung up. We had been on the phone for close to three hours, and it was time for me to eat as well.

I went downstairs to the kitchen, where my mother was putting the finishing touches on a roast for supper. "So who was that on the phone?" she asked.

"Nobody," I replied.

My father piped in, "Who were you talking to, son?"

Mom said, "Alex has a girlfriend, I think."

My dad was ecstatic to hear this. "A girlfriend? That's my boy!"

I sighed. "She's not my girlfriend, she's just a friend from school."

"Well, she's a girl, and she's a friend," my mother said, trying to act sly, "that makes her a girlfriend, I think."

I gave up on the conversation. Nonsense like this was the reason I never told my parents anything.

I thought that Saturday night was a one-time thing, but Marisa kept calling, twice the following day, then two or three times a week for a long while after that. I was the only one she would confide in about her abortion, even though Steve had personally spread the rumor to half the school. But Marisa pretended that nobody else knew, that it was a secret between her and me.

I knew it was a lie, but somehow, I didn't mind pretending along with her.

❖ ❖ ❖

January 30, 2000

Every year that I can remember, my father has thrown a Christmas party at our house for the people at his office and select clients. (This way you can have a big party and get a tax write-off at the same time.)

That year—1987—was no different. The second Saturday in December, my mother cooked all her usual "fiesta" party dishes—beef and chicken fajitas, some kind of chicken casserole that never looked appetizing but actually tasted very good, and various dips—supplementing the feast with food from a catering service. After spending the morning working in the yard, my father made the trek to the liquor store to pick up the gallon jugs of J&B, Cutty Sark,

Tanqueray, and no-name vodka—none of which would ever be consumed, as his party guests favored Jack Daniel's and Miller Lite.

He'd stash in the garage case after case of beer, chilling it in the four or five Igloos that never left the garage and were never used for anything else. It was impossible for the sixty or so people at the function to consume all that alcohol, but my dad's motto has always been "Better safe than sorry," and he always overbought, just in case.

When I was younger, I used to complain about having to help out by taking the beer out of the cardboard cases, filling the coolers with the bags of ice, and loading them up—a job that could take hours. But I didn't complain anymore. Here was our chance to get all the free beer we could carry. I figured my dad wouldn't even notice if an entire cooler vanished.

That evening, as the guests began arriving, I quietly excused myself and went to my room to tell Travis my plan. "Rally the troops," I said. "I'm bringing the provisions over."

No sooner had I hung up the phone than it immediately rang, practically still in my hand. I answered it and was greeted by a long pause and a sigh that could only mean Marisa was on the other end of the line.

Normally I would have had no problem chatting with her for hours on a Saturday evening—or reading a magazine while she talked—but tonight was different.

"Hey, Alex," she finally said.

"Hi, Marisa. Say, I can't talk now. I'm getting ready to go out."

"Where are you going?" She sounded hurt.

"I'm going over to my friend Travis's house. I have a cooler full of beer that I'm taking with me."

"Really? Where'd you get that?"

"My dad's having a party. Look, I gotta go before people get here and I can't get it out of the garage." I steeled myself to hang up on her, but she persisted.

"Wait!" A pause. "Well . . . can I come over there, then?"

Now this turn of events made me stop and think. Marisa had never met my geeky friends, and they certainly had never been in the presence of any girl on the It List, even if it was the B– It List where Marisa resided. "Are you sure you want to do that?" I asked.

"Sure, why not?"

She was going to force me to explain the obvious. I should've known as much. Marisa was pretty thick in the head. "Um, because you won't know anybody, and they won't know you."

"I like to meet new people."

"Uh, these *people* . . . Um, how do I put this? I don't think you're going to want to associate with these guys, you know? They're not, um . . . you know, you don't even like to wave at me at school."

"That's different, Alex. This sounds like a party."

I sighed, trying to figure out what to do. Finally I realized that there was no way I was going to get a 20-gallon cooler full of ice and beer out of the garage and a mile away from our house to Travis's without a car. A bicycle wouldn't even cut it—even if I sunk to riding one—so I finally relented.

"Okay, Marisa. Come on over, but get here as soon as you can."

I waited for her at the curb and finally she arrived after fifteen minutes, just as the party was getting started. "Sorry I'm late," she said. Obviously she had spent some time on her makeup and outfit, despite my assurance that that kind of thing wouldn't be necessary tonight.

Getting the cooler to her car was a two-man job, and I barely counted as a man, let alone Marisa, who counted for about half a man. She managed to carry her end of the Igloo about ten yards before dropping it on her foot, whereupon she collapsed in the grass crying. Hauling a cooler-full of beer through the yard was already the most obvious thing I could have been doing, and having a crying girl in bright red lipstick and a pink mini-skirt along for the ride was only making things worse.

I dragged the cooler the rest of the way to Marisa's car, and she finally pulled herself together enough to help me heave it through the hatchback and cover it with a blanket.

I slammed the trunk shut, pleased with a job well done, and took a cursory look back at the yard to survey the damage. In the morning, my dad would probably notice the gouges in the grass that the dragging end of the cooler had made, but I figured he'd chalk it up to general party mayhem, and that in turn would convince him that people had had a really good time the previous night. That would make him feel good—no matter how much he loved that lawn.

Minutes later, we had arrived at Travis's house. Marisa killed the ignition. "You're sure about this?" I asked.

"Of course," she insisted. "Now get out of the car."

We walked up the sidewalk to Travis's front door and knocked. Travis hated it when you rang the doorbell. The door swung open and Travis greeted us with his permanent smile/smirk. But his demeanor quickly changed to astonishment when he saw Marisa, who walked straight into the house without an invitation.

In the corner of the living room, James and Tommy were playing dice on the small table. They abruptly stopped their game in mid-roll and stared at the intruder in their midst.

It took a second before anyone said anything. And then it was James who leapt from his seat and nearly ran over to Marisa, standing at attention in front of her and extending his hand in greeting. I thought he was going to salute her for a second, but they just shook hands.

"I'm James," he said.

"I'm Marisa. The beer's in the car." With that, she gained our immediate respect. This was a girl who clearly had her priorities straight.

Travis invited her to have a seat while he sent James and Tommy to fetch a round of beers from the Civic. After learning of the size of the cooler, Trav had decided that bringing the entire thing into the house might not be such a great idea. In the unlikely event that his parents came in the room, hiding the cooler would have been impossible.

Two rounds later, we had all warmed up considerably, and Marisa had inserted herself as just another peripheral member of our gang, like James's cousin Johnny, who came by from time to time, or Travis's childhood friend Derek, who lived thirty miles away and rarely made it to our neighborhood anymore.

Of course, this peripheral person had blonde hair and extremely large breasts, which instantly made her the life of the party.

After two more rounds of beer, plus a visit from a bottle of gin, courtesy of Travis's closet, we were all the best of friends. Marisa wasn't even a strange girl anymore. She was just one of the guys, and she had an amazing capacity for alcohol. I don't know if she developed that before or after her trouble with Steve.

James impressed Marisa with one-armed push-ups. When Tommy said something rude, they wrestled on the floor until Tommy squealed Uncle, to Marisa's delight and to Travis's stern disapproval. (He promised swift vengeance if anything was broken.) Travis spun his favorite tunes for Marisa, who was shockingly unfamiliar with the classics. I just drank and took credit for being the one who brought the girl to the proceedings.

We stayed up until two or three and got stinking drunk, then Marisa went out to her car and fell asleep in the passenger seat. I

93

slept on Travis's bedroom floor, and around 8 a.m. I went outside to find Marisa still there, snoring with her mouth open and lipstick smeared all over the seat where she'd tossed and turned.

I woke her up and bummed a ride home, dumping the melting ice and water out of the cooler before we left. The beer was long gone.

Marisa dropped me off at my house, and I hustled the cooler back to the garage, upending it to dry, next to the others that my dad had already taken care of. The gouges in the yard were far worse than I had thought the night before; daylight really brings out tracks in the grass. But I was sure this would only make my dad secretly even happier, even if he grumbled about it aloud.

That was the only time Marisa came to one of our cocktail parties at the Pickford home, and she called me less and less after that. By February, she hardly called at all. The last I heard from her was that summer, and then it was as if she had disappeared.

I like to think that our party had been thrilling and cathartic for her, to the point that it finally broke the spell that Steve and the abortion had placed on her. She certainly seemed to have had a good time, and I never saw her smile as much as she did that night.

Then again, an equally likely scenario—made possible only after thirteen years of hindsight—is that she finally realized I was a dork, and exposing her to my friends was the thing that pushed her into that awareness. But she was too nice to simply stop calling. So she weaned herself from me gracefully.

I don't know which is the truth.

Whatever. The fall semester ended, and Christmas vacation came and went in a blink. Before I knew it, it was 1988, and school was about to start again.

❖   ❖   ❖

February 2, 2000

But, as it turned out, the school year would not start quite so soon for me.

Classes resumed on a Wednesday in January, and I showed up at 8:20 along with everyone else, going through the motions of the first day of the new semester, on which nothing much of anything ever happened, except the taking of roll and the issuing of new textbooks. Steve was even too preoccupied with high-fiving his buddies to give me a second glance, and I served their lunch with little commentary.

By the time I had walked home, I knew I was coming down with something nasty. After thirty minutes in the house, I was still shivering like I had crashed through the ice atop a frozen pond. I lay on the couch for a while, pulling a blanket over me and staring at the TV, and when I tried to get up an hour later I felt so dizzy I couldn't stand.

Mom got home around six and immediately knew something was wrong. Before long, I was carefully tucked into bed with three heavy blankets piled atop me, both a glass of water and a can of 7-Up on my bedside table, a sleeve of Premium saltine crackers, a small bowl of Cheerios, the remote control for the small TV at the foot of the bed, and assorted medicinal supplies, including a thermometer and various vials of Tylenol, NyQuil, and Robitussin.

I was sick for a while. Almost three weeks. Eventually I went to the doctor and was diagnosed with pneumonia, which meant taking massive loads of antibiotics that made me puke almost daily and just made me weaker and weaker. There was nothing to do but watch television all day long—though, fortunately, something saved me from the horror of watching soap operas: the 1988 Winter Olympics.

That winter, you may remember, the Olympics were held in Calgary, and the memory of the U.S. hockey team's dramatic win in 1980 was still the announcers' favorite topic. They were apparently hoping for a repeat despite a crummy 1984 showing. But once again, the United States didn't even place in the medal contention that year. As a matter of fact, they've never been in the top three since winning the gold in 1980.

All eyes were on the flamboyant figure skater Brian Boitano, one of America's sole hopes for Olympic glory that year after speed skater Dan Jansen fell down twice—right after his sister died of leukemia. The East German Katarina Witt repeated her 1984 victory in women's figure skating and continued her reign as a teen role model and Wheaties box stalwart. American Bonny Blair won a single gold in speed skating. And that was about it. The rest of the games were a blur of eastern European names and flags that I could never keep straight.

But I watched all the events. My dad brought me the sports page every morning, after he'd finished reading it, so I could keep track of statistics and plan around that day's events. For some reason, I found that I loved the biathlon and wanted to make sure I wasn't napping when it aired.

Reading was impossible, as I found it too difficult to focus my eyes and got a pounding headache anytime I tried. So when I got completely bored or there was nothing on TV, I passed the time by drawing reproductions of the photographs of the athletes that were printed in the newspaper. A ski jumper pointing his body into the sky. A four-man bobsled. A guy on a luge. I got pretty good after the second week, and I think my mother still has some of the drawings tucked away somewhere.

Those drawings make me think back to when I was in third grade and had to have my adenoids removed in a near-emergency operation, because I could barely breathe, they were so inflamed. I didn't get ice cream in the hospital, like kids who get their tonsils out. I got ice chips, like women in labor. What kind of a ripoff is that?

Back then, I was visited in the hospital by my teacher, Mrs. Mamula, who brought with her a stack of "Get Well Soon" cards that had been hand-made by my classmates using the artistic tools familiar to every third-grader: construction paper, glitter, and tempura paint.

The cards were sweet and thoughtful, born from the hands of children who had not yet learned how to hate. They featured crude pictures of birds, dogs, houses, airplanes, and cars—all meant to raise my spirits and make me anxious to return to school. Little Gretchen Cook had even written "I Love You!!!" in crayon. There was no hidden agenda among my schoolmates, nothing but genuine sweetness put onto paper.

But that was third grade. When I was sick with pneumonia in '88, I didn't get any such cards. Travis came by once, but he didn't stay long for fear of contracting my illness. He didn't bring any liquor this time, either.

I doubt anyone else even realized I was gone.

❖ ❖ ❖

February 4, 2000

It became painfully clear that I would recover soon enough. I would have been perfectly happy to stay in bed for the next two and a half years, never to return to Fall Valley High, but it was not to be. The Olympics were coming to a close, and as February approached, I returned to school, where I had to play catch-up for the rest of the semester.

I was still extremely weak. When I got home from school, a nap was always in order lest I fall asleep before dinner. On weekends, I rarely stayed over at Travis's past ten o'clock. Often I fell asleep on his couch, and they would just leave me there all night.

Steve greeted me the morning of my return in front of the school. He hadn't had anyone to serve him lunch for three weeks, and he was pissed. He'd let it go this time, he said, because he knew I was sick, but I better redeem myself with excellent service in return for this generosity.

I did my best, but that Friday I found myself more exhausted than ever. I carried over the first load of trays, each carrying two slices of pizza—the usual Friday lunch—then returned for the second. Balancing them on my forearms, I carefully walked back to Steve's table. But I was out of practice and so very tired, and I stumbled and fell right as I reached the table. Two of the trays ended up in Steve's lap, pizza-side down, an enormous mess on his new, pre-faded blue jeans.

The trays clattered to the ground as Steve leapt from his seat, and an ominous silence spread out from Steve's table, like the concentric waves of a nuclear blast, leaving dead everything in its wake.

All eyes turned toward us, and Steve stared down at me on the ground, where I was still on my hands and knees, paralyzed in fear. With so many teachers around, Steve didn't cut loose with his rage. Instead, he calmly sat back down, and I thought for a moment that everything was going to be all right. Conversations started up again, and lunch continued as normal. But Steve turned to his friends and muttered, "Clean up all the crap on the floor, and meet us with it outside, near the special ed building."

Steve then stood and hauled me up off the floor and put an arm around me so that it looked friendly. But he actually held me in a vise-like grip that I could never have escaped from. We briskly walked out to the special ed building, a few hundred feet from the cafeteria, while Steve's goons scraped up the mess. I didn't know what they had in store for me, but I was sure it was going to be awful.

I was right.

Steve pushed me into the mud to the side of the special ed building—the "D Wing," as teachers called it—and pushed his knee into my shoulder blades so I couldn't get up. I was so tired, I doubt I could have gotten up anyway.

I saw Dewie approaching out of the corner of my eye, a pink cafeteria tray in his hands. The other guys ran along behind him, laughing and hooting in anticipation of the events to follow.

Dewie arrived at my side and dropped the tray in front of me. It had been mounded with the food from the floor and the leftovers from the other trays. The mass looked like something out of *Close Encounters of the Third Kind*, a disgusting tower of once-edible food mashed together, pulverized pizza slices composing the core, with flecks of corn and carrot dotting its surface, and a sticky white sheen of milk covering the entire thing.

"Eat it," Steve said.

I resisted, trying to pull away, but Steve just pushed me down so my face was almost in the tray.

"Steve, I can't," I said, begging him.

"Yes, you can."

"Look Steve, I'm sorry. I've been sick, and I didn't mean to drop the—"

"Shut up and eat it . . . or we'll force-feed you."

Dewie, Lou, and the rest of them hooted again. They wanted nothing more than to shove the food down my throat.

I resigned myself to take a bite. It had all been reasonably edible food, I rationalized. So what if it was all mashed together. I tried not to think about the fact that most of it had been on the cafeteria floor.

Some tastes aren't meant to go together. Cold milk and hot pizza are two of them, I quickly learned. After one bite, I thought I was going to puke. But they made me keep eating.

Eventually, I did puke, throwing up all over the wall of the D Wing and the tray in front of me. Steve let me up after that. I think that's what they wanted in the first place. If I'd actually finished eating all the food and held it down, they wouldn't have been nearly as thrilled themselves.

The rest of the day is a blur. I cleaned myself up in the bathroom the best I could, which wasn't very well. Steve's stained pants drew a lot of attention from other students, but anyone who commented got a quick warning to shut up followed by a finger pointed at me. I was just as soiled as Steve was, with mud, food, and a bit of dried vomit staining my clothes.

Inevitably, Steve and whoever he was talking to burst into raucous laughter, and Steve's confidante, in turn, spread the story to someone else. By the end of the day, I could part the sea of people in the halls just by walking through them, leaving shrieks of mocking laughter in my wake.

I didn't know how much longer I could take it.

I ought to be grateful, I suppose.

I was only beaten up a couple of times. Embarrassing moments like the D Wing incident were relatively few and far between.

Others didn't fare as well. I already wrote about Tino, Arnold, and Pat Landers (of Pat Landers' Fag Palace fame), all of whom reached ends more bitter than mine. With each passing year, Steve found a new group of targets, carefully culled from the weakest of the freshmen entering Fall Valley High. As the species is a self-replenishing stock, Steve could spread his reign of terror simply by marking the passage of time.

And not only that, when you attack the weakest of the species and eliminate it from the food chain, a new weakest automatically takes its place. By the time he hit senior year, Steve Williams was regularly terrorizing over fifty individuals. At the same time he was more popular than ever; those fifty people represented less than one percent of the student body—one percent that the rest of the school would likely just as soon forget existed. To the "middle class" of Fall High, that one percent's persistent cries fell on deaf ears. I ignored them as well, too preoccupied with my own survival to stick up for people even lower than me on the food chain. But I would make it up to them. We would all get our revenge soon enough.

I think about those people from time to time.

Gene Thomson was a quiet, short, and not particularly bright kid two years behind me. As a freshman, he somehow found himself stuck with the responsibility of updating the big sign in front of the school every Monday morning before classes started. It was one of those backlit signs with black, plastic letters arranged to spell messages like "V-BALL FINALS FRI. GO RAIDERS!" or "CONGRATS SENIORS GRAD. 5/23" or even "BLITHE SPIRIT THIS WKND!"

Gene did his work at about five in the morning every Monday. Once, Steve and his crew decided to play a prank on him, so they sneaked up quietly and took the ladder, stranding Gene atop the sign. As the story goes, Gene started crying, and Steve said he'd put the ladder back if Gene changed the sign. Gene readily agreed, and on display for the entire school that morning was the message "GENE THOMSON IS SUPERGAY!" One of the S's was actually a 5—they only had two of each letter. The sign stayed up all day long because Steve hid the ladder in a ditch behind the school, and no one could find another one.

Gene complained to the principal and Steve got detention hall for one day. Later, he threw Gene through a plate glass window, which put him in the hospital for four days.

A guy named Tim stood up against Steve once. He was in my class, and he had taken so much of Steve's shit after three years that he finally snapped, screaming at Steve in the middle of the cafeteria. I actually witnessed this particular event.

Steve surprised everyone, even Lou, by not doing a thing to Tim. Tim stormed out, obviously feeling victorious, and everything went back to normal.

But that afternoon, Tim found all four of his Camaro's tires slashed. That weekend, his yard was covered in trash culled from the school's dumpster. Tim's family had to hire a professional crew to fumigate the place.

I remember another kid, Reid, who was a year behind me. He was a huge sci-fi fan, obsessed with *Star Wars* and *Star Trek,* and he would wear a yellow shirt in imitation of the *Star Trek* uniform, with the little crescent-shaped logo on it, at least twice a week.

He never did anything to make Steve mad—and neither had Gene Thomson, until he tattled—but Reid was definitely an outcast, and as such he was someone to vilify. Steve carefully typed a note on stolen school stationery informing Reid's parents that he could no longer wear *Star Trek*–style clothing to school. Reid's parents took this at face value and ordered it so, and Reid ran away from home that very night. His photo was plastered across the school with a huge "MISSING!" tagline, and daily announcements were made over the school's loudspeaker, begging for information as to his whereabouts.

Reid turned up a week later, but he'd never say where he'd been or what had happened to him. He never spoke about it at all, despite thrice-weekly sessions with psychiatrists after school. Whatever it was that happened to him, he never wore that *Star Trek* shirt again.

February 10, 2000

Easter 1988 was memorable for two reasons. First of all, it marked the final year, long overdue, that my parents made me play hunt the eggs along with all the attendant Easter Bunny nonsense. Second, it marked the arrival of a new addition to the family.

Despite hating the holidays categorically, my dad is big on tradition. He'll moan and groan about presents under the tree, how much money we're wasting on them, how I ought to get a job, and how inefficient it is to put up all these decorations and then take them down three weeks later.

But secretly he loves that stuff because it reminds him of his childhood and gives him a feeling of contentment, as if all is right with the world because there are mounds of presents under the Christmas tree—the tallest tree at the lot.

Easter was the same deal. Outwardly, my dad grumbled about how candy would rot my teeth, but he was the one who insisted that we continue the egg hunt, even going so far as to secret away a twenty-dollar bill in a big golden egg my mother had made out of an old L'eggs panty hose container and some metallic paint.

Easter didn't carry the excitement that Christmas did. My parents usually had to wake me up to get things rolling, unlike Christmas, which still saw me up before dawn, pacing around the living room in anticipation of a gift bonanza.

But candy? I could get that any day, and after fifteen years, you would think they would have figured out how to pick out better stuff. Not so. They still chose off-brand jellybeans, hollow milk chocolate bunnies, and Jordan almonds that threatened to chip a tooth. The few high points, like Reese's peanut butter-filled chocolate eggs, were few and far between. But the twenty-dollar bill was nice.

That spring, things were a little different. It had been pre-decided by my parents that this would be the final egg hunt, so they went all out. I went through the motions, looking for the twenty or so eggs hidden in the backyard, when finally I came upon the prized golden egg. Immediately I cracked it open, itching for the twenty, only to discover a slip of paper inside instead.

It was a note in my dad's handwriting, which read, "This year, the golden egg carries something better than cash. Check the garage."

I was too young for a car—I hadn't even taken Driver's Ed yet— but I high-tailed it through the house and to the garage to see what the surprise was. I swung open the door, but it was pitch black, so I flipped on the light. A set of beady little eyes on a streamlined white face greeted me.

My parents had bought me a pet rabbit.

"His name is Hopper," my mother said, appearing behind me.

"I thought I couldn't have a pet," I replied. My dad was allergic to cats and dogs, so we had been a no-animal household all my life.

"He's allergic to rabbits, too, so you'll have to keep him outside. And they make a big mess. You wouldn't want him in the house, anyway."

"Wow . . . thanks."

I went over to check out Hopper face to face. I'd never imagined owning a pet rabbit. They didn't really do anything. Dogs you could play with, and cats, at least, had personality. Rabbits just sat there and pooped all day. I didn't think I'd take to a pet rabbit.

I was wrong. Over the next few weeks, Hopper became a really good friend, mainly because he sat there in his cage and didn't make a fuss while I doted on him. He let me pick him up, and he was really soft. It was very comforting to sit outside after a bad day at school, behind the garage where Hopper's cage was, and stroke his fur. He enjoyed the attention, and it calmed my nerves a lot.

It suddenly made a lot more sense why Marisa had chosen to spend time with me.

❖　❖　❖

February 11, 2000

With Easter over, school persisted, the same way I imagine jobs at the post office or on assembly lines do. Time practically stood still, and only the ticking off of calendar days gave any evidence of its passing. We were in the home stretch to summer, and the halfway point of my high school career, but it seemed to last an eternity.

With football season over, Steve seemed more docile than usual. But I got lulled into a false sense of security. I should have realized that, with no outward target at which he could point his anger, he would bottle it up until the right moment presented itself.

I touched off that moment with a simple oversight. I was late with Steve's lunch by fifteen minutes. I had stayed after third period to discuss my final World History project with the teacher. This spilled well over into the lunch hour, and when I arrived at Steve's table, oblivious to the time, I found him sitting there patiently, waiting to be served.

I hustled through the lunch line, barging to the front and forgetting to take my change. Hurriedly, I set the trays down in front of Steve (first, as always), then the rest of his gang, apologizing all the way. They said nothing and proceeded to eat in silence, which was very strange, because they were always catcalling some girl or making fart jokes. The virtue of silence was simply foreign to them.

That afternoon I stayed after school in the library to do some research for that history project. It was seven o'clock before the library closed and I was forced leave, and I hurried home to see Hopper.

I went out back to his cage, and I found Hopper sprawled out there. Usually he sat in a little ball, so this was quite a surprise. I got closer, and he looked a little sick. He was breathing roughly, his body heaving up and down with each breath.

I ran in to get Mom, and after one look she hustled us both into the car to the emergency vet clinic.

Hopper died in my arms about halfway there, and I cried the rest of the way.

When we got to the clinic, we were ushered into an examination room, and a vet came in after a few minutes. After I told him what had happened, half-talking, half-crying, he felt around on Hopper's body to see if he could find any obvious cause of death. Finally, he asked, "Has the animal spent any time unsupervised outside of his cage recently?"

"No," my mom said. I shook my head, too.

"I think he's eaten something poisonous. He's had massive internal distress, I can tell."

The vet asked if he could do a quick X-ray, which would cost thirty-five dollars, and my mom agreed. A nurse came in and took Hopper's body away, and that was the last time I ever saw him.

Twenty minutes later, he returned with a film and popped it up on one of those X-ray viewing screens. By then, I'd calmed down.

"You see this?" he asked, pointing to the midsection of the picture. "I think he got into something metallic and ate it. Metal shavings, nails, and screws, by the looks of it. It just ripped up his insides."

"Alex," my mom asked, "how could he get into something like that?"

I looked at her, knowing all too well what had happened to Hopper. But I couldn't say that here. "I don't know, Mom. I guess they must have just fallen into his cage from the roof or something."

She looked at me with a sad face and said, "I'm sorry, honey."

We drove home in silence. Hopper was the last pet we ever had.

The next day at lunch, Steve asked me if I'd ever seen the film *Fatal Attraction,* which had come out the previous year. I said I hadn't. Steve told me it was really cool and that I ought to check it out on video someday.

❖   ❖   ❖

February 13, 2000

Saturday night we sat in the dark in Travis's living room, quietly drinking rum and Cokes, a beverage that can be hastily thrown together and consumed quickly to achieve the desired effect. Somebody had put *The Best of the Doors* on the tape player, and the melancholy opening lyrics to "The End" seemed particularly prescient.

I was wrecked—emotionally, and now, mentally, thanks to the rum—and after telling the story of Hopper, the normally jovial room fell silent.

It was the first time somebody mentioned the solution. I don't know who it was. I was too drunk to remember who said what. I don't think it matters, but regardless, I can't remember who said it.

And that was how it started: as a whisper in the air. It wasn't a plan. It wasn't a conspiracy. Just voices in the darkness, wondering how best to kill a perfectly hypothetical man.

Naturally, James, obsessed with weapons and the various modus operandi of killing, was bubbling with information on the subject. Before long, he launched into a monologue about the pros and cons of various modes of homicide.

"It used to be you could just shoot somebody, throw away the gun, and be done with it. No gun, no fingerprints, no proof that you did it. Now they'll dredge the Gulf of Mexico to find a gun somebody threw away. And believe me, they'll find it. I don't know how many times they've found pistols in the swamps of Florida. Guess there's a lot of shootin' going on there.

"It's too bad, too, because if you shoot somebody the right way, you can be sure he's going to croak. Take my father's piddly little .22 caliber handgun. Now this thing isn't much more than a good BB gun, but if you deliver a shot at point blank to the head, that .22

caliber bullet will rattle around inside that guy's skull until he's got nothing but pudding left in there. If he doesn't die on the spot, he's a vegetable for life—which may even be better than killing him."

We sipped our drinks, entranced.

"But you'd really want something that looks more like an accident or a suicide. And it's really hard to fake a gunshot suicide—you gotta do the note, the angle of the bullet has to be right, you've got to get the powder on his hands, and you only get one shot.

"So what else is there? Knifing is out. I mean, even though it's a satisfying kill and someone like *me* could do it—you know, a couple of well-placed slashes to the wrist—it's really messy and it'll take him forever to keel over. Unless you knocked him out first, it's just too hard to pull off properly without leaving a lot of evidence behind.

"Another good one is carbon monoxide poisoning. When he gets drunk and passes out, just start his car, close up the garage, and go home. But if he wakes up, you're dead. And you have to get him drunk, into the car, and into a closed garage. That's tough. Too big of a risk of eyewitnesses, also. I guess hanging is out, too."

I finally interrupted James's discourse. "Say it's a guy who's not the suicidal type. He's got too much to live for. You know, president of the company or something."

Travis piped in, "Yeah, but those are always the ones who do it. It turns out their lives are hollow and all that shit."

"Yeah, maybe so, but can you imagine the attention a big-shot suicide would bring? There would be a huge public outcry. And martyrdom, that's just no good. It has to look like an accident."

James went on, "Well, then you've got a couple of choices."

We listened.

"Auto accidents are the most common cause of death. Just cut the brake lines and send him downtown."

I shrugged off the suggestion. "Not a guaranteed kill, and we're a long way from downtown. Not to mention, they'd find the cut brake line and they'd suspect something was up."

James grunted his approval and continued. "A fall is good—no evidence."

"Yeah, but how would you get him someplace high enough to push him? This is Texas. We don't have any cliffs or ravines nearby, just fields and swamps and maybe a manmade hill here and there. The best you could do is the roof of a building, but you've got a witness problem again—and the access issue."

Travis piped in, "Ah, geography conspires against us."

James offered another. "Drowning? Take him down to Padre Island and haul his ass out to sea?"

"Say he's a good athlete. If he managed to swim to shore, you'd be dead."

"Hit him on the head, then."

"Wouldn't look like an accident. They can always tell if you hit the head with a rock, or if the head hit a rock by itself."

"Yeah," said Travis, "how do they do that?"

It was silent for a long while. James threw out some bizarre options. "Electrocution?" Too difficult. "Animal attack? Spider bite?" Not feasible. "Plane crash?" Not remotely realistic. "Set his house on fire?" Again, there'd be evidence.

James finally concluded, "I guess you're stuck with poison."

"That always looks like murder, though," I protested. "If you put rat poison or cyanide in someone's drink, they can detect that immediately, can't they?"

"True, but that doesn't mean it's murder. With strychnine and cyanide, yes. But what if he eats a poisoned mushroom? Or drinks a bottle of bleach instead of vodka? Or gets a bad bag of coke? It could look like suicide, but usually it looks like an accident. Especially if there's no way to tie someone to the crime."

Travis said, "There's always a way to tie someone to a crime."

"True," replied James, "but the game of murder is about *probable* cause and *likely* suspects. Police are busy people, and people die all the time. The cops don't go sniffing around for murder suspects when it's obvious there's been an accident. If a guy was to die of, say, mercury poisoning, they'll assume he's been drinking tainted water. No one is going to come looking for a murderer. Who has that kind of mind? And they're especially not going to come looking if the water really is tainted."

We were quiet for a long time, as Jim Morrison crooned the final words of "The End." James was right, maybe for the first time in his life. It was possible to kill someone and get away with it. With the proper planning, it would be easy. Trivial even.

And just that thought cheered me up. No one was really going to kill anybody. Hell, we were just talking about a hypothetical person that didn't really exist. And people talk about things all the time and never do them. That's what daydreaming is all about.

The conversation abruptly changed to lighter topics. Someone put a Police album on, and soon we were all happy-drunk instead of pitiful-drunk. There was no more mention of murder.

Still, it secretly comforted me to know that, from now on, Steve's life would be in my hands. I could end it anytime I wanted. And he would never know that I was in control.

Maybe someone should have told him.

❖ ❖ ❖

February 16, 2000

The rest of the year, somehow, didn't seem so bad. Not when Steve tripped me in the courtyard and I fell into a fresh pile of dog shit. Not when his buddies cut up my clothes while they were still on my body. It didn't really matter. I just let it roll off my back. If you're ever upset about something somebody has done, just imagine the many ways to kill them. It does wonders for the psyche.

By the end of the school year, Steve had been named Mr. Fall Valley, an award bestowed upon the coolest, most popular guy in school, even though he was only a junior. Steve made All-American as a football quarterback. He got invited to play in the big Texas vs. California game they had that year, and he won it for Texas. He was also an All-State baseball star, and as a starting pitcher, he went six innings in the state championship, shutting out the opposing team and giving up only four hits.

Put simply, Steve's popularity was never greater, which meant he was given the keys to the school, with free rein to do just about anything he wanted. No one did his homework for him anymore — because he was never assigned any. He was given straight A's in all his classes, whether he attended or not. He had whatever girl he wanted. All he had to do was point, and she became his. No chit-chat or awkward dating rituals. Local then national newspapers, magazines, and TV programs did profiles on him. *Sports Illustrated* gave him a full page. Fall Valley High had never before seen such a character as Steve Williams pass through its sleepy suburban gates. And few people dealt with him more often than I did.

Finally summer came, and it was time to forget about Steve Williams for a few months.

By the time our report cards arrived a week or so after the end of the year, it was clear my grades were headed down again. An A– eighth grader and a B– freshman, I was now a C+ sophomore, headed into what looked to be a C– junior year.

My dad gave me the speech late one night in my room. He said I was full of promise and potential, and how I needed to overcome whatever obstacles I was facing to get back to that A average. It was understandable, he said, to be an underachiever. Maybe school wasn't motivating me. I would have to learn how to motivate myself. Without better grades, I would never make it into a good college. And I wanted to go to a good college, didn't I? He would always be there to listen if I wanted to talk about it some more. And hadn't this been such a good chat? We should do it more often.

The lecture droned on and on, and all I could think about was getting out of there so I could head to Travis's to drown my sorrows for three solid months.

I had been working on some new drink recipes and couldn't wait to try them out.

❖ ❖ ❖

February 22, 2000

Dr. Carter and I have been meeting for eleven months now. He is extremely encouraged by the progress we continue to make, and today he asked if he could read my journal. I made it clear that that wasn't an option, and I've taken to locking this diary up in the fire safe I keep hidden deep within my closet, under the pile of decaying shoes that are worn beyond usability but which I'm too lazy to throw out.

I don't understand how this so-called "progress" has been achieved. I haven't told him what I did. I haven't even told him who Steve was. "It was just really rough in high school," I'll often say. He asks for details. I change the subject. He gets out the Rorschach blots or something. We dance around the issues.

I guess my progress can be attributed to the writing. And maybe that means I don't need Dr. Carter at all. But every time we meet, he asks me how much I've written, how I think it's going, how many words it is. I give him a rough count every time we meet, and he keeps a running tally with a graph, showing my progress. It's steady and solid, and it motivates me to keep working on it, for some reason.

If I didn't have Dr. Carter to egg me along, I don't think I'd have the patience and energy to keep writing.

Regardless, Dr. Carter says we will only have to meet once a week from now on.

February 23, 2000

The guys were soon impressed with my mastery of alcoholic mixology, with my ability to make Grasshoppers, Tequila Sunrises, White Russians, and homemade Bloody Marys, all from memory. Like all good bartenders, I even invented my own drink, the Warhammer (equal parts Jägermeister, 151-proof Bacardi, and raspberry liqueur), which nobody could stomach.

Tommy had a second cousin who was twenty-one. He attended the local junior college, and had moved to town a few months earlier. This made procuring hard liquor far easier than it had been the previous summer. However, he charged us more than we would have liked to pay, so unless somebody had an influx of cash, we stuck with beer and wine.

Tommy's cousin also had connections for more potent and less legal substances, and soon we found ourselves with enough pot to last the summer. From time to time, we also found ourselves buying magic mushrooms, LSD tabs, low-grade cocaine, various pills, and ecstasy, all of which served to really liven up the summer beyond typical wine cooler drunkenness.

Mind you, we were not heavy drug users. Alcohol just wasn't cutting it; we were simply experimenting with different substances to take our minds off of our otherwise boring lives.

To wit: For young and unmotivated guys, there's no job less rewarding or less interesting than canvassing your neighborhood for a Worthy Cause. Actually, I guess telemarketing is worse, but canvassing rates a close second. At least telemarketers get to stay inside on the 100-plus-degree days that are common during the Texas summer.

If you're not familiar with canvassing, it is a practice that many local, regional, and national political action groups use to raise awareness of their cause and money for their coffers. Canvassers, usually high school and college kids with no legitimate work to do during the summer, go door to door in a preassigned section of the city, distributing leaflets and asking for donations.

That summer, Travis and I signed up with the Clean Water Coalition, a well-known regional group with a rather obvious goal. One day, a week or so after school let out, we hitched a ride with Tommy's cousin to the Clean Water headquarters, which turned out to be an aluminum building in the back of an industrial park. We were greeted by a congenial secretary, who had us fill out an endless procession of forms, after which we were led into another room for orientation.

Orientation consisted of a brief but effective brainwashing about the importance of clean water. The orientation was led by a big-haired Texas woman who I would never have pegged for the hippie type these organizations usually attract. "Look at this contaminated water," she said, holding up a glass jar filled with an opaque liquid that might as well have been molasses. "This was taken directly from a Texas river."

Here are some statistics and gruesome pictures on how contaminated water can affect the babies of expecting mothers. Here is how our elected government officials have repeatedly voted against clean water. Here is what we can do to fix all of this.

They handed us brochures and other propaganda, and the woman explained the setup. We went door to door and asked for donations. We could find sample scripts in the literature, but we were encouraged to improvise. Anything to get them to donate—because we got to keep half the money. The rest went to the CWC to further the cause. We were encouraged to hit up friends and family, too, because they would always give money, she said.

Each Friday, we were to report to CWC headquarters, where all the canvassers gathered to see who the week's money winner was. The weekly winner would receive a prize, and the monthly winner would receive a bigger prize, and the winner for the entire summer would receive a mammoth prize. But she couldn't tell us what the prizes were.

Within thirty minutes we were out of there, and the big-haired woman said we could probably get a few hours of canvassing in before six, when CWC recommended we cease our efforts, because once the husband got home from work, the odds of getting money out of a house dropped dramatically. Our assigned region would be a roughly 8-square-mile area around our neighborhood.

On the walk home, we gave it a shot. We rang a few doorbells and stuttered through the poorly remembered and unrehearsed speech about the importance of clean water. Generally we got kind yet skeptical stares and doors shut in our faces. But some people gave us money. Not many, but some. By the time we got home, we had amassed sixteen bucks. With eight going to CWC, that was four dollars apiece. It had taken ninety minutes to canvass our way home. That worked out to $2.66 an hour. It made the concession stand look like executive work.

Travis and I talked about just keeping all the money, but we stuck out the canvassing for the rest of the week and showed up at CWC headquarters on Friday at five o'clock, as we had been instructed. For the first time we got to meet our co-canvassers. Most of them were lazy teenagers like us, but a few took the job seriously. These were the kids gunning for the mystery prizes. And one of them, a short kid named Eric who had curly black hair and a tie, won the week. His prize was a Scrabble game. Big Hair told us that the prizes would get better all summer, and that the monthly prize would be spectacular. Eric was named the official "Go Getter" of the week, and they shot a picture of him with a Polaroid camera and taped his smiling face to the wood paneling as a source of inspiration to us all.

Before long, Travis and I realized that we would make no progress unless we split up, and soon we were making above minimum wage but well below the Unlimited Potential we had been promised. Before long, I found the only way to get through the dull days was to carry a flask of liquor with me, so I could get quietly drunk as I wound my way down strange streets with a pack full of pamphlets. By the end of the day, I'd be so tired from the walk in the blistering sun that I could do nothing but lie down on Travis's floor and fall asleep. I don't know how people work on assembly lines and such, but I have enormous respect for them now.

Before long, the dream of riches had completely dried up, and Travis and I regularly traded off between last and second-to-last place on the weekly money tallies. We were dubbed the "No Getters" by CWC management, and we were constantly prodded, cult style, to see if we needed any help or if we were having personal problems, or if we'd like to tag along with one of the Go Getters to improve our standing.

We declined all of these opportunities, and before six weeks were up, we were invited to leave the CWC organization.

It wasn't a big loss. We'd made enough money to keep us in booze and drugs for the rest of the summer. And that would prove to be a whole lot more fun than soliciting money for clean water.

❖ ❖ ❖

February 25, 2000

Controlled substances make people do nutty things, things that in retrospect seem more stupid than funny. That's why they're *controlled*. I'm amazed we never got hurt or killed, but like I said, invariably it seemed like a good idea at the time.

When we were all highly toasted on weekend or even weekday evenings, we'd venture out into the suburban streets to create fun and excitement where we could. One favorite pastime was to find a nicely wooded piece of road and stretch thread or yarn across it. To each end of the string, we'd tie the empty aluminum cans generated earlier in the evening. Then we'd situate the string at the perfect height and scramble well out of view.

Soon enough, a car approached. When the car hit the thread, it would catch in the grill and yank the cans from the bushes. They made a huge clatter as the car dragged them along the pavement, and we'd roar with laughter at the sight.

What happened next depended on the driver. If he had his radio up too loud, he probably wouldn't hear the cans, and he'd drive off, usually losing the clattering contraption a few hundred yards down the road, or sometimes taking it with him for the rest of his journey. Sometimes, the driver would simply stop, get out, see the cans, remove the string, and drive off without a word.

And sometimes the driver got really pissed. This was the best. You knew you had a hostile victim when he slammed on the brakes and skidded to a stop, stormed out of his car, and starting yelling into the night when he discovered the cans.

One guy in a pickup truck was the best of all time. When he saw the little rig he screamed, "Come on out, you little shits! I'll kick your asses!"

He started searching among the trees, which got us a little scared, even though we were hiding a long way away from him. He was a big guy, too, with a shotgun in his rear window. We hadn't considered the possibility of armed retaliation. Fortunately, his white trash, big-hair girlfriend rolled down the window and yelled at him repeatedly to get back in the car, that she was tired, and that he was being stupid. After a couple of minutes, the guy gave up his search, threw our can-and-string rig into the bed of his truck, then peeled out. We all laughed so hard, my belly was sore from the hysterics.

When the Fourth of July rolled around, we splurged on Roman candles and other fireworks. Shooting Roman candles in an empty field is okay, but it's much more fun to have fireworks wars. The only problem is that they're impossible to aim, and they go really slow, so you never hit anyone. If somebody does get hit it's always luck. And even though they just bounced off you and plopped to the ground, whoever did the shooting usually claimed to be a great marksman and had to be given due respect for the rest of the night.

But fireworks were expensive. When they ran out, we'd often just hang out on the playground down at the elementary school. Usually we'd get beers, chips, cookies, and/or ice cream and just sit on the wooden fort or on the swings or on the see-saw and do nothing. There wasn't much you *could* do, as the air went from blisteringly hot during the day to bearably warm in the dead of night.

For weeks, we whiled away the days at Travis's or outside. All that changed, however, when an unexpected gift fell into our laps in the middle of July.

❖   ❖   ❖

February 26, 2000

I've written very little about Tommy mainly because there is so little to write about. He was one of those skin-deep people that rarely thought of anyone but himself, always looking to get rich and famous without doing any work, and thus destined to go nowhere in life.

We tolerated him for the reason most losers are tolerated: He made us feel better about ourselves. We might have been losers, too, but we weren't *that* bad. Tommy just took up space and never had a lot to say, and it was easy to put him in his place when he opened his mouth.

But one hot afternoon that summer, Tommy redeemed himself for years of idiocy when he announced that he had been asked by a friend of his father's to house-sit for the rest of the summer while the owners were gone on vacation. The homeowners had a son who was in our class, a tubby little guy everyone called Bean, even though his name was Mike. I don't know why. Bean's house was a few blocks away from Travis's, and we had the run of it for the next two months.

There is no better joy known to a budding alcoholic teenager than an empty house with no restrictions, and before night had fallen, we had relocated our base of operations to what became affectionately (if obviously) known as the Party House.

The accumulated stash from Travis's closet was carefully relocated, on foot. James went to the Safeway that afternoon to obtain beer, wine, and mixers. We threw out everything in the refrigerator to make room for our goodies. The stereo was quickly reloaded with our favorite tapes and discs, and the bass was turned up on the equalizer. The only job anyone took seriously was feeding Bean's dog Watson, a huge golden Labrador retriever that was very friendly and quickly became the summer's mascot.

That night, the Party House rocked like you wouldn't believe. A game of quarters in the dining room turned even more fun when James spilled a full mug of beer across the table, letting it drip onto the carpet without a care. We turned the music up all the way, just to see how far it would go. Travis used the spray nozzle on the sink to hose down Tommy, soaking most of the kitchen. And somebody threw up in the bathroom, missing the toilet entirely. Watson stank of spilled beer.

Bean had a plentiful wardrobe hanging in his bedroom closet, and when something spilled on our clothes, it was a simple matter to find one of Bean's T-shirts to wear. James started this trend on that very first night. First, he got wet in the beer spill. Second, he accidentally burned a hole in the first of Bean's shirts, prompting him to go fetch a second. By the end of the summer, Bean's closet was bare.

In fact, so was the rest of the house. Before long, we had ransacked every square inch of the place. He had the same computer as me, and I flipped through every one of his floppy disks and took the games I didn't already have. One drunken night, we opened up the machine and put pizza inside. We sealed it back up and left it that way for the rest of the summer. I don't really know why we did it, except that we were drunk and it was funny at the time.

It was only a couple of days before we found Bean's father's *Playboy* stash. Well, he only had two of them in the back of his closet, but it was like striking gold when we found them. Even better was finding his mother's vibrator, a little red streamlined number. We didn't even know what it was when we found it, but we figured it out when we turned the knob and witnessed the telltale buzzing.

Of course, the best part was that Tommy protested all of this. At first, he insisted that we keep the house in perfect condition. When we started raiding the closets, he got upset and tried to put his foot down, but that had all the effect of a friend's kid sister holding her breath until you gave her some candy.

Within a week, enough damage had been done that Tommy just gave up. He figured the worst was over and that we could always clean it up later.

Wrong again. One of our favorite pastimes quickly became

kitchen hockey, a game played with a real hockey puck on the lino-leum floor of Bean's kitchen. We played two per team or one-on-one with a referee and used brooms and mops for hockey sticks. Goals were marked off with tape, but we pretty much just slapped the puck around until we got tired. I don't think anyone ever suc-cessfully kept score to the end of a game, mainly because of the constant arguments over whether a shot had hit the wall on the in-side or the outside of the line of tape. Plus, there was the alcohol-fueled stupor we were all perpetually wandering around in, which didn't help us keep track of who was winning.

Anyway, the problem with kitchen hockey was the puck. It turns out that real hockey pucks leave big black streaks when they're used on surfaces other than ice. Especially linoleum. I remember trying to wipe up one of the streaks to no avail. They were like skid marks left by a car tire and they weren't going anywhere. I wager those streaks are still there to this day.

The house's fenced backyard made an excellent staging area for subversive pyrotechnics. Conveniently, a canister of gasoline had been left outside, next to the lawn mower. (Presumably, Tommy was supposed to be mowing the yard while he was house-sitting, but he waited to do it until the day before they came home and the grass was almost 2 feet high. This turned out to be an all-day chore.)

The gas wasn't being used, so it made an excellent catalyst for some great experiments with fire, my favorite of which was piling a mound of fireworks at one end of the back porch and drawing a line of gasoline around the porch to the other end. Light the far side of the line and watch it burn its way to the fireworks and *Boom!*—just like in the movies! Again, by the end of the summer, deep scorch marks crisscrossed the porch, the backyard, and even the fence. (As a side note, experiments with the fence were not so successful.)

But our finest hour came when word of our Party House spread through the community. The legend moved from some of the low-est echelons of coolness (namely us) to the next-higher level (the Key Club), to the next level (the Math Club), to the next level (the National Honor Society), to the next level (the Computer Club), to the next level (the United Literary Society & Latin Club), to the next level (the Fall Valley Singers), to the next level (the band), and to the next level (the golf team), which is about as far as the news had spread by the end of the summer.

Over the weeks, this built a steady progression of increasingly cool people who joined the Party House festivities. Before we knew it, *women* were showing up, without armed escorts. Without dates, even. Okay, they were girls. But they were really cute girls, for the most part, except for some of the butch ROTC chicks that James always brought around.

Fortunately, we'd had Marisa to practice on, so we could at least be semi-smooth when it came to behaving around the opposite sex. It's not like they came because they were interested in *us,* anyway. The girls came for one reason: free booze/drugs and no adult supervision. By the end of August, a weekend rarely went by when at least one poor girl didn't pass out somewhere in that house.

A typical Friday or Saturday night had thirty people hanging around. Not that these were huge parties like the toga party in *Animal House.* They were just excuses for people to get drunk, and people often came by on the weekends when they didn't have a better engagement.

We threw a good party. It wasn't hard, with no one around to answer to. Just crank the music, point the way to the refrigerator, turn down the lights, and your work is done. When the party's over, just shove the empties into a plastic bag and you're finished. No need for any fancy cleaning; it wasn't our house.

I usually worked as *de facto* bartender, which seemed to impress a lot of people, and I got to make plenty of rum and Cokes, which was about the only highball anyone knew how to order. Plenty of partygoers thoughtfully brought their own alcohol, and we often ended up with a bigger stash than we'd started with. We'd just roll that over to the next weekend and supplement it with that week's earnings from canvassing or whatever other jobs we'd scrounged up.

That was a typical weekend. To a moderate percentage of the Fall Valley student body, it had become cool to hang out with yours truly.

The weekdays were mellower, with the lights down low and quiet boozing in the living room. And believe it or not, it's your typical Wednesday or Thursday that I remember with the most nostalgia.

❖   ❖   ❖

February 29, 2000

The game was called Truth or Truth. It was an obvious variation on Truth or Dare, without the Dare part. I don't remember why we dumped the dares. I guess it was just too easy to embarrass one another with physical stunts.

Truth or Truth was always played with plenty of alcohol and with the lights completely out. Musical accompaniment was also a must, usually in the form of Pink Floyd.

It was the last Wednesday in August. School would be back in session next Tuesday, and I dreaded it.

We were trying our best to get through the massive stash of beer and wine coolers that we'd amassed and ignored in the Party House refrigerator. There was no way we'd have room for all of it back in Travis's closet, and we had to be out of the house by Sunday at noon, when Bean and his family returned.

Those games always started innocently enough.

Travis said, "Alex, truth or truth?"

"Truth."

"What girl do you like the most."

"You all know that," I said. "Alison O'Malley." I didn't know at the time that she had been dead for three weeks.

Travis went on, "Okay, but why don't you ask her out?"

"Huh," I scoffed. "Because she'd say no. It would be embarrassing."

James piped in. "Well, that would hardly be the most embarrassing thing that's happened to you."

"Shut up, asshole," I retorted, quickly changing the subject. "At least I don't go for those nasty bull-dykes like you do."

Everybody laughed. "They're not dykes, you jerks. They're honorable women."

That just made us laugh even harder.

"Okay, James. Truth or truth?" said Travis.

"Truth."

"What of these rumors that you have a bunch of porno magazines under your bed."

"False," replied James.

"And that those magazines relate to the subjects of overweight and pregnant women?"

A pause. "False."

"And that one of them is called *Whalers?*"

James started to crack. "Not true."

"And that Vaseline can be detected, smeared on the pages? And that a half-empty canister of said substance may also be found under your bed?"

James was getting heated, "Who told you that?"

Travis replied, "Your cousin, Johnny, of course. He's searched your bedroom high and low, and that's only the beginning of the depravity."

We all had a good laugh, and James was silent for a long time.

"And now, your punishment for lying—cheating at the venerable game of Truth or Truth." This was where the Dare portion of the game could still be found, although here it served as punishment. "Alex will mix a concoction of beer, ketchup, and chocolate syrup, and you will drink six ounces of it."

Everyone groaned, and I leaped to my feet to hustle together the foul potion. It was ready inside of a minute, and we turned the lights up to watch James choke it down. The look on his face was priceless. It was very rare that someone tried to get away with a lie at Truth or Truth. It was the best form of interrogation around. You always got caught.

The game went on as usual for a while, with typical questions and answers.

"Tommy, is it true you record yourself singing in the shower?" Yes.

"Tommy, is it true your mom caught you beating off while you were singing in the shower and recording the whole thing?" Um, yes.

"Can you come up with any way for us to get out of school this year and keep the Party House instead?" No, all around.

"Where are you going to college?" Answers: Don't know. Don't know. Nowhere, probably.

"What was your favorite part of the summer?" The Party House. The angry guy with the pickup truck who hit the string of cans. Watching James drink the beer-ketchup-chocolate mixture.

Eventually, Travis asked me what my least favorite part of the summer had been. While it technically happened while school was still in session, I answered, "Watching Hopper die."

The room was silent for a while, and "Comfortably Numb" from *The Wall* echoed through the house. The house felt empty, and in the dark, I felt alone. I was vaguely aware of the stench of garbage. We'd probably forgotten some discarded fried chicken bones in some corner or closet.

I finally asked Travis, "Truth or truth. What do you want to accomplish this year at school?"

Travis said, "I want to get through to May with as little hassle as possible."

"Tommy?"

118

"I want to start a new band and play a real gig down at the Speakeasy."

"James?"

"I want to earn the Compton Medal in ROTC and read *The Iliad* in the original ancient Greek."

Travis asked, "What about you, Alex?"

I said nothing for a long while. I was going to say, "Same as you, Trav." That wouldn't have been a lie, but it wouldn't have been the truth, either. What would it matter to say what I was thinking? I wasn't really going to do it.

But what did I want to accomplish, more than anything? Everybody already knew the answer, after all. It was as plain as day.

"I want to kill Steve Williams."

❖ ❖ ❖

March 1, 2000

That Saturday was our last hurrah at the Party House, and we were determined to go out in style. By nine o'clock, we had the biggest crowd yet, maybe fifty people crammed into the place. People who normally wouldn't give me the time of day were having a great time at my party. I made them drinks. I told them jokes. I was no longer a faceless, nameless geek.

By 1 a.m., the party was dying down, and people had pretty much left to go home to meet curfew or go park somewhere for illicit sex. Not that people didn't do that right in Bean's or Bean's parents' bedroom, too.

Travis, James, and I were still high from the party. Tommy had passed out on the couch, but we were still looking for more good times. The alcohol was about gone, and it was James who first mentioned that he was hungry. "Let's go to Denny's!" Travis exclaimed.

Now that was the best idea any of us had come up with in weeks. The only problem was that Denny's was more than ten miles away, and Travis's brother wasn't around to cart our asses to the all-night coffee shop on the Interstate.

However, Tommy had turned sixteen a few weeks earlier, and he had been given a crappy hand-me-down 1984 Toyota Corolla. The Corolla was parked out in Bean's driveway, just begging to go for a ride.

It was the end of the summer, and it just felt right to go out with a bang. We'd been breaking laws left and right for the last two years, so adding driving without a license wasn't a very big deal. We were confident that Tommy would not press charges even in a worst-case scenario.

Into the car we piled. James wanted to drive, Travis rode shotgun, and I sat in back. The drive out to Denny's was quick and without event. It was around 1:30, so the streets were pretty deserted, especially in the suburbs. We parked at Denny's and confidently strode inside to order coffee, pancakes, ice cream sundaes, and other late-night treats.

After an hour at Denny's, we started to get the sour glances from the staff, and rather than risk them calling a law-enforcement official, to whom we'd likely have to explain how three fifteen-year-old kids had arrived there and why they were so drunk, we opted to take our leave. We piled back in the Corolla and James peeled out of the parking lot as we left.

While the drive to Denny's had been fueled by alcohol-dulled senses, the drive home took that and mixed in three or four cups of stout coffee. When you're drunk and you've had a lot of caffeine, things just get weird and tense, and your stomach kind of knots up in protest of all the abuse it's getting.

Sure enough, James decided to take the scenic route home, driving down a back road through the then-undeveloped countryside. The problem was that while there were paved and divided roads, with grassy medians to boot, there were no streetlights. The roads sat waiting for the developers to get to work and throw up tract homes. Later, the municipality would put in the lights.

But for now, there was nothing but a wasteland of vacant earth, grooved with roads. At night, it was hard to know exactly where we were, and where the turnoff was that would take us back to the Party House in the 'burbs.

James blew right by the turn, and I spotted it first from the back seat. "James, this is it!" I screamed, trying to be heard over the blaring Bad Company cassette he insisted on playing.

James spun his head around, then, instead of stopping, he made a hard left turn. But we had long since missed the intersection, and a not-quite-sober James ran the car headlong, right into the divider.

The car bounced over the concrete curb and popped over the median, plowing up the grass. I held on for dear life as the car hit the pavement again on the other side of the road, where James finally slammed on the brakes and brought the car to a stop. It was readily apparent that something was wrong with the car as James eased it, lurching, over to the other side of the road. A moment of wits-gathering passed as Travis switched off the stereo and James killed the ignition. The only sound was the unmistakable noise of a stray hubcap rolling on concrete, and finally spinning to a stop.

After Travis lit into James with a few choice words about his doubtful heritage and his mother's unfortunate pedigree, which I won't reprint here, we got out of the car to survey the damage. It wasn't as bad as I had thought. The front right tire was completely flat, and the hubcap was nowhere to be found, but otherwise the car looked intact. On closer inspection, the wheel turned out to be pretty badly bent and would likely have to be replaced, but that was an expense we were sure we would be able to live with.

I went in search of the hubcap, while James and Travis looked for the spare tire and the jack. Fortunately, there was a jack, but it was one of those ridiculous, Japanese, screw-style things, and none of us had ever replaced a tire in the first place. Not to mention that it was really dark, with nothing but moonlight to see by. But by the time I found the hubcap (those things can roll!), James had the jack under the car and was slowly cranking the handle, inching the car off the ground.

Our adrenaline-infused panic had finally subsided to the point where logic dictated our actions once again. But this was all too short-lived. Another car was coming, and this car had three head-lights—the third light being the unmistakable hand-operated high beam of a police car, aimed squarely at us.

We were dead. The cop was going to want to see license and reg-istration. Then it would be a short ride down to a jail cell and charges drawn up for a half-dozen violations. Then my dad would come pick me up, probably beat the shit out of me, and I wouldn't leave my room for the next two years, forbidden from ever seeing the gang again.

The prowler eased up next to us and the window rolled down. It was a big guy with a mustache, but I could barely make out his face due to the ultra-bright light being shined in our eyes. "Any problem here?" he asked.

I can't imagine a more obvious question. Three people changing a tire in the middle of nowhere in the dead of night? Of course there's a problem. Travis gave him the obvious answer. "Just chang-ing a tire."

The cop surveyed the scene and said, "Okay."

And then he rolled up the window and drove off, leaving us alone in the dark again. For us, that was the most helpful thing that cop could have done.

It was three in the morning when we sheepishly pulled back into Bean's driveway. James killed the ignition, and Travis turned around in his seat.

"We need to come up with a story," he said. "Tommy's dad will buy him a new wheel, but that's got to cost a few hundred dollars, and I know James doesn't have that kind of money."

"Nope," James agreed.

"And neither of us is going to pay for this little incident . . . so here's what I've come up with," Travis continued. "We all know Tommy has a crush on Heather McManus, who lives about three blocks down the street. Tommy got drunk tonight. Really drunk. Around midnight, he was ranting about Heather and how much he was in love with her, and then he said he was going to go over there and tell her just that."

"He did?" asked James, unclear on where Travis was going.

"Just shut up and keep listening." Travis turned back to me. "He ran out to the car before any of us could stop him and took off down the street. But he only made it a block before slamming into the curb, which flattened the tire and bent the wheel.

"We ran after him and Alex and I took him back to the house, where he passed out on the couch. Then we went back to where the car was, and the three of us helped change the tire. We drove it back and parked it in the driveway. The end."

We were quiet for a moment. I finally said, "Do you really think he's going to buy that?"

Travis replied, "It's going to depend on how drunk he is. Let's go take a look."

We went inside, and, sure enough, Tommy was still passed out on the couch. In fact, he had thrown up in his sleep, all over the couch and the floor next to it. Watson the dog was busily licking it up upon our arrival, which was disgusting, but good, because none of us would have to clean up the mess.

"I guess he's drunk enough," I said. Then we all went to sleep. I got Bean's parents' bed that night because I had called it earlier, and I went to sleep to the droning of the Home Shopping Channel on their television.

Come morning, Tommy was more hung over than I'd ever seen him. By the time I got up, he was sitting on the kitchen counter, eating some stale cookies that had been lying around for weeks. "There's nothing else to eat. I need a gut sponge," he cried.

Travis came in after me, and he put his hands on his hips like a stern schoolmaster when he saw Tommy sitting there. "Someone had a bit too much to drink last night," he started.

"Tell me about it," moaned Tommy.

"You remember what you did?"

"No. What?"

"You wrecked your car because you wanted to tell Heather Mc-Manus how much you loved her!" Travis starting to laugh.

"WHAT!" yelled Tommy. He scrambled off the counter and outside, only to see his car in what appeared to be perfect condition. Travis and I followed.

"You asshole," he said. "It's not wrecked!"

"No, but you busted one of the wheels. The three of us had to fix it for you and drive your car back here."

"Oh. Really?" Tommy looked sheepish. "Well, thanks, I guess."

"Don't mention it," said Travis. "Anything to help out a drunken friend."

The lie had been almost too easy to pull off. If James could keep his mouth shut, we'd be in the clear forever. We were getting very good at telling lies. Travis, especially.

Tommy did get in trouble. He made up yet another story about being run off the road by an old lady, but his dad didn't buy it. Tommy was not a very good liar at all. He was grounded for the first two weeks of school on account of the car.

But when Bean's mother called Tommy's parents to complain about what had happened to her house, he was grounded for another ten.

❖ ❖ ❖

March 3, 2000

With school back in session, the legend of the Party House spread quickly, mainly courtesy of Bean, who whined to everyone who would listen about the wholesale destruction that had taken place inside his home.

At first, the stories were true. Typically, a tale would go like this: Tommy was supposed to watch our house for six weeks while we were on a long vacation. He invited his friends over, including

James, Travis, and Alex, and they proceeded to wreck our beautiful little house. There are stains in the kitchen and on the carpet and the furniture, half of my clothes are missing, and parts of the backyard are burned. My computer is messed up, and it smells like stale beer everywhere in the place, because of all the parties they had.

Fair enough, but over time, the stories began to sound more like this: Someone dropped a keg in the kitchen at one of those parties. The foundation is cracked, and it's going to cost $10,000 to fix. All of Bean's clothes were taken and given to the homeless. Bean's computer was stolen. Bean's computer was dropped off the roof. Somebody set the entire backyard on fire and grass will no longer grow there. The bathtub was filled with beer when Bean's family got home. The entire inside of the house was spray-painted blue. The carpet was removed throughout the house. The dog was shaved completely bare.

Now, none of this was true, but it had a couple of curious end results. Of course, Bean forever after hated the four of us, going out of his way to avoid us in the halls. But despite his vocal complaints, we never got in trouble. (Tommy's semi-indefinite grounding was the only real consequence of that summer.) But what was truly unexpected was that the four of us became small-time legends in school, and we suddenly found that we were no longer at the bottom of the geek food chain.

After that summer, we landed somewhere in the middle of the chain—maybe the lower-middle—bestowed the same wary respect given to habitual stoners and death metal enthusiasts. People nodded at me in the halls. They asked when and where the next party was going to be. They asked if it was true that we cracked the foundation or shaved the dog (I always shrugged in response), and they wished that they had been at the Party House on *that* night.

The more Bean talked and the more inflated the stories got, the more fashionable we became. Bean only made it worse for himself, but I guess he was just upset about his clothes. His mom had outfitted him completely in new attire from Wieners.

Don't tell anyone, but I was actually becoming cool.

March 4, 2000

And then we were back in the swing of school, my junior year.

The days flew by under a haze of indifference. Though I was two long years away from it, I guess I'd already graduated mentally. No one noticed that Alison O'Malley was gone until three weeks had passed. It was another two weeks before rumors started to spread about her suicide; the rumors were later confirmed by a "moment of silence" held during homeroom.

One of the first things a high school junior does is take the PSAT—the Preliminary Scholastic Aptitude Test, a precursor to the SAT college entrance exam. The PSAT is a three-hour test, just like the regular SAT, designed to neatly categorize you as smart or dumb, college-worthy or not. The questions are pretty much the same as those on the SAT, and the grading scale is the same, also. They give it to you as a junior so if it turns out you're not college worthy, they don't need to waste their time with you the following year.

James, Travis, and I all took the PSAT. Tommy didn't. He was grounded.

We had moved our weekend sessions back to Travis's house, and the night before the PSAT, we really did ourselves in on a bottle of Jägermeister. I don't know why we drank that stuff. It's disgusting.

Suffice it to say that come Saturday morning, we had universally raging hangovers, and I was probably in the worst shape of all. My head pounding, I climbed into Travis's mother's station wagon, and we rode in silence to the testing facility, my number two pencil in hand and four Extra-Strength Tylenols down the gullet.

The PSAT was the ordeal you would expect, compounded by my self-inflicted condition. However, the PSAT wasn't really that difficult. Even with half a brain, I muddled my way through the questions, finding the math section exceptionally easy.

By Thanksgiving, you get your scores in the mail. The verdict was in: 1330. 580 on verbal, 750 on math. You can only get 800 on each section. This was actually high enough to qualify me as a "National Merit Scholar Commended Student," which meant nothing except that I would be photographed in the yearbook with the thirteen other Commended Students from FVH that year.

My mother was ecstatic. A 1330 on the SAT pretty much guarantees you can get into any reasonably competitive college, even if your grades weren't that hot, like mine. The assumption was that I wouldn't get any dumber over the next twelve months, so my parents took me out to one of their favorite restaurants to celebrate my impending status as a college student.

But the minute we got home from dinner, I was told that it was time to start considering colleges. Once you take the PSAT, brochures and big packets start arriving from schools across the country, on a near-daily basis. You are encouraged to apply early so as to get "preferential consideration" from the colleges. Each application costs $25 to $100—and that was in 1988. The ambitious student could be out a lot of money by the time he applied to his thirty favorite institutions, not to mention the severe case of writer's cramp he's likely to have due to the prodigious amount of essay-writing involved.

Since I was an only child, my mom didn't have a little girl to dote over. I guess she saw helping out in my college selection as an opportunity for us to bond, and I suppose it gave her something to do that made her feel a bit more like a mother.

This was pure horror for me.

My mother loved college. She was in a sorority. Five of her sorority sisters were her bridesmaids. She made great friends that she still keeps in touch with. It was nothing but fun times, the best four years of her life.

However, she always pointed out, she wasn't as bright as I was. I had so much potential, it was really important for me to find a school where I could use all that potential that I was currently wasting.

And of course, she wanted me to stay close to home. This prompted tours of all the private colleges in a 150-mile radius, which is how we spent every weekend for the next several months, driving between little cities with no industry aside from education, looking for Just The Place for me to spend the rapidly approaching next four years of my life.

Eventually I just about lost my mind, and while we drove home from Trinity University in San Antonio, I told my mother I was going to Ohio State, the largest university in the country and well over 1,000 miles away. We had been arguing about this for a hundred miles or more, and we were almost home—in fact, we were in Fall Valley—when the argument came to a head.

"What do you mean, you're moving to Ohio?" she asked.

"I'm going to Ohio State. I've decided."

"What are you talking about? You've only seen a dozen schools. You've never even been to Ohio. You can't decide something like that."

"I already did. I want to go to a big school."

"But you won't get personal attention at a place like that. You'll just get lost in the shuffle."

"Good. Those small schools like Trinity make me sick."

"What? Mary Jo Wisenbaker's son goes to Trinity. She says he and his dorm buddies go over to his grandmother's house every Sunday night for dinner. They have a great time!"

I turned on the sarcasm full blast. "Ooooh, well that sounds like a lot of fun!"

The car lurched to a sudden halt. My mother was fuming angry. "Get out!"

"What?"

"Get out, I will not listen to your cynicism any more!"

I paused, but she yelled, "GET OUT!"

And for the first time ever, she really did stop the car and make me walk home.

It was only a mile back to our house, so I made it back in short order. When I came in, my mother was cooking dinner, and she didn't speak to me the rest of the evening.

I apologized for my attitude the next day, and she seemed to forgive me. We put the issue behind us, and moved on with our lives.

I'm only realizing this now, but that really was the end of the college search for both of us. True to myself, I ended up submitting only one application: to Ohio State.

❖   ❖   ❖

March 5, 2000

After the PSAT, the other big milestone early in my junior year was learning to drive. Being the youngest person in my class, I didn't turn sixteen until several months into the school year, well after everyone else was joyriding their asses off. Travis turned sixteen at the very end of the summer, so I caught a ride to and from school with him, instead of walking.

But now I was old enough for Driver's Ed, and since my sixteenth birthday was coming up on October 7, I wanted to be primed and ready for driving on Day One.

If I had taken Driver's Ed at school I wouldn't have finished until Christmas, so that was out. (My mother also complained that my grade point average would suffer, because low-level classes like

Driver's Ed were not worth as much as higher-level classes like Computer Math II.) So Mom let me sign up for Driver's Ed at the strip mall down the road. It was two hours a night, twice a week, for eight weeks. Road practice on the weekends.

I'm sure my Driver's Ed story is no different than anyone else's. A substandard building with wood-paneled walls, no climate control, and flickering fluorescent lighting. An endless series of videotapes from decades gone, unwatchably fuzzy with static due to their near-nightly viewing on a crappy VCR. Multiple-choice quizzes that were virtually impossible to fail. Bored instructors who looked like they'd rather be getting drunk at a bar than lecturing to a bunch of pimply teens. Driving practice in an ancient Chevy Nova, sticking only to undeveloped subdivisions so there would be no possibility of encountering traffic—or learning how to really drive.

On weekends, my dad let me drive around the Valley. I guess he was trying to make up for years of neglect by passing along his helpful tips about life on the road.

When I meandered too close to the side of the street: "Stay away from the curb! Do you know why motorcycles ride near the middle of the road? Because there are nails and glass near the side. You don't want to get a flat tire, do you?" (I have since learned that motorcyclists stay near the middle of the road in order to be better seen by drivers who only use their left-hand side mirrors.)

Or when I came to a bend in the road, with a little cul-de-sac on the right and the road continuing on to the left, and I didn't use the turn signal when I followed the continuation of the road: "You just broke the law."

But miracles do happen, and on October 7, I passed the driver's test with a score of seventy-nine. Apparently I did not look in the rear view mirror enough, and I couldn't parallel park for shit. Still can't.

The only problem after that: no car.

❖ ❖ ❖

March 6, 2000

And soon I learned the consequences of blowing all your earnings on liquor and drugs: no money to *buy* a car, either. And don't get me started on the cost of insurance. I was pretty much the only junior at FVH without a car. So what is a broke sixteen-year-old to do when his folks won't let him borrow either of their vehicles?

Beg. I started a campaign almost immediately to be given a car for Christmas. I didn't care what make or model it was, just something so I could get to and from school. Walking was out, and bumming rides was getting tiresome. I'm sure Travis was sick of my constant presence in the passenger seat, too.

My parents heard it pretty much nonstop. I circled ads in the classifieds. I left little notes out. I constantly asked if they needed me to go run any errands for them, and when they said yes, I always made a huge fuss about how I was going to have to borrow their car to do it.

Over time, this seemed to work. And pretty soon, I heard from my mom that I was going to get a car for Christmas. But I kept the pressure on, just in case.

On November 13, my pestering paid off. It was another Sunday morning, and I heard the lawn mower droning on as usual. Hung over, I tried to muffle the sound with a pillow over my head.

A knock came at the door, and my mother peeked her head in. Quietly, she said, "You know, you really should go help your father."

I knew better than to argue, so I silently pulled on some pants and a baseball cap to tame my unkempt morning hair. I went downstairs barefoot, and looking into the driveway I knew something was amiss. There was a red Camaro parked outside. It was old and faded, and the big blue bow on the hood gave it away.

I ran outside and noticed my mother was behind me. "Holy—is this for me!?" The mower cut off somewhere near the side of the house, and I hopped in the car. It was an old Camaro from 1981, and it had more than 85,000 miles on it, but it was still a cool car. Better than Steve Williams' Jeep, even.

My dad approached. "You like it?"

"Yeah!" I practically squealed.

"Well, take it for a spin."

He didn't have to tell me twice. I started her up and tore out of the driveway, speeding around the block. The sense of freedom was incredible. There is simply no better way to feel like you're in control of your own life than to drive really fast in a red Camaro with the windows down and the radio turned up.

When I got back home, I parked in the driveway, and got out and gave my dad a rare hug. "Do you like it?" he asked.

"I love it. Thanks a lot."

"It's the kind of car I would have wanted when I was a kid. Be sure you take good care of it. And stay away from the curb."

"I will."

I loved that car. It wasn't long before people recognized me by the Camaro alone, and they would wave and honk their horns on the way to school. It was the best present I ever received.

The three of us stood there quietly, looking over the car with pride and contentment. I inspected every surface, getting to know the contours and the little dents and dings. My parents were obviously happy that they'd been able to get me excited about something—a rarity that always made them feel good about themselves, like they'd succeeded as parents, for once.

For my dad, the car was a way for him to recapture a bit of lost youth. He secretly drove it sometimes early in the morning. I always knew he had driven it because the radio would be set to an AM station. If we had one thing in common, it was love of that car.

I have never felt closer to my father than I did that morning.

❖ ❖ ❖

March 8, 2000

The semester flew by. Steve ignored me, except at lunchtime, and despite a drinking habit that would kill a small elephant, my grades were better than ever.

Christmas came and went with little fanfare. The car was my retroactive present, a fact of which I was reminded on a twice-daily basis.

Earlier in December and much to everyone's surprise, Travis starting dating a girl who had been a semi-regular at the Party House during the summer. Her name was Jennifer, and all I can remember about her was that she liked country music, had long brown hair, and had a really huge ass. Not that that's a bad thing. I like a big ass.

New Year's Eve was coming, and Jennifer suggested we rent a hotel room and revive the Party House tradition for one night, having a dozen or two people in for an impromptu celebration. Sounded good to me. It beat driving around the neighborhood for hours, mocking people who'd found something better to do.

So a hotel room it was. Early on the 31st, we drove from hotel to hotel, trying to find someplace that both had rooms available for the night and would rent one to us. Jennifer had a fake ID that said she was twenty-one, but it wasn't a very good one, and most of the respectable places sent us packing without a second look.

After a half-dozen tries, we found a Motel 6 out on the highway that would rent us a room, and we forked over the $24.99 in advance.

We checked in at three and filled the bathtub with ice from the motel ice machine, making trip after trip with that little plastic bucket, which is apparently designed to prevent you from filling the bathtub with ice from the motel ice machine. But with unlimited time, you can do just about anything.

Then we got as much beer as we could, icing it down in the tub, plus hard stuff and mixers, and whatever other controlled substances we could find late in the day on New Year's Eve. Meanwhile, Travis put the word out about the party, and by ten o'clock, people had started to arrive.

Our guests emptied the tub of beer quickly and drained the liquor bottles. Midnight came and went. The ball dropped, and 1989, the year my life would break in two, was ushered in.

But that night I was on top of the world. My miraculous transformation into semi-popularity had been completed months earlier. People said "Hi" in the halls. Girls stopped to talk to me and sometimes they gave me their phone numbers, writing them on my hand along with their names, using little hearts to dot the i's.

By the time two or three rolled around, the room had cleared out except for a half-dozen of us, boys and girls, and I had broken out the good liquor I had stashed in the nightstand next to the Gideon Bible. I was collapsed on one of the beds, drinking a gin screwdriver the best I could.

Naturally, the party chat turned serious, and a roundtable game of Truth or Truth broke out among us.

Someone started with the obvious, "Who do you secretly have a crush on?" The answers came back: I picked Erin Lince, a giggly blonde who I didn't know very well, just to have an answer. Some girl said John Montgomery, the school's star golfer. Or Carin Airhart, on the tennis team, with whom James was currently infatuated and who, years later, came out as a lesbian. My favorite answer came from some other girl, who offered Mr. Echols, the art teacher.

But it was only after the "What do you want to do when you graduate?" "What is your favorite city?" and "How old were you when you lost your virginity?" questions that someone said, "Who do you hate more than anyone else?"

I thought about it for a long time. Steve had done nothing to me all semester. Forcing me to deliver his lunch wasn't grounds for hatred, and I got the impression that even if I suddenly quit doing that, he might have forgotten all about me. Maybe I should have. Maybe my daily presence only served as a subtle reminder that he would someday need to put me back in my place. At that moment, I certainly didn't like Steve Williams, but I wouldn't—and didn't—say I hated him.

In the end, I didn't answer. Instead, I just pretended I had passed out from the booze, and eventually, I really did fall asleep.

❖ ❖ ❖

March 9, 2000

That winter was the coldest on record for Texas in the last fifty years.

Every morning would bring on the arduous process of scraping ice off the windshield, warming up the car, and carefully coasting through the streets on the 2-mile trip to school—all habits familiar to those in colder climes but utterly foreign to us southerners.

It was so cold that in January, school was canceled altogether for two days during the first week of classes. When it gets below 32 degrees in Texas, the state just shuts down, unable to cope.

It also messes up people's lives. You have to bundle up in lots of clothes to go outside, then unbundle once you're back indoors. You waste hours and hours just warming up your extremities. Your face turns red—or purple. Things break. Plants die. The world slows to a crawl.

Cold weather makes you bitter. If you're into sports and you can't play them on account of the cold weather, it makes you even more bitter. If you're a senior and this is your last chance at high school greatness on the baseball diamond before you go off to college, this is tantamount to getting cancer. With the season postponed indefinitely, Steve Williams must have felt like he was on chemo.

Steve spoke to me for the first time in months. It was a Friday, and about a third of the student body had stayed at home because of the freezing rain that was pelting the area that day. As I dropped off his lunch—a hoagie and a double order of French fries—he grabbed me by the arm. "We're going to the quarry this afternoon," he said. "I want you to come."

"The quarry?" I protested. "In this weather? I don't think I can drive out there today. It's like an hour away."

"It's forty-five minutes, and there won't be any traffic today," he replied. "You'll be there, or I'll fucking kill you."

I toyed with the idea of blowing him off, but I'd done that before with extremely unsatisfactory results. So I drove the forty-seven miles to the quarry, an enormous hole in the earth for mining marble that had long been abandoned and had now filled to an unknown depth with rainwater. This winter, the quarry was frozen over.

The rain had stopped, but huge, gray clouds hovered ominously. It looked like the storm could start again any time. Steve and Co. were already there when I arrived. They left their cars running: Steve's Jeep and Lou's giant pickup truck idled, trying to keep warm. Steve and his friends were huddled in a little circle, talking quietly, their breath leaving little steam puffs in the air as they spoke. Vogon, Steve's usual right-hand man, was noticeably absent.

I killed the engine and got out. We were all bundled up in multiple layers, padding ourselves up into unlikely girths. They actually didn't look much bigger than me with all the clothes I had on.

I approached. "You're late," Steve yelled at me.

"You didn't tell me what time to be here," I replied, getting a little smart-alecky with him (not a wise move).

"Shut up." Steve's friends made a circle around me. This did not bode well.

"What do you want?" I asked.

"I said shut up! Dude, you don't understand *shit*, do you? I thought the fucking bunny would knock some sense into you, but no. You must be some kind of damn special-ed moron, huh?"

I said nothing. I hoped that was what he wanted.

"Good. Now I don't think you understand what's been going on, do you?"

I shook my head no.

"I didn't think so. We've got a big problem. We've got a really big problem. You see, ever since your little party days this summer, people seem to think you're not the sissy-fag-pussy boy that you really are. They seem to think you're cool. And last week, a couple of chicks saw you bringing lunch to me, and you know what? They wanted to know if we were *friends*. Can you fucking believe that? *Me* friends with *you*? I mean, I set them straight and all about how you were a voluntary servant and everything, but like, dude, that was just *sick*."

Steve paced around and threw some rocks into the quarry before he went on.

He spoke facing away from me. "We're going to have to do something about this before it gets way too out of hand."

"What do you want me to do?" I said, getting nervous.

Steve spun around. "I said SHUT UP!"

He nodded to his henchman Dewie, and Dewie flexed his arm and punched me hard in the stomach. It hurt, but not as bad as it could have, since I had on all those layers of clothes. I doubled over anyway.

"Now you've got this car," Steve went on. "I happen to know it's a piece of shit, but some people think it's cool. I would tell you to get rid of it, but I don't think you would."

"Why don't you just leave me alone? No one will have to see us together ever again!" I argued.

He nodded to Dewie again, and Dewie, sensing the first punch hadn't had the right effect, decked me in the jaw. I fell on my back, blood gushing from my mouth. It hurt like hell. A tooth had been knocked loose. Not out, but loose and wiggling in the socket.

"This is the way it's going to be with you, isn't it, Fag Boy? I can see I'm going to have to teach you a lesson, and that really disappoints me." He turned to Lou, and said, "Get the car."

I tried to protest, but Dewie stood on my neck, pinning me down. My head was spinning so badly, I couldn't have done anything, anyway.

Lou drove the car up to the edge of the quarry, killed the engine, and got out. The keys were in it, and he left the door open. For a long time, the car's chime of "ding, ding, ding, ding" was the only thing I could hear. It was so remote out there. There weren't even animals rustling around.

Steve thought about what he was doing for a long time. I don't know if it was guilt, or if he was just thinking about covering his bases. I know how it goes: It was probably a combination of both. Finally he said something to his cronies. "Everybody got their gloves on?"

Lots of reluctant, nervous murmurs.

But Steve pressed on with his orders. "Then *push.*"

Dewie let me up so he could help, and I sat up in time to see four guys pushing my dinging red Camaro over the edge and into the water-filled pit of the quarry. When it hit the ice, it sounded like a thunderclap, followed by a quick gurgling as the car rapidly filled

134

up with water and sank.

In a daze of disbelief, I stumbled to the edge to see for myself. The car had left a perfect semicircle in the ice where it had fallen through, and I could no longer see it in the murky water below. That night, I knew the ice would close back up, and no one would ever find that car again, even after the thaw.

Steve pushed me back to the ground and stood over me. "I hope this is clear to you now, Alice. Is it?"

"Yeah, it's clear," I said, spitting blood.

"Good, because I don't want to have this conversation again. Besides, it looks like you're out of cars."

Steve turned to his gang. "Let's get the fuck outta here."

Realizing my predicament, I pushed through the pain to get back to my feet. I called out to Steve, who was headed to his car, "You're not going to leave me here!"

Steve turned around. "I don't see how you'll learn your lesson any other way! Besides, I can't be seen with you. You're a pussy, and pussies don't ride with me!"

His crew giggled, and they piled into their two vehicles.

"*Wait!*" I yelled. There was no hope of catching a ride out here, and it was so cold my feet were already a little numb.

They just ignored me. They slammed the car doors and shifted into gear, kicking up gravel under the wheels as they drove away. I was alone, miles from civilization.

I knew it would get dark soon, so I started walking. It was about twelve miles to the Interstate, and I figured that if I hustled, I might be able to get there by nine o'clock when it might still be 15 or 20 degrees out. It would be dark—very dark—by then, but at least I'd have a chance at hitching a ride on the well-traveled highway.

I did not make good time. Thanks to the rain, the ground was very icy, so I had to walk deliberately to avoid falling. It was twilight before I made it even four miles, and I knew I was going to be lucky to get to the Interstate by midnight.

Is it possible for someone to be as shallow and one-dimensional as Steve Williams? People would say I'm only writing bad things about him, that anyone as popular as he is must have some good in him. We don't put evil people on pedestals, do we? Of course we do. Most people just choose to overlook the bad in things, whether it's a TV show, a meal, or a football star. All is forgiven, and forgotten. The good is made up, pulled from thin air.

But, as I found, it really *is* possible for someone to be completely superficial. Most people have layer after layer of personality. They're shy on the outside, but burning with creativity on the inside, and under that, they secretly fantasize about short girls with black hair and pale skin, and under that, they are afraid of rejection and won't talk to the girls, and under that, they resent it. But Steve Williams wasn't like that. What you saw was what you got.

I walked and stumbled and walked some more, but my worst fears came true shortly after 8:30. The ominous clouds opened up and freezing rain began to pelt the Texas earth. There was no shelter in sight. My only option was to continue walking, keep the muscles moving lest they freeze up altogether. I pulled my hood up to cover my face as best I could, but it didn't help much. I was freezing.

By 9:30, I knew my mother would be panicking. I was panicking, too. The rain was getting worse, and I could barely keep moving.

I don't remember when I fell. I don't know if I hit my head, but I don't think so. I don't know if I fell on the road or on the shoulder. I don't remember passing out. I don't know if I was face up or face down. And I don't know who found me, or when.

❖ ❖ ❖

March 11, 2000

I do remember waking up in a hospital bed, covered by what must have been a dozen wool blankets. My face was bandaged, and the room was oppressively warm. An IV was stuck in the back of my hand. It was after 2 a.m.

I looked around for a call button, which I pressed repeatedly until a nurse arrived. She was a large blonde woman with too much makeup, not one of the buxom young girls you see on medical shows on TV.

"You're up! That's so nice. Your parents are on the way," she said, checking my IV and getting a thermometer to take my temperature.

"Where am I?" I asked.

"You're in the hospital," she said, giving me that obvious look.

"Yeah, but *where?*" I barely got the words out before she jammed the thermometer in my mouth.

"Pinwood."

I was in the little town near the quarry, still forty or so miles away from home. I didn't even know Pinwood had a hospital.

I knew exactly what my parents were going to say when they arrived, and I had rehearsed the dialogue in my mind a good half-hour before they showed up.

When they walked in, my mother rushed to my side, and my father hung back by the door. By then, the nurse and a doctor were in the room as well, ready to explain what happened.

"Oh my God, honey!" my mother practically yelled as she ran to hug me. "What happened? We were worried *sick*!"

My mother kneeled on the ground and caressed my hand, trying to comfort me. Of course, she was the one who was agitated and needed comforting, not me.

The doctor spoke up. "A local rancher brought him in about an hour ago. He was unconscious, cold to the bone, and obviously beaten up."

My dad said, "How did you get way out here to Pinwood?"

I was ready with the answer that would shock them all. "I got car-jacked."

"What!?" my mother exclaimed. "In *Fall Valley*!?"

"Yeah. Two guys, at the intersection of Royal and El Dorado. They were wearing masks, and they jumped into the car at the stop light."

"Oh my Lord," my mother whispered, wishing it not to be true that criminals regularly cased the Valley to prey on hapless kids.

"They took the car?" my father asked.

"Yeah. They put a pillowcase on my head and threw me in the back. One of them hit me in the jaw pretty hard. They said they'd shoot me if I moved or made any noise."

The doctor said to the nurse, "We'll need to call the police in on this one. Can you call the station?" She agreed and left in a hurry. Obviously, Pinwood just doesn't see a lot of carjackings or kidnappings.

I went on. "They drove for about an hour. Finally they said they needed to get rid of me, and that this would be a good place. Then they yanked the pillowcase off and tossed me out of the car and drove off. I didn't know where I was or what to do, so I started walking. Then it started to rain and I was really cold . . . I guess I passed out, I don't really remember." It was a real effort to tell the story, and I made it seem even worse than it really was.

My mother was crying, and my dad was shaking his head. He believed the story, but I don't think he could accept that the Camaro was gone.

The Pinwood police were local schmucks, unlike the state and Federal guys I'd have the pleasure of meeting later that year. Basically, they took my statement, asked what the carjackers looked like ("six-foot, tan complexion, never saw their faces") and wrote down the details about the Camaro. I knew they'd never find the car, and they'd never find the guys. My case would vanish into a file in the basement of the Pinwood Police Department, and that would be the end of it.

The doctor said if I looked all right the following afternoon, I could go home, but now I needed to rest. My parents were sent to the nearby Super 8 Motel, with instructions to return the next day at 3 p.m. to arrange for my release.

It wasn't until after my parents left that I realized that the little toe on my left foot had been amputated. The doctors later told me it was frostbitten beyond repair.

❖ ❖ ❖

March 12, 2000

I was finally left alone, and for the remainder of the night I just stared at the ceiling of Room 121 in Pinwood General Hospital, unable to sleep at all.

Put in my position, I'm sure many people's thoughts might turn to suicide, and I honestly can't blame them. It's certainly a way out of a life full of pain. It crossed my mind, but I dismissed the idea, mainly because I doubted Steve Williams would feel responsible for causing my death if I killed myself. He wouldn't even notice, so what kind of revenge would that be? Instead, my thoughts turned to someone else's death.

I didn't and still don't think it's unreasonable to blame Steve Williams for three full years of personal agony. As an exercise, I made a mental tally of all the tortures he'd put me through, from beating after beating, to daily embarrassments, to killing my pet, to destroying my car, to nearly killing me the night before. The process made me more and more angry, and by the end of it, my blood was boiling.

There was no way I could revisit Steve Williams with the same amount of pain he had caused me. Add in the pain of dozens, maybe hundreds, of other kids in the same predicament as me at some point or another, and Steve had clearly caused enough suffering for ten people.

Was Steve going to change his ways when he went to college in the fall? I didn't think so. I had even heard a rumor that Steve might not go to West Point like he was "supposed to," his dad being an alumnus and all. He was actually considering Ohio State, where he had already been offered the starting quarterback position as a freshman. If I went to Ohio State, too . . . well, I was never going to be able to handle another tour of duty with him, and I knew it.

It was about three in the morning when I made my decision. Steve Williams was going to die. I was going to kill him.

❖   ❖   ❖

March 13, 2000

A week had passed, and I was as drunk as I'd ever been. After a near-death experience, some people take stock of their lives and make dramatic changes in the way they see the world. Some people just get really shit-faced. I was one of the latter.

I didn't drink to forget. I drank to put myself in another place for a while. A place where nothing could hurt me except the next day's hangover.

James and Travis were pretty far gone, too. I'd told them about the incident at the quarry and how I made up the story about the carjackers. So we kept the evening on a light note, as usual.

But that changed when I finally got up the nerve to make my drunken announcement. "I'm going to do the world a favor and kill Steve Williams."

The room fell silent. "Shut up," said Travis. "Be serious."

"I am serious," I said. "I'm going to poison him, like James said."

"I never said to poison anybody!" James protested.

"No, I mean your idea about poisoning someone's food and making it look like an accident of some kind."

"Well, I'm not taking credit for any idea like that. I only speak in theory."

Travis remarked, "If you're going to kill someone, you're going to need a better plan than just 'poison him.'" Obviously he was challenging my willpower and testing my seriousness. It was a challenge he would lose.

"I'm working on that. Steve's parents are going to be gone for like a month in the spring, on some training trip to Hawaii with the football team. I'm going to do it then, when they're not around to see him get sick or call 911 for him. Since I still serve him lunch, I figure I'll just put something in his food."

"You're going to kill him at school?" asked James, incredulous.

"Yeah."

"Heavy."

"What are you going to poison him with?" asked Travis, continuing his interrogation.

"I don't know. Something they can't trace back to me. Like I said, I'm working on it."

"If you serve him the lunch that kills him, you're going to be a murder suspect immediately."

"I've got a plan for that, too. I'll rig it so it looks like the poison came from someplace else instead of from the lunch. I may not be as strong as Steve, but I'm sure as hell a lot smarter. I've got plenty of time to set up the red herring."

"I can't believe you're serious, Alex," said James. "You're talking about murder—for real."

"I'm talking about justice."

"There's no honor in poisoning someone. That's cold-blooded killing. You should stand up to him, challenge him to a real duel like a man."

"Don't you pay attention, James? I've stood up to him more times than I can count, and every time I do he beats the crap out of me. Next time he'll probably break my neck."

"Why are you telling us this, Alex?" asked Travis. "Wouldn't it have been a lot smarter to do this yourself, in secret?"

"Yeah, I thought about that. The problem is that I don't think I can do it alone. I know I'm going to need some help and support, and I have to be sure you two will go along with it. You guys are the only people I really trust in the entire world, and I know that even if you decide not to help, you'll at least swear to keep this a secret. Will you?"

James and Travis solemnly nodded. That was one thing we had. Absolute trust.

"I also doubt I could keep this to myself without going crazy. I knew if I didn't share it with somebody, I would just explode."

Travis snickered, "I can see how that would be a problem."

"So I guess I have to ask now. Are you guys in? I will actually do the deed—feed him the mushrooms or the Drano, whatever it takes—so you won't be guilty of murder, only I will. You would be guilty of conspiracy, I guess, but we're all under eighteen, so even if we got busted, we wouldn't get any real jail time. But there's certainly a risk involved."

I paused to look at their faces. I couldn't read them at all.

"So, will you help me?"

No one spoke for what seemed like a really long time. Finally, Travis, my best friend in the world, replied, "Yeah, whatever it takes, I'm right behind you."

I looked to James, who eventually said, "Whatever it takes, man. One for all, and all for one."

"And we're all sworn to the utmost secrecy?" I asked. "This has to be a pact on your word of honor, the details of which will never leave this trio. Especially not to Tommy."

"I swear," James said.

"Yeah, I swear," said Travis.

We shook on it and all took a shot of tequila to seal the oath.

After recovering from the low-grade tequila shot, Travis said, "If you're really going to do this, Alex, you should know: There's no statute of limitations on murder. You better get your alibi perfect. If Steve Williams dies, it's going to be a front-page story."

I replied, "That's exactly what I'm hoping for, Trav. I want the entire world to know that Steve Williams is a dead man."

That was it. After that night, no one ever said "go" and no one said "stop." The plan took on a life and a momentum of its own, and over the next two months, it steamrolled ahead, virtually unstoppable.

As simple as that, I had launched the plan.

March 14, 2000

You'd be surprised how much stuff in the world is poisonous. Anything in sufficient quantities can kill you. Aspirin can kill you. Apples can kill you. Onions can kill you. Coffee can kill you. Water can kill you.

The trick to poisoning someone is that you have to get them to consume something that they wouldn't normally consume, or to consume so much of something that they die before they can seek medical help.

Today, researching this kind of information is painlessly simple. Just fire up your computer and jump on the Internet. Hundreds of

Web sites devoted to poisoning information are at your fingertips.

But back in 1989 it was a different story. The computer bulletin boards of the time carried some information about poisons in their file sections, but the information was dated at best, and accuracy was always a concern. Filled with bravado, slang, and typos, it was impossible to tell what information was based on real, medical fact, what was based on the writer's personal experience, and what was bullshit. But one of the files, "How to Kill Friends and Influence Dead People," was kind enough to include a bibliography of additional reading, which sent me off to the library to do further research.

To avoid suspicion, I did most of my research at another high school's library, borrowing Travis's beat-up Ford LTD or bumming a ride off of him or James. I always hid the books inside larger books as I studied them, and I always parked myself in the most remote corners of the building, out of view of any nosy staff members. I never took notes, memorizing everything I needed to know. I even wore gloves whenever I handled the poisoning books to avoid leaving fingerprints, and I always returned the books to their original locations at the end of my research sessions.

I would take no chances at getting caught before the deed was done. It would only make Steve even more popular if I got busted in the act.

It's probably safe to say that I am one of the most knowledgeable laypersons in the country when it comes to poisons. For example, most poisonings are suicides, almost 70 percent, in fact. The other 30 percent are accidents. Somewhere in the cracks between the two, maybe 0.5 percent of all poisoning cases, are homicides. Of course, you never know how many of the 70 percent and the 30 percent are really murders dressed up to look like suicides or accidents, and I was hoping to be part of that unknown group.

There are three classic poisons in literature and history: cyanide, arsenic, and strychnine. These poisons are all relatively simple to procure, very easy to administer, and very, very deadly. The problem with all of them is one that I would wrestle with for weeks: creating the appearance of an accidental poisoning.

Cyanide works by messing up your blood so it can't absorb oxygen. It occurs naturally in some fruit seeds and pits, including peaches, apples, and apricots, and cyanide compounds can be found in bug spray and metal polish. I couldn't come up with a way to get Steve to drink metal polish, and I didn't want to mess with pure cyanide, but the seed idea had some promise. You don't need much cyanide to kill a person, so I figured maybe I could slip him apple seeds since they were so small. But upon further research, I discovered it would take thousands of apple seeds to kill someone, all consumed in a short time span, since there is so little cyanide in each one. So cyanide was out.

Arsenic is a fun metal, often showing up as a white powder that you can dust on someone's food or blow into his face. Arsenic really screws up your digestive system: In chronic arsenic poisoning cases, the body swells and goes numb, but the hands and feet burn. You get violently sick, your hair falls out, and finally you die when your heart stops. It sounds very painful. The problem with arsenic is that it's harder to come by these days than it used to be. Napoleon may have died from arsenic present in the wallpaper of his day, or from an intentional poisoning. Arsenic is still found in some wallpapers, paints, and weed killers, but none of this stuff is easy to get someone to consume. I can just imagine force-feeding Steve Williams a roll of wallpaper.

For a while, I was set to kill Steve with strychnine. It's a classic poison, interfering with your central nervous system. When you take it, your body goes into agonizing seizures until you finally kick off. The only place you'll really find it today is in rat poison. I figured I could get some rat poison, grind it into dust, then spread it around in Steve's gym locker. Maybe line his football helmet with the stuff and let him breathe it in during a big game, then keel over in the middle of the football field at halftime. It would be a memorable and exciting way to go, but in the end, I figured it wasn't really feasible. There was no way to ensure he would inhale enough strychnine that it would kill him, and it would be fairly obvious that he was murdered when they found the dust. But there was one detail that finally took strychnine off the list: Football season was over.

The Big Three weren't going to work. So I kept looking.

Household chemicals commonly lead to accidental deaths, especially among children. Would it be possible, I wondered, to trick Steve into consuming a cup of Drano, some Ajax, or even Downy fabric softener? Steve might be a fool, but he wasn't a baby. Whether or not I took the "Mr. Yuck" sticker off the bottle, I didn't think he'd fall for it, and I wouldn't be able to force him to down it.

Gasoline and turpentine presented the same problem: highly

toxic, but very obvious. I can smell gasoline 100 yards away.

What about medicines, then, with no real taste? Aspirin and Tylenol are toxic in high doses, and I could ground tablets up and slip them in his milk, I thought. Unfortunately, the dosage requirements are so high that it would take something like 100 tablets to do him in. That's like a pile of powder the size of your fist. Prescription drugs like Vicodin, morphine, and Percodan are toxic at lower levels. The problem, though, would be getting a prescription, and that prescription would leave a paper trail that was too risky.

Sleeping pills were at the top of the list for a long time. Lots of people die from sleeping pill overdoses—they're readily available over the counter, and the fatal dosage isn't terribly high. But once again, setup was a problem. People don't accidentally take too many sleeping pills. They take them on purpose so they can fall asleep and never wake up. Why would Steve Williams take twenty sleeping pills at lunch? He wouldn't. I would have to sneak them to him at his house in the evening, and the prospect of going to his home just left open too many opportunities to slip up, leave evidence, and get caught.

What would work in low doses that would look accidental and could be done at school? Poisonous mushrooms or berries were strong contenders. I even went on an expedition into the woods to see if I could find any of the species that were photographed and illustrated in the popular literature. I found some mushrooms and I found some berries, but they didn't look exactly like anything I found in the books. In the end, I couldn't tell if they were poisonous or not. I couldn't take the chance on a guess.

Other poisonous plants, like the hemlock, oleander, rhododendron, and foxglove, were easier to identify and obtain. Getting Steve to actually eat rhododendron was going to be a problem, though. Like herbs and flowers, it would be easy to taste and see. Dosage would be another problem. Who knew how much foxglove it would take to kill a guy?

Eventually, recreational drugs came up. Steve could easily OD on heroin, cocaine, or even alcohol. I could even track down some ether or nitrous oxide, enough to kill a cow, I figured. But getting him to take it would be a huge problem. If he was going to West Point, he was going to have to clean up. He didn't even drink or smoke anymore. If I had any heroin, I could try to surreptitiously inject him with a huge dose and stage the scene to look accidental, but I wasn't confident that I could pull it off. (And I didn't have any heroin, either.)

Same problem with botulism. That would have been a real coup. The school cafeteria would have been implicated, there would be a scandal, and I would never, ever be suspect. But how do you get botulism? They don't exactly sell it at Walgreens.

Still, the idea of a workplace hazard acting as the poison was very enticing. People would immediately assume it was an accident. I figured most cops are lazy, and if the cause of death turned out to be something like botulism, they were likely to close the case without much of an investigation. So what else would make the cops instantly blame the school? Asbestos would be great, if it didn't take twenty years to kill you. Mercury is pretty good, as a common industrial toxin. A little mercury will go a long way, but getting ahold of a sufficient quantity would be tough and suspicious.

In the end, there was lead, the timeless toxin in paint and pipes. I didn't know exactly what kind of dose it would take to kill a person, and somehow I'd have to stash some lead on campus to be used as a decoy during the inevitable investigation. It wouldn't be easy, but lead would be untraceable and wouldn't require an enormous quantity to do the job. It would also be easy to find plenty of the stuff, and with minimal precautions it wouldn't harm me at all.

Lead wasn't perfect, but it would do.

❖   ❖   ❖

March 15, 2000

Lead is a curious metal. One of the first elements discovered, lead was first used in ancient Egypt and Babylon. It's still very common today. Lead-acid batteries power your car. You wear a lead vest when you get X-rays at the dentist. Most bullets are still made of lead, and the use of lead in roofing materials is actually on the rise. Lead is so common that it is often found in the dirt outside your house and in everyday dust. Lead is everywhere.

Until recently, lead was a common component of paint and gasoline, and it was the *de facto* material for plumbing pipes. Old buildings frequently have both lead paint and lead pipes. This is a fact I would use to my advantage later.

Unfortunately, lead is toxic, especially for children. In 1978, lead paint was banned in America. In 1995, leaded gasoline was prohibited from sale. Its effects are the same whether it is inhaled or ingested. If swallowed, lead accumulates in your organs, including the brain and kidneys, causing severe damage and, ultimately, death.

Lead poisoning is an ugly disorder. In adults, it affects body strength and weight, it messes with your ability to sleep, it screws up your gastrointestinal tract, it can wildly affect your blood pressure, and worst of all, it can permanently destroy your central nervous system. I find it amazing that people painted their walls with this stuff for centuries. Today, one in six children has some kind of lead poisoning, making it the most common environmentally produced disease in the world.

Lead is a cumulative poison, meaning it stays in the body, and each incidence of exposure adds to prior incidences. This means you can start off with small doses and build upon them with larger doses. Lead has no taste or odor. Its grayish-blue color is often the only hint of its presence.

Slow lead poisoning often drives people crazy. They don't get better until they're out of their lead-infested homes and safely locked away in a mental hospital.

Steve Williams wouldn't have that option.

❖   ❖   ❖

March 16, 2000

The following weekend, James arrived at Travis's house with a large paper sack. It was full of a bunch of little somethings rattling around, and he dropped the sack on the table, where it landed with a dull thud.

"What's that?" asked Travis. The two of us had just opened a beer to kick off the weekend, and James went to the kitchen to fetch one for himself.

"It's your lead, Alex," he said, twisting off the top and chugging half the bottle.

I looked in the bag to discover hundreds of lead miniature figurines. Pieces from an old chess set. Minutemen and army figures designed for war-game simulations. Collectable figurines from James's old Dungeons & Dragons stuff. It was all dusty and discolored, and most of the pieces were bent beyond recognition, to the point where they couldn't stand up any more.

"They're all junk. Just grind them up and you'll have all the lead you need," James said. He was right. It was enough lead to kill an elephant.

"I got you something else, too," James continued. From his back pocket he fished out a thick, iron file. "I figure you'd just get lost in a hardware store and you'd look suspicious. Just use this to shave off whatever lead you need."

"Cool, thanks," I offered. "I owe you one."

"Don't mention it," replied James.

Travis spoke up. "Yeah, please don't mention it . . . ever."

"But hey," James remembered, "I'm gonna need that file back when you're done with it."

Sunday morning came around and I happily mowed the lawn without even being told. It was March and I'm not even sure the yard needed mowing, but I did it anyway. That way I knew I'd have the rest of the day to myself to work on my project.

Mom and Dad left for some charity function around noon, and I staked out a spot in the garage for my project. I figured that if any nosy investigator found a little lead dust in the garage, no one would think twice about it, and it certainly wouldn't be traced back to me.

I took all the precautions I could against inhaling the dust, but I knew from my research that lead dust can penetrate any filter or mask, so instead I rigged up a little shield with some bricks and a sheet of Plexiglas I found in a corner of the garage. I figured this would keep most of the lead contained in a small area.

First I put down several sheets of newspaper, then dumped a few of the miniatures out onto it. I then slid the paper into the shielded area, and using the file James had given me, I started grinding.

The lead was soft and pliable. It only took a couple minutes to grind a miniature into a fine, gray powder. I did as many as I could before my hands got tired and chafed from nipping my fingers with the file. I should have worn gloves, I thought. That had been a mistake.

I worked for about an hour. The pile of powder that accumulated was sizable—about the size of a coffee cup, and I figure it weighed more than a pound. I started to use the little scale that had come with my childhood chemistry set to weigh it out, but the scale only went up to 100 grams, and transferring the powder back and forth got too messy, so I abandoned that detail.

I took an old mayonnaise jar from the kitchen, made sure it was perfectly clean and dry, and I carefully transferred the lead powder from the newspaper to the jar, sealing it tight.

Then it was time to clean up. I hosed off the bricks and the Plexiglas, washing the detritus into the street and leaving the bricks to dry. The newspaper I double-bagged with grocery sacks for later disposal in a far-away dumpster.

The remaining miniatures and the carefully cleaned file I returned to the recesses of my closet, also double-bagged in grocery sacks. There wasn't any risk of contamination from the miniatures. I just didn't want anyone to find them.

Within an hour, the bricks and the Plexiglas had dried. I returned the bricks to the stack behind the house and put the plastic back where I'd found it. I washed my hands for what felt like five minutes. My fingers had turned gray and black where the lead had rubbed off on them, but it all seemed to come off with no problem. Still, I didn't eat with my fingers for a week after that.

The first phase of my job was done, and I collapsed on my bed, realizing that my heart had been pounding at over 100 beats a minute for the last two hours. My handiwork sat in front of me, a jar of grayish-blue powder with a blue lid reading "Hellmann's."

I couldn't believe it was deadly. It looked as harmless as a coin collection. It was inert and dull. Boring, even. I guess that explains why for centuries people didn't take lead seriously as a health risk.

Soon enough, I would find out that it would take as little as a few tablespoons of the powder inside that jar to kill a grown man.

❖   ❖   ❖

March 17, 2000

My next dilemma soon became readily apparent: how to get the lead into Steve's body.

I had banked on easy access to his lunch tray every day as the most convenient way to introduce the poison, but actually getting it into the food undetected would be a problem.

The journey from the lunch line to Steve's table only took about thirty seconds, and usually it involved one or two trips back to the line to get all the food that Steve and his friends ate at one sitting. This was always a rushed and confusing process, and I knew there would be little time to coordinate the actual insertion of the lead.

A bigger problem arose when I tried putting the lead on some sample foodstuffs.

First, I raided the refrigerator for all the leftovers I could find. My mother was the best at saving any last scrap of food that we might possibly eat at a later point in time. However, we rarely, if ever, consumed the leftover food, which was fine by me, but as a side effect, our refrigerator was a mysterious boneyard of Ziploc bags and Tupperware containers.

I made myself a plate from a bit of everything in the fridge: cold and congealed macaroni and cheese, a slice of pizza, a few green beans, a scoop of Mexican casserole, and a sliver of Key lime pie. I took the plate to my room and locked the door, carefully retrieving the jar of powdered lead from its deep-in-the-closet hiding place.

I carefully sprinkled a tiny bit of powder over the food on the plate. Wherever it landed, it was obvious. The silver-grey flecks shined like glitter. One glance and you would know it was tainted. I'd only used about an eighth of a teaspoon over the entire plate, too. I didn't know what the required dosage would be to kill someone, but it would be more than that. Maybe over the course of a year or two I could drive Steve insane through the lead buildup in his brain, but that wasn't the goal. Besides, I only had a month.

I tried mixing the powder into the food, but that didn't help much. The macaroni and cheese looked like it had been doused in pepper; the casserole was smooshed into an unrecognizable mess that no one would eat. No matter what the original food looked like, the leaded version was obvious.

Back to the drawing board. My only other lunchtime option was the beverage. Steve drank either milk or Coke—whatever I brought him, as he rarely gave a preference. Milk is no good at all, though. It's actually used as an antidote of sorts for heavy metal poisoning because it works as a binding agent to scrub the metal out of your system. It would take double or triple the dosage to get the same effect if I spiked his milk with lead.

But soda was another story. Coca-Cola and lead would not interact inside or outside of the body, and the can would make the lead invisible, no matter how much lead I put in it.

I tried it out with a sample can, popping the top and putting a full teaspoon of lead inside. Swirl it around for a second and spill a little bit on a white paper plate. The lead was invisible. You'd need a magnifying glass to spot the little flecks inside the brown liquid. It was virtually undetectable.

And so it was decided. I would buy a Coke for Steve every day and dope it with lead. The only sign that something was amiss would be the fact that the can would be opened by the time it reached Steve. But I figured he'd be too oblivious to notice.

I quickly destroyed the evidence, washing the poisoned food down the sink and scrubbing out the basin with Comet. The paper plate and various other utensils were double-bagged for later disposal by the usual method, making sure to never use the same trashcan or dumpster twice, and that they were always at least fifteen miles away—farther, if I could convince James or Travis to keep driving.

My next problem was how to get the lead into the Coke can. You can't exactly take a mayonnaise jar full of powdered lead into the cafeteria and measure out a portion into a soda can in full view of the student body. So how to devise a way to surreptitiously introduce the lead into the can?

In the movies, they always have those fast-dissolving pills that you can just drop into a drink. That would be great, but I didn't really have the capacity to create lead tablets in my bedroom. The lead would have to stay in powder form from beginning to end.

I thought for a long while about it, and finally I decided on the following plan: I would use the alcohol lamp from my chemistry set—basically a very small glass jar, about the same size in circumference as a quarter. The lid is metal, with a hole drilled through the top so the string that's used as a wick can stick out. Throw away the wick, then get a heavy-duty plastic straw that's the right diameter to stick through the hole. Glue the straw in place with super glue, seal the connection with two layers of epoxy, and snip off the ends of the straw to the desired length. The resulting contraption is just a jar with a long snout.

To fill with lead, just unscrew the cap (with snout attached), and spoon in the powder. Put the lid back on, nice and tight, and dispense the powder through the straw by simply tilting the contraption. I retrofitted the alcohol lamp and found it worked very well. To seal the end of the straw, I took a wine stopper from the enormous jar of corks my mother had collected over the years, and carefully whittled it down the appropriate size. It didn't take much more than twenty minutes to get a perfect seal on the dispenser that could still be removed and replaced inside of three seconds.

Despite the nightmarish heat of Texas, I wore long sleeves all the time, and still do. This made it easy to secret the dispenser under my clothes. All I had to do was tape it to the underside of my forearm so the end of the straw was just hidden beneath the sleeve at my wrist. I usually used a couple of athletic wristbands to make sure the contraption stayed in place and invisible.

Practice makes perfect, as my dad always says, so of course I spent a lot of time dispensing the powder into my test Coke can. After a few days of practice, I could uncap the dispenser, pour out powder into can to within an eighth of a teaspoon in accuracy, and recap the dispenser, all within fifteen seconds. I could do it standing up, while walking, and with barely a glance. I practiced in front of a mirror and made sure that no one would be able to tell I was introducing something into the Coke can. To the untrained eye, it would simply look like I was opening the can and wiping off the top as a gesture to sanitize the container.

Of course, that was about as far from the truth as you could get.

❖   ❖   ❖

March 18, 2000

I knew the next stage of the plan would be the most difficult.

While lead is a relatively common industrial and residential hazard, I had no idea if Fall Valley High had any level of contamination at all. The school building was old, but it had such great funding I found it hard to believe there would still be any lead paint or pipe in the place.

Then again, it would be that very disbelief that would work to my favor. No one had checked FVH for lead in decades, I was sure. So when the silent killer turned up again, a public outcry would be the natural response, not accusations of murder.

And so the question became, where to plant some lead on the school campus?

Lead paint was an obvious first choice, but repainting part of the school was an unlikely proposition. It's *too* obvious, it leaves too much evidence—especially if you drip paint on your clothes. Anyway, it would have been impossible to find lead paint at a store, since it was illegal. Mix my own lead paint? A possibility, but not one I wanted to explore. So I focused on another solution.

Namely, lead pipe, which at the time was still very easy to obtain at scrap metal shops in a variety of shapes and sizes. I figured all I'd have to do would be to replace a few water pipes—say, the pipes leading into a couple of water fountains—and the decoy would be set.

It was time for some recon, and I enlisted James and Travis to give me a hand.

We arrived at Fall High at midnight on a Saturday, rolling up discreetly behind the school in James's shitbox of a car, which he'd bought off the scrapheap and rebuilt in his driveway. We had dressed in black and wore baseball caps instead of masks. If you get busted wearing a ski mask, the cops know you're up to something nefarious. If you're just wearing a hat, it's still hard to make out your identity, but you look like you could be dressed normally. The rubber gloves might be harder to explain, but fortunately we never had to.

Travis stayed outside as a lookout, with instructions to honk the horn if trouble arose. If anything went wrong we would immediately abort the mission, split up, and rendezvous later at Travis's place. Since schools are common targets of vandals and graffiti artists, the cops made periodic stops at FVH. This little visit, I knew, would be an extremely dangerous one.

James and I half-ran through the courtyard to check out the building. The school was locked up tight, but the locker room was not. I guess there wasn't anything worth stealing in there, so they figured, why bother? This way, dedicated athletes could come by on weekends or after hours and still get into their lockers.

The boys' locker room had two water fountains. They were the old kind, with white porcelain basins and exposed pipe underneath. James, an old hand at do-it-yourself home repair, took one look underneath the basins and said, "Oh yeah, this is going to be a piece of cake."

A length of pipe led from the wall to the nozzle on the water fountain, with connectors at each end. All we'd have to do would be replace that length of pipe with one made of lead, and the job would be finished.

James took exact measurements of the pipe. The other water fountain had an identical setup, but James measured it as well, just to be sure. With the necessary dimensions written down, we hustled back to the car, where Travis was waiting.

"You get what you needed?"

"Yep, no problem," I said.

"Good, let's get outta here. This place gives me the creeps."

And outta there we got, all without incident.

James and I took a trip the following day to Al's Metal and Scrap, a good forty-minute drive down the highway toward Mexico. Al's was rumored to be a place where drug lords went to quietly and permanently dispose of bodies. Whether that was true I'll never know, but I was pretty sure that two teenagers buying a couple of old pipes would generate little more than a grunt and the exchange of two or three dollars.

Back in Al's pipe alley, we scoured through mound after mound of old plumbing equipment. It took hours of disgusting, dirty work, but eventually we came up with a pair of pipes that perfectly matched the intake pipes in the water fountains at Fall High. They looked like they were at least thirty years old, so they'd match perfectly with the aging infrastructure of FVH. I tested the pipes with my pocketknife. The metal curled off perfectly, leaving behind shavings of the soft gray color I knew so well. They were lead, 100 percent.

I pulled my baseball cap down over my face to pay the $2.80 for the pipes. The clerk said nothing during the exchange, and neither did I. The pipes were concealed in brown paper bags under the front seat of James's old Mercury, and it would be one more week until the following Saturday, when we'd install them on the locker-room water fountains.

I never tell anyone, but I'm sure I could forge a brilliant second career as a plumber.

❖   ❖   ❖

March 19, 2000

Another week came and went while I steeled myself for what I was about to do.

I served Steve his lunch as usual. I started buying him Coke instead of milk, just to make sure he wouldn't freak out or anything. He didn't. I don't think he even noticed; he just sucked down whatever food and drink I put in front of him. I tried to avoid saying anything in his presence. I just did my job and listened to him prattle on about how great his life was going be after he graduated.

I didn't bother to correct him.

A few things did come out of that week of patient listening. First, I learned that Steve finally had been accepted into West Point. But I don't think he realized that West Point has something like only one female for every nine male cadets. Those are not good odds. Nor am I sure what he'd think about a college full of driven, mili-

153

tary-minded chicks—not quite the submissive wallflowers he was used to at FVH. Steve never struck me as someone who'd get on well in the military, but with an Army Major as dad, I figure he didn't have much say in the matter.

Also, I learned that Steve was poised to repeat his position as the starting pitcher on the All-State baseball team. If he made it, he'd be the first Texan ever to achieve such a feat, and the sports magazines were dying to do a cover story on him if he pulled it off. Can you imagine what that would have done to his ego?

I put this information in the vault, for later use.

The week flew by. On Saturday night, Travis, James, and I drove to the school and parked in the same place we had the week before. James was in charge of the two pipes; I was in charge of tools and the jar of lead dust.

All three of us wore yellow rubber gloves. These clashed with our all-black outfits, but we weren't about to take any chances. Before we had left, I thoroughly wiped down both lead pipes with rubbing alcohol, to ensure that no trace of fingerprints was left.

Outside the school, Travis stood guard, while James and I hustled into the locker room. The first order of business: Replace those pipes.

After shutting off the water main, James laid down on his back under the first water fountain, peering up at the tangle of pipe. "Wrench," he ordered.

I handed him the heavy-duty pipe wrench we had taken from his father's toolkit. James put the wrench to the connector and pulled, but it didn't budge. Decades of sediment from the area's hard water had sealed the pipes together.

James pulled again, grunting, as hard as he could. I was holding the flashlight and I tilted it up to see his face, which had turned beet red from the effort. But the pipe didn't move.

"Damn it!" he yelled, getting up off the ground. He left the wrench stuck on the connector, sticking out obscenely.

"Hammer," he sternly ordered next.

I gave James the big claw hammer we'd brought just for this purpose. He got down on his knees and carefully lined up the hammer to the wrench handle. He gave himself a mental one-two-three count, tapping the handle each time, then lifted the hammer high above his head and slammed it down on the wrench. The clang was so loud that I was sure Travis had heard it from 100 yards away through the concrete wall.

Still, the pipe didn't move.

Again, James slammed down the hammer on the wrench. A third time he smashed it as hard as he could, and finally the connector on the pipe gave up. Though it wasn't easy going, James was able to twist the connector the rest of the way off using only the wrench.

The other end of the pipe required the same treatment, but this one only took two whacks.

Finally the original pipe was free, and we carefully replaced it with our lead pipe. The fit was good, not great. The lead pipe seemed to be a tiny bit smaller around than the original, so the threads on the connectors didn't catch perfectly, but it went on. It blended in perfectly with the other pipes. After it was installed, we gave it a try. Whenever you activated the water fountain, the pipe leaked, just a little, dripping slowly on the floor. It hadn't leaked before, but there wasn't much we could do about it aside from welding the connection, and we didn't have the time or expertise for that.

"Besides," James pointed out, "the water that leaks onto the floor will be contaminated with lead, too. It will get on people's shoes and they'll track it all over the locker room and all over the school. Soon enough there will be lead traces all over the campus."

"Maybe I should spread some lead dust around the gym and in the courtyard. Seed the whole place with it," I said.

"That's a good idea, but won't it get a lot of people sick?" asked James.

I laughed. "No way. You'd have to ingest this stuff for it to hurt you. And even if someone licked the entire floor of the locker room, they wouldn't get enough in their system to get *that* sick. But they'll get some . . . enough to show up if they test people for lead."

"Gotcha."

"Besides, once Steve bites it and they find the lead, they'll clean this place from top to bottom and you'll be able to lick the floor of the locker room."

We laughed, and while James worked on replacing the pipe for the second water fountain, I started dusting the locker room with lead shavings from the jar.

Clang! James was trying to get another stuck connector open. The clanging went on, four, five times. This one was really stuck. "Damn it!" I heard him once again curse from across the room.

"Keep trying!" I exhorted. Meanwhile, I had carefully removed the lid from the jar of lead powder and was sprinkling it around on the floor as if I was feeding chickens with seed.

Another clang.

"*What the hell is going on in here?*" The voice came from the entrance. It was loud and sudden, and I almost dropped the jar. My heart leapt to my throat. We were busted, I was sure.

But finally my mind caught up. It was Travis, investigating the noise.

I rounded the corner to face him. "Jesus Christ, Trav! Don't do that!"

"You're making enough noise to wake the dead. I'm sure they can hear that at the Circle K a mile down the street."

"No one can hear it," growled James. "Besides, there's no other way to get this fucking pipe off except through force. Now shut up and hold the flashlight so we can get out of here."

"Fine." Travis grudgingly picked up the light and shined it on the target for James's hammer blows.

It only took two more hits and the pipe came free. The other side was freed in just a couple of knocks.

As the two of them replaced the pipe, I found myself in front of Steve Williams' locker. I knew it well. It was one of the jumbo-sized lockers, with plenty of room to hang up your clothes and store bats, balls, pads, and jock straps. Non-jocks had lockers the size of a shoebox. The front of lockers like Steve's were covered in lattice-work, presumably to let the contents breathe and avoid mildew.

It also made it easy to toss a few pinches of lead dust straight in. I even managed to get a little in his football helmet. However, since football season was long over, I knew that Steve would never be wearing that helmet again.

I stood there, staring at the locker. You couldn't see the flecks of dust inside or on the floor. They were invisible.

"Let's go, we're done," said James, tapping me on the shoulder. I didn't know how long I'd been staring at the football helmet. I broke out of the daze and did a quick double-check to ensure we had everything we'd brought with us: tools, flashlights, jar of lead, and gloves, plus the two pipes we'd taken from the water fountains.

On the way out, I quickly sprinkled the gymnasium and the courtyard with the dust. I paid special attention to the entrance-ways to the school, which I knew would be heavily trafficked on Monday, spreading the lead dust throughout Fall High. Over the course of the plan, I would periodically drop dust—and lots of it—from my wrist dispenser at random locations in the halls during the school day. This would continue to spread the lead dust around the school as well as increase its overall concentration.

We disposed of the gloves and the original pipes in the usual way, bagged and tossed into a far-off dumpster. The tools were cleaned and carefully replaced, and the jar of lead dust went back into my closet.

Our frame-up was set. If anyone got sick from lead, the evidence would point to the school as the culprit.

And someone was about to get very, very sick indeed.

❖   ❖   ❖

March 20, 2000

Then, suddenly, I found myself carrying Steve Williams' lunch tray across the cafeteria.

It was noon on Monday, April 17, 1989. The lead dispenser was firmly attached to my forearm with tape and elastic armbands, and Steve's meal—two slices of pizza, two orders of onion rings, a chocolate brownie, and a can of cold Coca-Cola (opened)—was safely in my hands.

Time stopped, I was sure of it. The effect was bizarre, the kind of slow motion you only see in action movies. Steve's table stretched away from me, and he seemed to shoot farther and farther into the distance, as if I'd never be able to deliver his meal to him. My feet grew heavy to the point where it felt like I could no longer lift them at all, and my hands started to shake uncontrollably.

In that moment of missing time, my mind fought back and tried to take control of the situation. It was half-successful. Operating the lead dispenser was almost a matter of habit, and I began the deft movements that would dispense the tiniest flecks of lead dust into Steve's Coke can. Despite the unsteadiness of my hand, and much to my surprise, the grains of lead slid right into the open mouth of the can. Quickly I corked the dispenser and somehow my feet unstuck themselves from the cafeteria floor.

Everything gradually got back to normal, and with each step I took toward Steve at the end of his table, he zoomed closer to me. Now that the package had been delivered to its intended, I found the shakiness subsiding. My heart rate slowed to all of 150 beats per minute.

Would this dose of lead kill Steve Williams? Absolutely not; I

157

knew that. What effect would it have? That I couldn't say. Low dosages of lead can have unpredictable effects on people. That's why I knew I had to start small and work my way up. If he was going to have some bizarre reaction at a low dose, getting violent, say, or jumping up on the table and spouting *Hamlet*, I wanted to be prepared for it.

Confidence slowly returning, I strode the last few feet toward the smiling Steve, who was leaning back on the rear legs of the chair, his hands behind his head.

But my wobbly legs got the better of me, and with only a few feet to go, I tripped.

Down I went to the tile floor, my heart jumping back into my throat as I tried to save the tray.

The tray hit the ground flat on the base, letting out a loud *thwack!* as it hit. Because it didn't hit at an angle, though, the food just kind of rose up off the tray then landed back down, basically in the same place. The Coke can, however, spilled.

My eyes widened, and I reached for the can, but it was too late. The can toppled over, and Coke began to glug-glug-glug out onto the floor. I grabbed it as fast as I could, but not before a third of the soda had spilled. All the while, Steve and his cronies raucously laughed at the sight of me scrambling on my hands and knees to rescue Steve's lunch.

I saved the rest of the can and carefully placed it back on the tray. Then I got up and finished the remaining couple of steps to Steve's seat at the head of the table, carefully placing the tray down in front of him.

He surveyed it, and the food looked intact. Normally he would have sent me back for a brand new tray, even though nothing had spilled, just to boss me around. But he must have been extra-hungry that day. "This'll do, Alice. But go get me another Coke." I silently nodded and scurried back to the lunch line, and Steve called out behind me, "That comes out of your own money!" I didn't acknowledge him but paid for the extra Coke, also picking up two more lunch trays for Steve's crew. But as I walked back to his table, I saw that he was already drinking out of the partially spilled can, the can I had spiked with lead.

Unconsciously I broke a smile. I dropped off the food and the spare Coke, which I left unopened and uncontaminated, and Steve looked up at me. "What the fuck are *you* grinning about?"

I forced myself to stop smiling immediately. "Nothing," I said.

"Good," he said, "then go get the rest of the food for these guys."

I hurried back to the line and retrieved the three remaining trays for the bottommost goons in Steve's group.

By the time I had delivered all the lunches, Steve had finished the original, half-emptied can of Coke, and he popped the top on the second. By the end of the lunch period, he had finished that can, too. The spilled Coke was mopped up by a custodian within about five minutes. Any traces of lead would be washed away with the dumping of the rolling yellow bucket.

I watched Steve as well as I could for the rest of the day. He appeared as normal as ever, grabbing a sophomore girl's tits in the hall, beating up a freshman in the locker room, peeling out of the parking lot on his way home after school. Nothing out of the ordinary.

Sure, I was disappointed that the lead hadn't had a noticeable effect. But part of me was happy, albeit still nervous over the uncertainty of how this would all play out and not really ready to join that small club of people who have killed in cold blood. I knew this was going to be an endurance race—against myself.

I don't know if a sane person can ever really prepare to be a murderer. All you can do is keep telling yourself that you're doing humanity a favor. The notion of the ends justifying the means becomes a huge part of your moral code. And it helps if you ease yourself into it. Or go insane.

As such, my first day as a poisoner came and went without incident.

❖   ❖   ❖

March 22, 2000

"I still can't believe you went through with it," Travis said, after I relayed the story of that day's nearly disastrous lunch. The two of us were sitting in his backyard. Monday nights were no good at Travis's place for a good boozing: His parents stayed up late, and if you wanted to sneak some liquor you had to do it discreetly.

I took a pull off my beer. "Neither can I," I replied.

"How are you feeling?" he asked.

"I'm not really sure. At first I was too nervous to know how I felt at all. Now I'm just kind of hanging out there, wondering if this whole thing is going to work at all."

"Well, you can't quit now," Travis said. "What would your dad say?"

In unison, we chanted, "Quitters never win . . ."

We had a good laugh at that one. I was determined to see this through. And Travis was right, considering the amount of planning, fortitude, and courage this venture required. Had this been any other project, my father would have been proud.

After a long silence that lasted the time it took to consume half the contents of a beer bottle, Travis spoke again. "So what do you do now?"

"I guess I keep on trying. It's going to take a while to figure out the dosage. I'll just keep it small for now and slowly increase it until something happens."

"Well, if you need a hand," Travis said, "don't ask me."

We laughed some more and hurriedly finished our beers. Sneaking just one beer was tough enough with Travis's parents right inside the house.

"I better get home," I said. And with that I left to prepare myself and my lead dispenser for the following day.

Sleep came in fits, on and off. It was hardly anything you'd call rest. But eventually the sun crept up and the clock flipped over to 6:30, and I knew my mother would be yelling for me to get out of bed.

I showered and dressed quickly, then carefully situated the dispenser on my wrist and took a couple of practice runs, making sure my skill with the device was still intact. It was. In fact, my arm barely shook at all. Although this wasn't the real thing, maybe I was coming to accept what I was doing.

School droned on as usual, and the lunch bell finally called me to my daily duty with Steve. Again I went through the lunch line (today's special: Salisbury steak) and again I bought him a Coke, popping the top as soon as I plucked it from the cooler.

Again the long walk to Steve's seat stretched out before me, and again the time seemed to pass in slow motion. But this time, my hands didn't falter as I balanced the tray on one arm, removed the cork with a free finger, and deftly waved my hand over the top of the can, as if I was wiping a bit of grit off the surface, depositing my tiny dose of lead into the dark liquid within.

The cork went back on, the dispenser carefully disappearing up my sleeve. I set the tray on the table in front of Steve and quickly returned to get lunch for his friends. This time, the delivery of the lead had gone perfectly and without incident.

I watched from afar as Steve finished his Coke, crushing the empty can in his hand to prove his manliness, growling as he did so.

Steve never bussed his tray, always leaving his mess for some poor custodian to clean up. After Steve left with his crew, I stayed behind in the cafeteria and watched as the janitor cleaned up after them. The can went into the trash, followed by the remainder of his food, scraped into the wastebasket like slops into a pig's trough.

Later, I watched Steve as closely as possible, but nothing seemed to be happening. He was his usual asshole self, acting like he was king of the school and we should all clear a path for him and bow our heads whenever he passed by. The sad thing, I realize, is that some people really did this whenever he was around.

Wednesday and Thursday were the same. The lead went into the Coke, the Coke went into Steve, and nothing happened. At the time, I was working with a dosage of about one-eighth to one-quarter gram of lead per day. This is about the same amount of metal contained in a regular metal staple.

On Thursday afternoon I decided to do a little more research. From my earlier investigation, I had expected some immediate behavioral effects even at that low dosage, but perhaps I was underestimating Steve's weight. And who knew how anyone's unique metabolism would react to the lead? In poisoning, every case is different. Some people can even build up immunity to arsenic if they undergo constant exposure. Maybe Steve was a freak genetic specimen who was resistant to lead.

James gave me a ride to the other high school where I did my research, and I searched through some of my favorite reference manuals on heavy-metal poisoning. All signs seemed to indicate that I should up the dosage. At a quarter-gram per day, I figured Steve may eventually be driven insane, but it would take months to build up in his system to cause the results I was looking for.

Come Friday, I boosted the dose to a full one-third gram. It sounds like nothing, and if you look at a third of a gram of lead powder on a piece of paper (which I did that evening), it looks like nothing. It's tiny. Blow on it and it disappears into the wind.

But coming out of the spout of my homemade dispenser, that tiny mound of lead looked like a tsunami of gray sand, an unfathomable flood of poison that would inevitably kill its intended.

March 25, 2000

By Wednesday morning of the following week, I was starting to get nervous again. I had been dosing Steve's Cokes for seven days, and nothing had happened. With fewer than four weeks left in the school year, if the poison didn't take effect soon, the summer would arrive and I would lose my chance for good.

At the time, and I still think about this now, I asked myself why I didn't just let him go. In less than a month the torture would end. He wasn't going to Ohio State after all. He was going to vanish off to West Point, out of my life forever. Why kill him? Why not let him go? I still ask myself that question.

I had upped the dosage slightly, every day. And finally, the first effects of the lead began to show themselves.

It was lunch on Wednesday and, after popping the top of Steve's Coke can and sliding about a half-gram of lead into it, I gently set the tray down in front of him.

For the first time in the years I'd been serving him his meals, he did something I'd never seen before: He hesitated. Normally Steve would tear into his lunch, no matter what it was or how unappetizing it appeared. But this time, Steve just stared at the chicken pot pie in front of him with a glazed look on his face.

My heart went up into my throat. I thought he was onto me. I thought for sure I was busted, and he was hesitating because he knew his lunch was poisoned. I just stood there, paralyzed, waiting for him to kill me.

But he didn't. He slowly picked up a fork and stabbed it into the pot pie, devouring it by the time I could return with trays for his friends. He drank the Coke, oblivious to its hidden contents. And finally I realized that, in all likelihood, it was the lead that was finally taking its subtle effect.

The plan was working.

❖ ❖ ❖

March 27, 2000

By Friday, Steve's daily lead intake was up to two-thirds of a gram, a little less in mass than a small paperclip. It was obviously impacting his mood, making him slow and sedated.

Dewie would crack a joke, and normally Steve would burst out laughing, high-five his friends, and throw a little food at a passing freshman. But Steve didn't laugh. He would just stare back at Dewie, looking slightly annoyed, then he wouldn't say a thing. He'd just look down at his food and quietly continue eating.

Their meals took on a somber mood, and I watched carefully from my seat two tables away. The Fall Valley Raiders baseball team played its final game of the regular season that afternoon. I heard that Steve got yanked after two innings, having given up seven runs.

That night I met with James and Travis over an old bottle of rot-gut tequila that had turned up under Travis's dirty clothes. We even splurged and bought limes—not because we were sophisticates, but because we simply couldn't down the shots without something to cut the awful taste.

Despite the promise of a real alcoholic hammering, the mood that evening was sober. In fact, I felt like Steve among his friends, quiet and distant, unable to express myself because I didn't really know what to say. For Steve, he couldn't articulate what was happening to him because he didn't know. For me, my apprehension focused on the future, and what would happen to me after my deed was completed.

"I don't know what I'm doing, guys," I explained, downing my fifth shot.

"What do you mean? You know what you're doing. You have it planned out to the second," said Travis.

"No, I mean I know what I'm doing. I just don't know *why* any-more."

In character, James stated the obvious. "Maybe because of all the horrible things he's done to you over the past three years. If you were anyone else, you would have done this two years ago instead of waiting so long."

"I know, but I still can't justify it to myself. Something is discon-nected. I want him to die, but I don't want to kill him. Does that make sense?"

"Of course it does," said Travis. "No one wants to be a murderer. That's why firing squads use one blank among all the regular bul-lets: So the shooters can rationalize to themselves that they didn't fire the fatal shot. But you're methodically killing a person, slowly poisoning him day after day. There's no one else you can blame. You're going to drive yourself crazy like that."

"What do you recommend?"

"You either have to quit, or you have to get it over with soon."

"But I can't up the dosage too much, too quickly. It will look suspicious."

"Then quit."

I paused for a long while and didn't look up. "I can't."

Travis downed another shot and grimaced, and I finally caught his eye. "Then you're just going to have to deal with it."

❖　❖　❖

March 28, 2000

The plan was slowly killing me, along with Steve.

While Steve was experiencing a buildup of a toxic heavy metal in his brain that was driving him insane, I was driving myself insane thinking about it.

I resolved to get this over with as soon as possible. Besides, I said, there were only three weeks left in the school year, and I had to hurry.

Steve's daily dose of lead was now a full gram per day. In that third week, I also began to sprinkle a tiny amount of lead dust on the meals of Steve's friends. I did this only when the food was dark in color and the lead couldn't be seen: meatloaf, Salisbury steak, and hamburger patties were all prime targets for the lightest dusting.

Why? Conversations with James and Travis had convinced me that the two lead pipes plus the lead dust I was still spreading through the school might not be enough to convince an investigator that environmental lead had killed Steve Williams. Others should be dosed with the lead to make the story believable.

I suppose I could have taken down a couple of Steve's friends along with him, considering I had every opportunity. While Dewie and Vogon were exceptional thorns in my side, *all* of his annoying friends were jerks. The world would never miss them.

But my beef was with Steve. He was their leader, and they would all learn valuable lessons from the death of their master.

A gram of lead slid into Steve's Coke on Monday. Steve was just sitting there, slouching in the ugly, plastic, molded chairs typical of educational institutions around the country. Although I had feared otherwise, the weekend had done nothing to change his mood, a condition I knew could be traced to the lead building up in his brain.

He didn't touch his food for a long time. His friends were almost done eating by the time he picked up a fork. But when he finally ate, he ate quickly, as if his body and his mind were fighting a duel: the mind unwilling to exert any effort, the body starving for food. Eventually, the body won out, as is always the case with people like Steve.

This continued until Wednesday, when I gingerly set Steve's tray down in front of him, careful to avoid agitating him in any way. Dewie was pulling a typical stunt—drinking milk (taken from the tray of a passing girl) through a straw up his nose and spitting it back out onto the floor, through his mouth.

Vogon and the rest of the crew busted out laughing, but Steve just stared at Dewie, white liquid dripping down his chin. After the laughter died down, Steve spoke. "You're such a moron," was all he said. Dewie looked back at him, very sober. "Aren't you tired of being you?" Steve asked.

I was thrilled. Steve would normally have been cutting up with the rest of them. He probably would have tried the stunt himself. But the lead was breaking down his tolerance for idiocy. In a sense, he was becoming a normal person.

But by Thursday afternoon, any hope of normality was pretty far gone. Steve's irascible attitude and perpetual silence were one thing, but the physical effects of the lead were unmistakable.

In a matter of days, Steve had turned a ghostly shade of pale—a shade you don't normally see except in the complexions of the geekiest of computer programmers who never see the light of day. His head was starting to swell just a bit, the result of cerebral edema that was still nascent, but which would be massive by the time Steve died. Had anyone looked, the most telling symptom of Steve's poisoning was that his gums had turned a bluish tint, a dead giveaway of lead in the system. Thank God the baseball season was over, or Steve's coach would have taken him to a doctor personally.

Had Steve done something as simple as visit the school nurse, the game would have been over. But Steve never went to see a doctor. Why? First, if a doctor found him sick, he would have been ruled ineligible to play with the All-State baseball team, which was scheduled for its traditional big game in early June. If he wasn't on that team, he wouldn't get his place in the record books. He probably figured he could stick it out until after the game, that he'd get better sooner or later.

Second, any kind of illness could jeopardize Steve's admission to West Point. Military organizations and institutions don't want applicants with any kind of disability. Steve didn't have a "fallback" college, and if West Point changed its mind, he'd be out of luck for the fall. That would mean, at best, a one-year gap between high school and college, which wouldn't look very good on a résumé.

Steve's hubris was to blame. Brainwashed all his life by sports clichés insisting that he could rise above anything, power through the pain, "walk it off," and just be a man, Steve would never accept that a little illness could keep him down. Steve surely thought: What does a little pain now matter if it guarantees me a place in history? I'm sure he thought about the flashing cameras, the cheering crowds, the fawning fans, and the line of girls. It was easy to forget about a little stomachache when celebrity was on your mind.

Of course, as history has proven, heavy metal always wins out over trite aphorisms.

❖　❖　❖

March 29, 2000

By Friday, Steve was getting very sick. He walked with his arm pressed against his stomach, a futile gesture against the intestinal disturbance that worsened every day he drank from the poisoned cans of Coke.

He and his friends ate lunch in silence, his closest friends afraid to make him angry for fear of being cast out of the inner circle. Steve looked really sick, and Vogon even suggested he go to the nurse, but Steve just told him to mind his own fucking business — or else Vogon would have to go see the nurse himself.

I caught a glimpse of Steve in his last class of the day. In a bout of either pity or self-defeat, my teacher had let us go a few minutes early. I took the opportunity to hustle over to Steve's pre-calculus class for one final check on him before the weekend. Peeking through the little window in the classroom door, I spotted Steve huddled in the far corner of the room, both of his arms pressed against his stomach and his chin down against his chest.

He looked bad, and he was obviously counting down the seconds until he could go home and sleep through the weekend, hoping to recover.

When the bell rang a few moments later, he hopped up out of his seat. His backpack was already fully loaded. He had never even taken out his binder, math book, or even a pencil during the class.

Steve rushed his way through the crowd to the door, and before I could even think of getting out of the way, the door swung open

166

and smacked me in the head.

I lay sprawled out on the floor and felt a little bit dizzy, my eyes straining to focus. A hand reached down and grabbed me by the shoulder, pulling me up into a sitting position.

"You okay?" It was Steve. He was staring me right in the face.

"Uh, yeah." I didn't really know what he was asking, I was too busy staring into the distorted face of a dead man. Pasty and sweating, he looked like a flash-frozen corpse in mid-thaw.

"Then get up and help me. And hurry."

Steve shambled off toward the parking lot, and I jumped to my feet, hastily following.

The parking lot was still empty. School had only been out for a minute. On a Friday afternoon with the summer nearly upon us, the lot would very soon be crawling with students, creating an impromptu traffic jam.

I caught up with Steve as he reached his car. "Drive me home," he ordered. "I'm too sick."

If I hadn't known that he really was too sick to drive, I wouldn't have believed my ears. Drive Steve's Jeep? As far as I knew, *no one* but Steve had ever driven Steve's Jeep. Had circumstances been different, I would have lingered around and let the entire student body see me behind the wheel of the most recognizable vehicle at Fall High. But I figured if I was spotted now, that would mean even more questioning when Steve croaked, so I tore out of the parking lot as quickly as I could get the key in the ignition.

My eyes were glued to the road. For a long while I was too scared to look at Steve. I was somehow sure that when our eyes met, he would know what I had done.

We were halfway to Steve's house (I knew where he lived, though I'd never been there) when I finally took a quick peek at him. He was hunched, almost in a fetal position, curled up against the door, his arms huddled around his legs. His face was covered in sweat, and he was shaking a little. It looked like he was trying to keep warm, though I doubt that was the case.

I don't know what made me talk to him. I was scared to death, but the sadist in me wanted to push it farther. I wanted to see what he would be like in the last days of his life. Call me a monster. I deserve it.

"What's wrong with you?" I asked him, feigning ignorance.

"I'm sick, you little fuck. What do you think?"

"No, I mean, I know you're sick. What's the matter?"

"My head hurts, my stomach hurts. I've got the fucking jitters. I'm sick."

"Sounds like the flu. That's funny, though, 'cause it's not flu season."

"Yeah, well, I'll be better on Monday, I'm sure. I just need to sleep."

"Yeah, sounds like it."

We pulled up to Steve's house: a pristine, white, plantation-style home in the heart of the suburbs. I parked in the driveway, as far out of sight from the street as I could.

I got out of the car, but Steve didn't. I waited thirty seconds or so, and finally went around to the other side of the car to help him out. It was like trying to pick up a quadriplegic baboon, getting him out of the Jeep. Finally I managed to get him to his feet, and he used me like a crutch to get to the door and inside the house.

"My room's upstairs," Steve muttered. Obviously that was his way of asking for help to the bedroom.

Inside the Williams home it was like a museum. It was obvious that a maid visited at least three times a week, and every crystal bowl, every candlestick, and every houseplant had an assigned spot atop an antique.

The staircase curved around the entry hall, depositing us on the second story after an agonizing trip up the risers.

At the end of the hall was Steve's room. Someone else obviously kept it clean for him. The man was a slob, and didn't know the floor from an ashtray. But his room was nice and clean. It was simply decorated, lacking the girlie posters and sports memorabilia you might expect of other kids his age, obviously a mandate from the parents so his room could be kept appropriate for local home tours or the occasional magazine photographer.

Steve collapsed in his bed in the same fetal position he'd assumed in the car. He didn't even get under the covers. I had to pull them up for him. He was as helpless as a baby, and I started to wonder if he would make it through the weekend. Without additional lead in his system, though, I figured he would get a little better each day until Monday. He'd still feel like crap on Sunday evening, but he would probably feel like he was turning the corner, finally kicking the "flu" that had been nagging him for a couple of weeks now. I laughed out loud, thinking about this.

"What's so fucking funny?" Steve asked.

"Nothing, nothing. It's just funny to see you sick like this. You know, you're so tough and strong and all."

"Shut up and leave me alone."

"When are your parents coming home? They can take care of you."

"They're out of town. They're on vacation and won't be back for two weeks. My little sister's staying with her friend while they're gone."

I had completely forgotten about the parents. With the folks out of town, no one would be able to intervene and rush him to the emergency room. He was all mine.

I played along. "Well, maybe you can throw a party tomorrow night." It was all I could do to keep from laughing. There would be no more parties for Steve Williams.

"Yeah, maybe." The idea seemed to cheer him up.

"Okay. Well, you call me if you need anything this weekend." I thought better of that right after I said it. The last thing I needed was phone records tracing me to Steve in his dying days. But it was too late. Steve didn't reply. He just lay there, shaking, feebly willing his illness to go away. I left, trying to rub away any fingerprints wherever I thought I had touched. I walked home the back way, so no one would see me.

Thank God Steve never called that weekend. I doubt he had my phone number.

I kept away from Travis and James for the first weekend in recent memory. I didn't know how they would react, knowing we were near the conclusion of the plan. I didn't want any naysayers, any nagging voices of reason, any doubt. Not now. It was too late for that. So I went home and sequestered myself in my room.

I stayed there for most of the weekend, preparing myself for the end.

❖ ❖ ❖

March 30, 2000

I didn't really expect Steve to show up at school on Monday. I knew he would feel a little better as a tiny bit of the accumulated lead slowly worked its way out of his system, but I figured he would try to take it easy and skip, coasting through the end of the school year, as seniors often do.

But Steve Williams was a man of outrageous conviction. He had been told that you could overcome anything, and a little flu wasn't going to stop him from finishing out the school year—or more importantly, the baseball season. Later I learned that Steve had already maxed out his absences for the semester, the result of too many days skipping class to sleep late or go to the beach. If Steve was out of school even one more day, he'd be disqualified from sports for the remainder of the year.

Steve took up his usual place at head of the lunch table that Monday. He sat there, never speaking. And though it was a violation of the school's dress code, he wore a baseball cap pulled down low over his brow. That cap never came off again. He also kept his letterman's jacket on all the time, despite the fact that the temperature outside pushed into the 90s. Still, he was conscious and alert. But not for long.

I popped the top on a fresh can of Coke and set it down on Steve's lunch tray, next to something billed as "tamale bake," a Mexican casserole of unrecognizable content. As I carried it toward Steve, I deftly removed the cap from my dispenser, which I now kept filled to capacity, just in case.

Into the can slid about a gram of lead. I hadn't really planned in advance how big that week's dose should be. Steve had been surviving on a gram a day for the last week, so in the few seconds I had to think about it, I figured we were too far gone to risk some nosy teacher sending him to the nurse's office. It was time to double up as we entered the home stretch.

I dropped in a second gram of lead, which sunk quickly into the brown depths of the soda. He sipped at the drink, and by the time lunch was over, the can was empty. I didn't see Steve for the rest of the day.

On Tuesday, I reported to Steve's table to collect lunch money and take any special orders—my usual routine—only to discover that Steve was absent from his seat.

This was unfathomable. Did he stay at home, too sick to come to school? I thought I knew Steve better than that: He wouldn't risk his chance to be immortalized in the record books. I'd heard talk that Steve was running up against the maximum number of school absences. No sports, no All-State baseball team. I was sure he would suck it up and finish out the measly nine days of school left. It was simply not possible that he'd quit at this point.

But something was off at Steve's table. His friends were just sitting around, looking like they'd just lost the homecoming game, bummed out and flicking paper balls back and forth at each other. There was no laughter or crudity, the usual hallmarks of the table. The mood was somber.

With trepidation, I approached. "Where's Steve?" I asked, to no one in particular.

Vogon looked up, just as he was forming a small ball from a straw wrapper. "He's outside."

"What do you mean? He's late? What does he want for lunch?"

Vogon replied, annoyed with me. "No, I mean he's eating his lunch outside with the stoners and geeks like you." There was real contempt in his voice. "You'll have to go out there to feed him."

The table snickered, unsure if Vogon had made a joke and unwilling to give up on their fearless leader just yet. I shrugged and walked outside into the sprawling courtyard of Fall Valley High, looking for Steve.

I found him near the shop building—where they "taught" wood shop, metalworking, auto repair, and A/C maintenance. These rooms didn't see a lot of action during the day. Usually the courtyard area near this building was populated with guys sneaking cigarettes or pot, but Steve's unexpected appearance had probably made them scatter.

There he was, his back to a nonfunctional phone booth, out of view of anyone who might be looking his way. His hat was pulled down low over his face. It looked like he was sleeping, or trying to, at least.

I kneeled down in front of him, looking up at his eyes. The sight was shocking. Steve's skin was even worse than I'd seen before: a pasty bluish-white, although his hands and his face were all I could see. Steve was so bundled up that he was sweating profusely, and a trail of drool running out of the corner of his mouth indicated that he was having a hard time controlling his bodily functions. It smelled like he'd been throwing up, and a crusty stain on his shoe confirmed my suspicions. He kept one arm constantly pressed against his stomach. The abdominal pain must have been severe. But he was still alive.

"Hey, Steve," I said quietly.

He slowly looked up to meet my gaze. His eyeballs seemed like they were about to pop out.

"Are you okay? You look like shit," I said, playing dumb.

"Yeah, I'll be all right," he said, in what sounded like the very voice of Death.

I tested him. "Do you need to go to the doctor?"

"Can't. They'll keep me out of the game."

"I don't think you're going to be playing any game."

"Yeah, well what the hell do you know?"

"Are you hungry?" I asked.

He shook his head no.

"Thirsty?"

After a while, he nodded yes.

"Okay, I'll go get you a drink."

I started to walk back to the cafeteria, but I heard Steve quietly call out for me before I got very far. "Hey, wait."

I turned. "Yeah?"

"Maybe I shouldn't have a Coke today."

"Okay, what do you want?" My stomach turned. I was sure he would say milk. Or worse: water.

"Maybe a Sprite."

A relief. "Sure thing, Steve."

❖   ❖   ❖

April 2, 2000

Somehow Steve made it through the week to Friday. He ate his lunch, or rather, drank his lead-doped Sprite, outside by the shop building. His goons ate inside in silence, looking at me with contempt as I passed by with a can of soda for the friend that had forsaken them.

Every day he drank two or three grams of lead. A weaker man would have died long ago. I know I would have. I don't know why his teachers let him stay in class. I guess the faculty didn't want to ruin his chances for baseball glory either.

There was no longer any need for secrecy as I mixed the poison into Steve's drink. Steve and I were invariably alone, and he was so far out of it that I probably could have spoon-fed him powdered lead and he wouldn't have known it from applesauce.

I dropped three grams of lead into the can of Sprite as I walked to Steve's new lunch spot.

He had fallen asleep by the time I got to him. A trail of drool was running down his chin onto the baseball jersey he wore, forming a discolored pool where it landed. It was a pathetic sight, and I woke him up by shaking his shoulder.

Steve's eyes flicked open. They were bulging out underneath the lids, and seeing the whites appear so suddenly shocked me so much I almost dropped the can of Sprite.

But I regained my composure and sat down beside Steve. We had a little heart-to-heart.

"You don't look so well," I told him.

"I know. Only one week of school left, though, then I can rest."

"What about the All-State game?"

"Yeah. After that, then I can rest."

"I don't know . . ." I said with skepticism in my voice. I enjoyed toying with him. "I don't know if you're going to be well enough in time."

"Yeah, I feel like a pile of garbage. But I'll get better. I'll push through it."

What a naïve asshole. He wasn't going to work through anything. The motivational speakers of the world have tricked people into thinking they can overcome any obstacle if they just have enough willpower. Stop kidding yourselves.

Steve sipped on his Sprite, slowly killing himself with each gulp that actually made it into his mouth. He had only managed a few sips when I figured out he was never going to finish the entire can. I rudely took it from him and added more lead.

I dumped in the entire contents of my dispenser, about ten more grams, which I figured was enough lead to kill a very large animal.

As I handed the can back to Steve, I took our conversation to another level. "Are you happy with the way your life has turned out, Steve?" I asked him.

Despite a swelling brain and massive internal pain, Steve was still proud of himself. "Shit yeah," he mumbled. "I can have any chick I want, I'm the school hero in two sports, I'm going to an awesome college. I've done everything perfect."

Steve's voice was raspy and his speech was halting. Getting out each phrase was an effort, punctuated by long gasps for air, coughing, and moments of silence where you thought he might have died. But he didn't. He kept on breathing. Kept on living.

I continued the interrogation. "But what about all the people you've stepped on, Steve? You didn't get to where you are by being a great guy. You did it by treating most of the world with contempt. You did it by being a selfish asshole, if you'll pardon my language."

It was a long time before Steve answered. Finally, he spoke, "Maybe you're right. I guess maybe I could have been nicer to a lot of people."

"You know when you left me out in the quarry, after you pushed my car in, I got frostbite. They amputated my toe."

He tried to lift his head to look at me but was only partially successful. One eye met mine. "Really? I didn't know that."

"You didn't know or you didn't care?"

He let his head drop back down.

"I'm sorry, Alex. I never meant to hurt anybody like that." It was the first and last time he ever called me by my real name. And even though he sounded drunk when he said it, I thought I felt a glimmer of hope for the humanity in Steve after all. Maybe he wasn't a monster. Maybe he could be redeemed. Maybe he had learned his lesson.

Steve went on. "I'm sorry for a lot of things. You've been so good to me, and I've treated you like shit. None of my friends are out here with me. Only you. You must really care about people." I thought I was going to tear up until he finished, "I hope you're not a fag or something."

I just stared at him after that. Now would be the last chance for me to call this whole thing off. I could take the can from him and leave him there to sleep it off. Over the next few months he'd slowly get better as the lead left his body, then he'd be back to his old self—almost as good as new.

Or I could have gone to the principal and confessed the whole thing. They have all kinds of drugs that can speed your recovery from lead poisoning.

Either way, Steve would get well. And maybe he would have been a better person when he made it back to full consciousness, learning from his near-death experience, as many people often do. Maybe I was the one who was the asshole now.

I mean, is it fair to take someone's life in exchange for a pet rabbit, a Camaro, and a pinky toe? I started to feel sorry for the guy, but I pulled myself back and reminded myself I wasn't Steve's only victim.

I thought of Alison O'Malley, driven to suicide by Steve's callous treatment. I thought of Gene Thomson, whom Steve had tossed through a window and who now had a speech impediment and a limp as a result. I thought of Pat Landers, the guy who got kicked out of his house because of Steve, and who, according to the rumors, had been kidnapped and murdered while trying to live on the cheap in Mexico. I thought about dozens of kids, just like me, none of whom had the ability to stand up against the tyranny, and none of whom were willing to forgive and forget.

But did that make it right for me to be the angel of death? Shouldn't I have turned the other cheek and let him live? I'd proven my power. Whether he knew it or not, Steve now owed his life to me. I was smarter and better than Steve Williams would ever be. And maybe that was enough.

I was torn, but I didn't have the luxury of endless hours to reconsider the plan. In fact, I figured I only had a few short minutes until the bell rang and the courtyard flooded with kids en route to their next class. This was my last chance. Steve's parents would be home on Sunday night. They'd rush him to the hospital on first sight. It was now or never. In the space of thirty seconds, I made my decision.

Solemnly, I looked to Steve and said, "Why don't you have some more Sprite? It'll make you feel better."

❖ ❖ ❖

April 8, 2000

Steve Williams died on May 12, 1989 — a lifetime in the past. It was about 12:35 in the afternoon. I don't know exactly because I don't wear a watch. When he went, he didn't say anything. He just kind of choked and gurgled, and then his head fell back against the phone booth. Then he stopped breathing altogether, and his body went limp. I checked his pulse: Steve Williams was dead.

I grabbed the can before it could spill. That would be evidence that I'd have to get rid of quickly.

There wasn't a lot of time to feel sorry for what I'd done. Not yet. I just bid a silent farewell to Steve Williams, the now-martyred hero of Fall Valley High, and leapt into the cleanup phase of the plan, which I began to fear I hadn't thought through well enough.

I poured the rest of the Sprite onto a nearby patch of grass, then I crushed the can and carried it with me as I strode across the courtyard toward the main campus. I reached the doorway into the C Wing, the building farthest from the location of Steve's body. I turned around to take a last look at the scene of the crime. From here you could only see a couple of feet poking out from behind the phone booth. It was difficult to see the feet at all, and even if you did notice them, it just looked like someone had fallen asleep, probably some stoner who'd had too much to smoke.

175

I turned back around and pushed my way into the school, jamming the crushed can into my pocket. I didn't look back again.

Quickly, I stashed the lead dispenser and the Sprite can in my locker, filling the receptacle with pencil shavings I had collected expressly for this purpose, my hope being that a casual observer would see the dispenser as a fancy pencil sharpener and nothing more. I hid the dispenser deep inside one of those zip-up pencil bags along with a bunch of pens and pencils, then shoved that down into the bottom of my locker.

I spent the next half-hour in agony. My plan was to let someone else discover the body, let them deal with the cops and the hassle. I was just waiting nervously for the voice of Principal Patterson to come on and announce "A Terrible Tragedy" or some such nonsense. But that's not what happened.

Angela Sharp's piercing scream could be heard throughout the school, though it was barely an echo by the time it reached my classroom on the C Wing's second floor. Mrs. Flores put down the chalk and her teacher's-edition physics book and told us all to stay in our seats. Such interruptions happened all the time at FVH, but the sound of a girl screaming that loud usually drew the attention of the more civic-minded teachers.

Mrs. Flores went out into the hall. From our seats we could hear the twittering sounds of gossip among the faculty, and teacher after teacher passed by our door, run-walking toward the courtyard to get in on the action, to get the good dirt on what was going on before anyone else.

Our classroom erupted with chatter. What was going on? We didn't have any windows so we couldn't see out. And although I knew what had made Angela Sharp cry out in horror, I desperately wanted to see what was going on in the courtyard below, where the echoes of murmurs, screams, chatter, and gasps were growing louder by the second.

Gordon Eisenstein, a perpetually inquisitive kid, was the first student in our class to rush out into the hallway. Mrs. Flores had been gone close to three minutes and he just couldn't stand it any longer. Neither could I. Our class streamed out in a rush of bodies, flooding the hall in a surge toward the stairs that led down to the exit and the courtyard.

When I made it outside, there were already close to a hundred people in a massive crush near the shop building. Some of the voices were hysterical, screaming "Call 911! Call 911!" but most of them stared awestruck at Steve's corpse. Obviously he was too far gone to bring back, but what the hell would some teacher know about that?

I played like I didn't know what was up. We tried to push through to the front of the crowd, but some of the larger male faculty held people back. One of the girls in our class got up on Gordon's shoulders to see what was going on. She yelled out, "It's a body! Somebody's dead! It's covered up with a blanket, but it's definitely a dead body! *Omigod*!!!"

And with that a new uproar erupted from the crowd. I turned around to look back at the school building. Students were pouring out in droves, as if the place was on fire. As if *they* were on fire. In minutes the courtyard was filled to capacity with thousands of students, all with one question on their lips: "Who died? Who is it?"

Angela Sharp, a couple of teachers, and I were the only ones who knew. And none of us was talking.

❖   ❖   ❖

April 10, 2000

It took fifteen minutes for Principal Patterson to push his way through the crowd to the body. By then, a couple of cop cars had also arrived, but these were suburban traffic cops, unskilled at dealing with the discovery of corpses and certainly unfamiliar with how to handle near-riot situations. They just milled about like everyone else, pleading over their radios for more officers to come to the scene.

Eventually one of the cops made it through to the body. He spoke to Principal Patterson for a few minutes, then peeked under the sheet. Not even bothering with looking for a pulse—it must have been that obvious—the cop wrote something down in a little book. I can only assume it was the official pronouncement that Steve was dead.

I looked around the courtyard for a friendly face, but Travis and James were nowhere to be seen. All I could really see were the dozen or so people from my Physics class, pressed up against me, all straining to get a look at the corpse, and all repeating, over and over, "Who is it? Who could it be?" I was trapped where I was standing.

Someone passed a handheld loudspeaker to the principal, and after about five minutes of pleading and through the judicious use of screeching feedback, he managed to silence the mob. The principal addressed us.

"Students of Fall Valley High, I regret to inform you that one of our star scholars has passed on. Steve Williams—" At this, the crowd erupted with shock and horror, drowning out the next sentence. It took another few minutes to quiet the crowd again, and the principal continued, "Steve Williams died earlier today of unknown causes. Classes will be canceled for the remainder of the day. You are all asked to immediately collect your things and leave within the next fifteen minutes. That is all."

By this time, at least a dozen cops and men with jackets reading "coroner" had arrived. The cops made a circle around the courtyard, while the coroners worked their way to the body.

Few people followed the principal's orders immediately, but slowly I began to make my way back to the C Wing to get out of there. I didn't want to stick around to see what happened next. Every person I passed was talking to someone else about the latest news from the crime scene: The coroners put the body in a black bag. They loaded it onto a gurney. They wheeled it out to an ambulance waiting behind the shop building. The ambulance drove off. And then there was nothing left to see, but people stayed there, just looking, waiting for the punch line to a truly sick joke.

The halls were still fairly empty, even by the time I made it inside. I returned to the Physics classroom and grabbed my backpack, then made a quick dash to my locker for the pencil bag, with its dirty secrets.

The cops soon started to work their way through the school, ordering kids to leave immediately. I was lucky I had already been to my locker by then. "Leave it," they commanded to most people who started dialing their combinations. "You can get it next week. Go home."

I had no desire to stay to watch the circus. It would be on TV at five o'clock, anyway. I pushed through the doors to the parking lot and broke into a run. I couldn't control myself, I just had to get away as quickly as I could. As I passed through the rows of vehicles, I even spotted Steve's Jeep, which had been parked haphazardly across two spaces with one wheel up on a concrete divider.

I wondered what would become of that car.

178

April 11, 2000

It was barely one o'clock by the time I got home. The house was empty, of course. My dad was at work and my mom was at some social function, surely enjoying herself at what would be the last "happy event" of the year. For the remainder of 1989, there would be no more cocktail parties or charity fund-raisers. Instead, Fall Valley would become a morass of candlelight vigils, memorial services, and potluck dinners "to help the Williams family through their time of crisis." Disgusting.

I ran up to my room and shut the door, trying to think. I just didn't know what to do. I had practiced the murder until it was practically a reflex. But I hadn't given much thought to the aftermath. I was paralyzed with indecision. A mountain of evidence seemed to fill my bedroom. I had to get rid of it.

I sprung into action. I quickly found a garbage bag and loaded it up with all the evidence that was left: the jar of lead shavings, the dispenser, the killer can, the metal file James had lent me but wanted back (sorry, James), various rubber gloves, lead-smudged newspapers, and sundry other trash that could be linked to the crime.

I called Travis. Thank God he was home. Before I even asked, he said he was on his way over to pick me up.

I waited outside, concealing the trash bag in the bushes, out of sight. I paced around the yard anxiously, agonizing over each minute that passed. By now, my mother must have heard what had happened from one of the other parents. Hell, it was probably on TV already. I knew that my mother would arrive home soon, then my father would come home early, and then we'd have an unfathomably awful "family chat" about the day's events.

Travis beat her, thankfully. I grabbed the trash bag and jumped into his car. He knew where to drive: the incinerator behind the meat-packing plant, about thirty miles south.

Neither of us said a thing until we were about twenty miles out of town. I told Travis to pull over, so I could scatter the rest of the lead in an overgrown field. I got back in the car and shut the door. He pulled back onto the highway without a word.

The meat-packing plant was always busy, but no one ever bothered you behind the slaughterhouse, and it was extremely easy to get into the back room where you could just dump your trash into the hopper that fed into the enormous furnace. Outside the back room, I swung the bag into a concrete post, smashing the glass inside into unrecognizable bits. Then I tossed it into the hopper, and up, up, up it went, into the fire.

It was never a good idea to linger around the slaughterhouse lest you arouse the suspicion of a security guard, so I hustled back to the car, and Trav quickly drove off, his tires spitting gravel from the unpaved road, taking us back the way we came.

We were well away from the meat-packing plant when Trav finally spoke.

"You really did it, huh?"

I didn't look at him. I just stared at the flat road ahead and a landscape devoid of features. "I guess I did."

"Do you think you're going to get caught?"

"Probably. Cops are smarter than we give them credit for, I think."

"Yeah."

"The school's going to be a madhouse. It's going to be horrible. Girls are going to be crying."

"They'll probably put up some stupid picture of him near the front office."

"God, that's going to be awful."

"Yeah."

It was quiet for a while until Travis finally said something else. "You going to turn yourself in?"

"No. I don't want to go to jail. They're going to have to work for it if they want to catch me."

"Never plead guilty. That's what my dad says."

"Your dad's pretty smart."

"Well, I don't know if this calls for a celebration or not, but we should get a drink."

"Definitely."

We drove straight to Travis's house. We knew his parents wouldn't be home. They had real jobs in the city. I would have been surprised if they even knew what had happened yet, much less left work early (unpaid leave, no doubt) just to see how their kid was coping.

We had a few shots of rum and listened to some music before I went home to the inevitable. By then, my parents would be home, and they'd be worried sick. They would have called the school at least three times, looking for me. Head down, I walked home, ready to face what I already knew would be a mushy smothering of emotion designed to overcompensate for years of neglect.

April 12, 2000

"How awful this must be for you."

It was a refrain I would hear again and again, from relatives close and distant, from school counselors, from police officers, from other students, from reporters, from people I didn't even know.

Of course, good old Mom and Dad wanted to hear the whole saga. They'd read about Steve Williams' prowess in sports in the papers and had seen him play a few times. My dad occasionally asked if I knew this god of the athletic field, but I never mentioned Steve by name around my father. As far as my parents knew, the bully who had tormented me for years was a nameless ogre, not the school hero.

"He was that baseball player, right? Did you know him?" my mother asked, the corners of her eyes drooping into a caricature of motherly concern. She had already forgotten my tearful confession to her from a year earlier, after Steve and his friends had pummeled me senseless following the *Blithe Spirit* Fag Show.

"Yeah, Mom. Everybody knew him."

"So tell us what happened," my dad said, the vicarious rubbernecker.

"I don't know. It was really confusing. A girl screamed from the courtyard and all the teachers went to see what happened. By the time I got there, there was a huge crowd of people. Some girl had found him dead near the shop building. Then they sent us home. That was it."

"How did he die? I heard he got shot," said my mother, trying to hide her excitement.

"No, Mom. He didn't get shot. He just died. I don't know what the cause was. I'm sure it will be in the papers soon enough."

"I bet it will. On the way home the school was crawling with news crews," my dad interjected.

"Well, honey, you know we're here for you if you want to talk about this."

"I know, Mom. Thanks." I reassured her. I gave them both ample time to express their remorse and regrets, but they appeared to be done.

"So," I asked, "what's for dinner?"

April 13, 2000

Saturday morning arrived without the knock on the door I had expected. I had spent the previous night sleepless, staring at the bumps on the ceiling, trying to make patterns of the textures to little avail. I was dead tired, but, as is the case any time you have insomnia, the harder I tried to will myself to sleep, the farther out of reach it slipped.

I was up before my parents that morning, something that almost never happened. I couldn't sleep and wanted something to occupy my mind. I even considered mowing the lawn but thought better of it.

For breakfast, I ate what I could of a bowl of cereal before my stomach turned against me. Then I just sat in the kitchen in silence, waiting for the doorbell to ring and my life as I knew it to come to an end. It wouldn't be long, I figured, until the cops pieced together the mystery; I should try to enjoy myself while I still can. But like it is with insomnia, the more you tell yourself to relax, the less relaxed you are.

By noon, I was pacing around the house like a mental patient, driving my parents crazy, I'm sure. I couldn't watch TV. It seemed like every time I turned it on there was some "special report" or another about the tragic death of a young hero at Fall Valley. But no one knew any actual facts about his death, so the stations just aired a ton of grainy home-video retrospectives about Steve Williams, sold to them by locals looking to make a quick buck. I turned off the TV and left it that way, but I could not stop dreading the fate I felt sure was in store for me.

Finally I asked if I could borrow my mom's car to get out of the house, and they agreed. Mistaking my panic for sorrow, they pitied me. Plus, I figured they were ready to do about anything to get rid of me.

I drove the speed limit to Fall High. They say most criminals are caught when they return to the scene of the crime, and I always laughed when I heard that. What kind of stupid criminal would go back to the place where the authorities were most likely to be? Now I know. It's impossible not to go back. Any criminal worth his psychosis wants to see the consequences of his actions. It's an obsession. It's what makes us criminals.

You can't see much from the road that passes in front of the school, but you can see enough. The news crews were gone. Most of the cops had left, too, but I counted two cars and a big police truck, like the kind you see in the movies for hauling people away from a riot or something. They had hung yellow tape everywhere. Every entrance to the school and the grounds—especially the courtyard—had been blockaded with that yellow "POLICE LINE DO NOT CROSS" ribbon and those wooden barricades they use for road construction.

On my third or fourth drive-by, I finally spotted the cops, one inside the school and two in the courtyard. They were on their hands and knees, carefully investigating the ground, one square foot at a time. One of the cops was taking pictures of everything. He'd point a camera at the wall, snap a photo, move a couple of feet to the right, then repeat. Over and over again. I knew Steve's suspicious death would result in an intense investigation, but this bordered on obsession. A witch hunt.

Woe unto the witch.

❖ ❖ ❖

April 15, 2000

Come Monday, my mother had no idea whether I should go to school or not.

I got up, showered, dressed, and ate as usual, but no one had said whether or not school would be in session.

In the end, it was decided that I should indeed go to school that day. If there were no classes, my mother said, I could come home.

I walked to campus, and upon my arrival, it was clear that classes had been canceled. Hordes of students in my predicament milled about in the parking lot, outside the campus. The yellow tape was still up, the doors were locked, and a squadron of police patrolled the area. A handful of newspeople worked the crowd, trying to get fresh quotes and squeeze some more juice out of a story that had largely played itself out over the weekend.

Though the autopsy report had still not been released, the media assumed there was no foul play. The story was simple: Local sports hero dies of sudden and mysterious, but natural, causes. A community grieves. Next segment. Repeat. The only news crews left were the third-tier players: twelve-page community newspapers and local cable TV reporters.

I milled about with everyone else. I didn't see a friendly face, so I just sat down on the back of someone's pickup truck, waiting for someone else to decide that we should all go home.

Almost twenty minutes after the bell normally would have rung, Principal Patterson came out to address the crowd. He had the same loudspeaker he'd addressed us with in the courtyard only three days earlier. Some aide brought a little stepladder for him to stand on, and again he used screeching feedback to silence the chatter in the parking lot.

When he finally earned a rough approximation of silence, he told everyone to go home. "Classes are canceled for the rest of the week, pending an investigation into the death of Steve Williams. The final week of classes will resume next Monday, and final exams will be administered next Thursday and Friday. So you've all got an extra week to study. Use your free time wisely.

"During the investigation, please *do not* come to the school campus unless you are specifically asked to do so. The police will be interviewing acquaintances of Steve Williams as part of the investigation. Many of these interviews will be held on campus, and the authorities will notify you individually if your presence is required.

"Again, please *do not* come to school unless you are called. Now, everybody please return to your homes until next week. Thank you."

The loudspeaker cut off with a chirp and the principal uneasily stepped down from the wobbly stool. People were disappointed that he hadn't provided any more insight into Steve's death, but as they realized they'd just been handed a week off from school, they started leaving. School was the last place they wanted to spend a free week of vacation.

I walked to the road, dodging the cars creeping their way out of the parking lot. But something made me turn around. Off in the distance, beyond the parking lot, near the main entrance to the school, some intrepid ROTC freshman was raising the American flag, a job he'd probably been doing daily since the beginning of the school year.

The ROTC kid was raising the flag like nothing had happened. He was "just doing his job," as they say. Principal Patterson and one of the coaches saw this and ran over to the flagpole. A lot of shouting ensued, though I was much too far away to hear any of it. There was yelling and pointing and what looked like physical threats.

Finally, his eyes downcast, the ROTC kid slowly lowered the flag to half mast. He tied off the cord, as the crowd dispersed. The flag fluttered in a sudden brisk breeze. I could even hear it whipping back and forth, slapping the aluminum pole angrily. But the mast was much stronger than the flag. No matter how loud it protested, the mast remained steady. The flag's complaints were lost to the wind.

The flag in front of Fall Valley High flew at half mast for the rest of the school year, and the entire summer.

❖   ❖   ❖

April 18, 2000

The call came that afternoon. My mother answered the phone. She didn't even mention it to me until hours later, while we were waiting for my dad to get home so we could eat dinner. She just looked up and said, "Oh, honey, the police called and they want you to come to school tomorrow at ten, so they can talk to you about that boy who died."

That was it. I guess to her it sounded pretty innocent. You know, "just routine." I'm sure they said that on the phone. And maybe the police didn't suspect a thing. But my stomach sank. I was certain they were on to me. I just didn't know why they weren't going to arrest me that night.

For the fourth day I didn't eat and for the fourth night I didn't sleep. Morning took its time coming. By 6:30 I simply couldn't stay in bed any longer so I showered and dressed.

I watched cartoons and game shows until 9:45, then drove to school in my mother's car, prepared for the worst.

The yellow tape was still up, and the parking lot was empty save for a half-dozen cop cars and an equal number of civilian ones. But more curious were the large, white vans with an unfamiliar seal on them. Upon closer inspection I could read the text: Environmental Protection Agency. I didn't make the connection at the time.

A uniformed cop who looked bored out of his skull greeted me at the entrance to the school. He asked my name and checked a clipboard. He then lifted the plastic about a foot and waved me toward the courtyard. I still had to duck to pass under the ribbon.

Being back in school was surreal. I passed the gym and a few classrooms. The place looked haunted.

In the courtyard, a few cops in uniform and a number of plainclothes officials were scattered around. Most were idly chatting, drinking coffee, or otherwise wasting taxpayer dollars.

On the far side of the courtyard I could see a card table had been set up near Steve Williams' place of death. A couple of cops were sitting there, and when they saw me, they waved me over. I hurried over to them.

When I got to the table, I could see behind the phone booth where Steve had been sitting. White tape stuck to the ground, the phone booth, and the adjacent wall, outlining the position of Steve's body when he was discovered. Despite the lack of blood-stains or bullet holes, the image was ghostly and disturbing. Fall Valley really was haunted.

"That bothering you?" One of the cops, a well-manicured man in his thirties, with a trim moustache, was speaking. He startled me, pulling me out of a dazed stare at the tape.

"Huh?" I muttered.

The cop jerked his thumb toward the tape outline. "The tape. It freaks people out sometimes. We can cover it up if you want."

Finally I averted my gaze. "No, that's okay."

"All right then," he said. "Have a seat." He pointed to a folding chair opposite where he and the other cop, a pretty redheaded woman with a concerned look, were sitting. I sat. "I'm officer Lemons."

"Officer Lemons?" I asked, skeptical.

"Yeah, Lemons." He looked bored . . . waiting for a joke that I was too nervous to make.

The woman cop spoke. "I guess this must pretty hard for you." That phrase again.

I nodded, playing along. "Yeah, it's hard for everybody."

She continued, "I mean, for you. You were the last person to see Steve Williams alive, is that right?"

I replied to the question, "Well, I don't know. Maybe."

It seemed like they already knew a lot, and I immediately began to worry that they were trying to trick me into spilling the beans. Still, this didn't seem like an interrogation. I hadn't been offered a lawyer or been read my rights—the legality of which I'm still trying to figure out. This, apparently, was just a friendly chat, albeit with curious overtones.

The two cops looked at each other, trying to size me up, I guess. Surely they were expecting someone different, someone more in line with Steve's other friends.

Officer Lemons asked, "So he was alive when you left him."

"That's right."

"You're sure."

"Pretty sure. He was moving and all."

"Did he say anything to you?"

"Not really. Just a lot of mumbling."

"Where did you go when you left him?"

"To class, of course."

"I see." He flipped through his notes. "Physics, right?"

"Yeah." I strained to see what he had written about me in his files . . . my class schedule? My grades? The parking ticket I got after I'd only had my car for a week?

Lemons went on. "We were told that you used to get Steve's lunch for him, is that right?"

"Yes."

"And during the last week he couldn't eat, so you just brought him Cokes. Is that right, too?"

"Yes. He was drinking Sprite, mostly."

"I see. And I also understand that you and Steve Williams had some problems. You got in a few fights over the last couple of years?"

"Sure, I guess."

"So you weren't friends."

"No, I wouldn't say we were."

"Enemies?"

"No, I don't think so. I was just another guy in his path. There are tons of kids like me that didn't really get along with Steve."

"Was getting his lunch a kind of punishment for you?" The cop looked concerned, more frantic. But he was grasping.

"No, I wouldn't say that either. I did it as a courtesy, not because I had to."

"A courtesy." He looked skeptical.

"Right, a courtesy." I just stared at him coldly for a while as he sized me up, wondering if I could possibly be a killer. The woman whispered something in his ear, and finally he kept going.

"Do you know how Steve Williams died?" the male cop asked me.

"No, how?"

"He died of lead poisoning. Does that surprise you?"

"Sure. I mean, I thought lead wasn't a problem anymore."

"Well, yes and no. Lead is all over the place, and getting rid of it is tricky. But it's very rare for anyone but small children to actually die from lead exposure."

"Wow," I deadpanned. "Is that why the EPA people are here?" I was getting good at playing the game, and I could feel my confidence coming back.

"That's right. You're a smart kid, aren't you?"

"I'm pretty average, I think."

The woman asked, "Where do you want to go to college?"

"Ohio State." I practically spat it out.

"That's a long way away," she replied. "Why do you want to go there?"

"It's a good school. I like Ohio a lot." Truth is I'd never even been to Ohio.

Lemons took over again. "You saw Steve every day during the last few weeks of his life, correct?"

"I guess so, yeah."

"How sick did he seem to you?"

"Well, pretty sick, you know?"

"Sick enough to go to a doctor?"

"Sure. I told him all the time he needed to go to a doctor, but he wouldn't."

"Why's that?"

"Because he couldn't have any more absences or he wouldn't make the All-State baseball team."

The cop did a double take. "He told you this?"

"Yeah, sure."

The two cops did another whisper huddle and flipped through their papers.

"Steve's friends and teachers have all told us that Steve didn't seem that sick to them. That they had no idea how bad off he was. Why do you think that is?"

I thought about it for a while. I didn't really get the question and had no idea how to respond. Finally, I replied, "I'd say they were covering their asses and trying to make themselves feel better. Steve was really sick."

Lemons looked me in the eye. "That's what I'd say, too."

Lemons tapped a pen on the table. I kept looking at the outline of Steve's body. No one said anything for a while. I figure it was some dumb police tactic to make suspects spill their guts.

"You know what I think?" asked Lemons, finally breaking the silence. "I think Steve was intentionally poisoned. I think someone killed him."

I tried to look shocked. I had never expected them to get this far. The cops really were smarter than I gave them credit for.

"Wow. Really." I just kind of nodded, pretending to think about what he said.

"You don't know anyone who would want to kill Steve Williams, do you?"

"No."

"And there was no reason you would want to kill him."

"No. I don't even like to eat meat." I threw that in because I thought it would sound especially pathetic. I think it did.

Officer Lemons sized me up for a long while, taking a mental picture of me. But finally he tidied up his stack of papers and closed a manila folder. "I guess you can go home, Alex. We can call you if we have any more questions, right?"

"Sure. Hope I was some help."

I got up and turned to leave when he called out, "Alex!" I turned back around. "One more question."

"Yeah?"

"You brought Steve a Coke on the day he died, right?"

"A Sprite."

"A Sprite, right."

"What about it?"

"I'm just curious. What do you think happened to the can?"

Immediately I knew I was still looking at an uphill climb, that the cop thought I could be the quiet murderer they feared. But I was ready for the question and crinkled up my face, the way I'd practiced. "I don't know. I guess it got lost in all the commotion."

"I guess so." The cop smirked at me. "Thank you, Alex."

I walked out the way I came. It was uneventful except for passing a couple of EPA guys leaning against the outer wall of the gym, taking a smoke break.

They didn't pay any attention to me as I went by, and I overheard a tiny portion of their conversation.

It went like this, "I can't believe these guys are treating this as a homicide case. What kind of person would murder somebody with *lead?*"

It is a very reasonable question.

April 20, 2000

When the phone rang the following morning, I was certain it was going to be the cops, asking me to come back for a second round of questioning and offering me a court-appointed attorney.

But it wasn't the police. It was an unfamiliar voice, a woman whose sadness could be heard right through the wire. Though we'd never met, I knew it could only be one person: Steve's mother.

"Is this Alex?" she asked, in that quavering whimper.

"Yes."

"I'm Bonnie Williams." She paused. "Steve's mom."

"Hi, Mrs. Williams."

"I hope you don't mind my calling. I know you did so much for Steve over the last few weeks that I'd like to meet you in person. Do you think you could come by this afternoon?"

This was most unexpected and sounded just awful, but I felt so guilty and sorry for this woman that I couldn't refuse. "How about two o'clock?" I asked.

"That would be fabulous. Do you know where we live?"

"Yeah. I know."

At two, I drove Mom's car to the Williams house, where I'd visited a little over a week before to put the dying Stevie to bed.

Much to my surprise, the house was abustle with all manner of visitors: cops, delivery people, relatives, neighbors, reporters, and, most intriguingly, EPA officials. Cars lined the street around their house for hundreds of yards. For a moment I feared some kind of setup, but I quickly dismissed it. Steve's mother wouldn't be smart enough for that.

I rang the bell and she answered. I knew her from the social pages in the newspaper, a frail-looking woman with too-high cheekbones and an expensive blonde dye job. "Alex?"

"Yeah."

She smiled politely. "Come on in."

Inside, the house was a mess. For starters, it looked like a flower shop. All over the foyer were weepy flower arrangements, some simple, some outrageously elaborate. Photos of Steve were scattered all over the place, most of them featuring him in some kind of posed sporting stance—ready to throw the winning pass, ready to knock in a home run—you know, "the way they wanted to re-member him."

People filled every room of the house. Cops and EPA officials with strange-looking devices scanning floors and walls. Another policeman dusting an old pair of gym shoes for God knows what. Relatives comforting other relatives. And people in the kitchen, cooking, always cooking.

"Can I get you something to eat?" Steve's mom asked.

"No, I'm fine."

"Okay. Well, why don't we go someplace quieter so we can talk?"

Visions of *The Graduate* dancing through my head, Mrs. Williams led me upstairs to Steve's room. She shut the door behind us.

I couldn't believe it, but there were even more flowers up here than there were downstairs. All over his bed, his desk, the floor, the dresser, everywhere. In fact, there was no place to sit, so Mrs. Williams cleared some space on the bed by piling up the flowers in a corner of the room, where the once-pretty arrangements became a tangled mass of vegetation. "I'm sorry for the mess," she said. "Steve's father and I had to cut our trip short, and with all the deliveries we just haven't had a chance to get tidied up."

She sat on the newly cleared edge of the bed and patted the area next to her, indicating I should sit. I did. Then she hugged me briefly. I was so confused and unprepared, I didn't even hug her back. I just leaned against her cold, hard, and bony body and let her get whatever comfort she needed out of the embrace.

Finally she let go, sat up, sniffed back a few tears, and talked. "So I guess you and Steve were good friends?"

"I don't know. Not really."

I don't think she was paying attention to me at all. She just kept on blathering. "We don't really know what to do with his things. Steve doesn't have a little brother, just a sister. She really isn't interested in sports or athletics."

"Really?" I asked. I vaguely remembered the sister but knew nothing about her. "How old is she?"

"Ten. She's an angel, but she's not like Stevie. She won't come out of her room, but I guess that's okay, for now. You'll meet her at the funeral."

"The funeral?"

"It's on Saturday at Woods Prairie. One o'clock. I hope you can come."

"Yeah, sure, I'll be there." I don't know why I said it. I just didn't want her crying on me.

"That's wonderful. It wouldn't be the same without you."

This woman was too much. She'd never even met me, and already I was indispensable. Then again, I guess I was of more comfort to her than Steve's real friends, none of whom I figured had even spoken to her since Steve died.

Mrs. Williams got up and made her way through the maze of flowers to Steve's closet, where she vanished for a minute or so. Then she appeared with an armload of stuff, which she presented to me.

"Steve would have wanted you to have these." One by one, she handed over a football, a football helmet, a football jersey, several pairs of socks, some blue jeans, and a well-worn jock strap. One look at me and it would have been pretty clear that not only was I not going to fit into these hand-me-downs, but I simply didn't have a football physique. And a used jock strap? Grief can blind you pretty severely, I suppose.

"Uh, thanks," I said, my arms full of Steve's old clothes.

"This way you can remember Steve every time you wear them."

"Yeah, that'll be great."

We sat there for a few minutes more, in silence. Finally Mrs. Williams spoke, "Well, I guess I won't keep you any longer."

"Okay." I awkwardly got up to leave and stumbled my way to the door and down the stairs, with Mrs. Williams following behind me.

She called out as I left the house, "We'll see you on Saturday!"

"Okay!" I yelled out, not even turning around. I didn't close the door behind me, hurriedly walking back to the car. I drove home as fast as I could, putting as much distance between myself and the Williams house as possible.

When I arrived home, I opened the garage door and parked the car. My first order of business was transferring all of the crap Steve's mom had given me from the back seat of the car and into the bottom of a large trashcan near the door to the house.

I feel bad about that. I bet that stuff would have been worth something today.

❖   ❖   ❖

April 21, 2000

Steve's funeral was even worse than I ever imagined.

My mother took me. She made me wear the navy blue suit that never fit right but was the only formalwear I owned. My dad tied my tie for me because I'd never learned how. Then he left for a Saturday of work, and Mom and I headed for Woods Prairie Cemetery.

We were late, as usual, and the service had already started. A huge throng of people in black surrounded a mound of dirt, a large wooden casket, a minister, and two assistants. A half-dozen photographers stood in a herd behind a small barricade, hoping the news of the dead sports hero would go national, thus making their exclusive pictures worth a fortune.

We had to check in with a security guy before we could approach the service. He checked for my name on a clipboard then waved us in. We stood at the back.

It was the usual graveside service. Nobody from Steve's family spoke, just the preacher. Ashes to ashes and all that business. The whole thing was over ten minutes later. They didn't even put the casket into the ground. They do that later. I don't know if that's normal or not—to this date, Steve's is the only funeral I've been to.

The family was seated up front. The rest of the crowd had to stand. I guess they seat the family in case they get woozy and fall down. Can you imagine if someone fainted and fell into the grave?

Steve's mother looked like she was straight out of a movie, with a black dress, a broad-rimmed black hat, a black veil, the whole mourning suit. She was sniffling and sobbing the whole time. Steve's dad was practically busting out of his Army uniform. He had obviously put on a lot of weight since he'd last worn it and hadn't had time to get it altered. He just sat there staring at the casket the whole time, never showing any emotion, other than what I might call stoic boredom.

Steve's ten-year-old sister sat between them. Her legs were too short to reach the ground so she kicked them back and forth, periodically hitting the bottom of her own chair, making her jump a little. This seemed to encourage her, and she'd do it harder and harder until finally her dad would break his stare and, teeth clenched, order her to stop.

I wished that the funeral had been open-casket. I wanted to get one last look at Steve before they buried him. I was mainly curious about how he looked. I was sure they could revive the color and get rid of the disgusting pastiness, but I kept wondering if makeup could make his swollen head look normal again. I would never find out.

At the end of the service, the minister said there would be a reception at the Williams home, and that all were invited to attend. Steve's father saluted the casket, and everyone moved slowly to their cars, chatting in low murmurs as they went. Then, one by one, people left, each car following the last on the twisting drive to the Williams house.

Despite a week to prepare for the event, Steve's house looked exactly the same as when I'd been there on Tuesday. The flowers were in the same place, except there were even more of them, and people were still cooking in the kitchen.

We were there early, so we had time to get something to eat. My mother chatted with an aunt or a cousin or something while I nibbled from the deli tray. There wasn't any bread to make sandwiches, so I just ate the cold cuts with a fork.

Soon enough the house filled with people and the din of conversation was almost as unbearable as the smell of thousands of flowers just starting to rot. When my mother met Steve's mom they went on and on. Parents can always find some common ground, it seems.

Notably absent were Steve's friends—his usual crew—none of whom attended the funeral or the reception. I don't know if that's surprising or not.

We'd been there an hour, and I found myself sitting in the living room, having cleared a space on the couch for myself to sit among the flowers. I ended up reading a month-old copy of *People,* the only magazine I could find, anywhere.

I had finished reading a Grace Kelly retrospective when Steve's little sister came running through the room for the fifth time. No one had been watching her, and I had caught her sneaking Cokes, at least three in the last hour.

And this time, when she came running through, dodging the furniture, the people, and the flower arrangements, she tripped, and when she hit the ground, she slid a few feet along the carpet before coming to a stop against the leg of a table with a thud.

The cry she let out silenced all conversation, and within seconds her mother was in the room, picking her up and hoisting her over a shoulder, patting her back and saying, "There, there, it's okay," while the kid screamed quite to the contrary.

The girl's emotions finally caught up with her, and the angst that comes with the death of a family member came rushing out. "You . . . killed . . . my . . . brother!" she howled, crying between the words. Again and again she howled, "You . . . killed . . . my . . . brother!"

"Shhhhh, it's okay sweetie." Steve's mom could see that the visitors were getting uncomfortable.

The girl only screamed louder. Finally she wriggled her way out of her mom's embrace, fell to the ground, and started running again.

In a bit of a daze, she ran straight into my leg and fell down. I jumped and sort of kicked her by accident, and she grabbed my ankle and held on for her life. She looked me in the face, screaming at the top of her lungs, "*You killed my brother!*"

My eyes bugged out and I started to lift myself off the couch, but with the little girl holding my leg I couldn't really get up.

"You killed my brother!" She was shrieking, and I was about to lose it. Did she know something or was she just upset? My heart started to race, and my brow started to sweat. By this time virtually everyone in the house had congregated in the living room to gawk. Steve's mom was pulling on the girl, but she wouldn't let go of my leg, creating a writhing, human chain with three links.

I panicked. "Get her off me! Get her off!"

Steve's mom screamed as she pulled, "Somebody help me!"

"You killed my brother!" The accusation echoed through the house, a piercing wail of unimaginable shrillness. The girl wouldn't let go of my leg. Her cries pierced my brain. I thought I was going to pass out.

That was the moment when I first felt I was going crazy.

❖ ❖ ❖

April 22, 2000

All weekend I waited for the cops to catch up with me. Every hour was agony. I couldn't watch TV, couldn't read a newspaper without the specter of Steve rising from the grave. I paced in my room, back and forth, back and forth.

Night fell, and the sun rose. I didn't sleep, and the phone never rang. That late-night knock on the door never came. There was nothing, and the silence was unbearable.

I knew that, logically, I ultimately had nothing to fear. There were no witnesses to the murder, and there was no evidence tying me to the crime. One of the great things about lead is that it truly is everywhere. If I'd been found with, say, some lead fishing weights in my locker, what would they do about it? Nothing, unless they found one in Steve's stomach. No evidence, no conviction. Hell, no probable cause, even.

But evidence was a legal requirement. Homicide investigators work on instinct. I'd seen it in Lemons the other day. I knew he smelled a rat, and I played the best opponent I could. I just acted like myself. I showed him why Steve Williams picked on me and thirty kids just like me: because I was *nobody*. I was a person of no consequence. I was the guy whose name you forget right after you meet him, because there's no reason you'd ever want to recall who he was.

I was the kind of person who can just slip right through the cracks.

❖ ❖ ❖

April 23, 2000

Come Monday, Steve was buried and we were back in our seats for the final week of school, tying up loose ends and taking our final exams. I hadn't seen Travis since the day Steve died, when he drove me out to the incinerator. I guess he and James knew better than to check up on me.

The cops were all gone, the doors were unlocked, even the tape outline had vanished from the courtyard. But the American flag still flew at half mast. If it hadn't, I might have thought that Steve Williams had already been forgotten.

When I sat down at first period, I realized that was far from the truth. For starters, hastily written and typo-ridden fliers had been deposited on every desk in the room:

> ATTN FALL VALLEY HIGH STUDENTS
> In this time of grief and truama plese be aware that we have made counseling services available to you all free of charge. If you or someone you know is condemplating suicide or entertainng negative thoughts of any sort, help is available!!! You are not alone! Again, all services are free and anonimous and they are available 24 hours a day.
>
> Together we can all overcome and persivere in this time of crisis!!!

There was a phone number and a name indicating the creator of the memo, an FVH guidance counselor I'd never heard of.

I crumpled up the flier and shoved it in my backpack. I still have it now, which is why I know exactly where the typos and bad grammar are.

When the bell rang, Principal Patterson's voice crackled over the P.A. system. He might as well have been reading from the flier.

"Students of Fall Valley, thank you for bearing with us and pulling together during this time of grief and trauma. We will all miss Steve Williams, who passed away on Friday, May 12th, a day that will hereby be remembered as *Steve Williams Day* here at Fall Valley High School."

I couldn't believe my ears. Steve Williams Day? What an insult.

Principal Patterson went on. "You have all received information on our counseling hotline, which is available twenty-four hours a day, free of charge. Or feel free to come talk to one of our specially trained student counselors, who are always available to discuss any feelings you may have about this incident.

"As you know, this will be the final week of the 1989 school year, and I hope you will all be able to concentrate on your studies and preparations for final exams. If you are having trouble keeping your mind on your schoolwork, please see a counselor or come see me personally. My door is always open."

With a click, he was off the air. The classroom was immediately abuzz. Why? Because the principal had not specified Steve's cause of death, and with the exception of a very small number of people who had spoken with the investigators, nobody knew. I certainly wasn't going to say anything.

It took the teacher five minutes to quiet people down. She was so frustrated by the end of the process that she told us to read silently for the rest of the period. It was pretty much like that for the rest of the day. But I didn't read. I stared out the window at the flag, fluttering in the breeze, halfway down the pole.

❖   ❖   ❖

April 24, 2000

When I got to school on Wednesday, I was prepared for a day of laziness. No one really teaches the day before finals (which were to be administered on Thursday and Friday). You just chat with your teachers, listen to them talk about life or college or getting a job or something, and then people get all weepy because they suddenly think they had the greatest teachers of all time, and then you go home and get ready for finals.

But when I approached the school, on foot, I saw immediately that this was going to be anything but a boring day.

News crews surrounded the school in a mad crush. It was far, far worse than the initial media frenzy right after Steve's death. This time, big, national news trucks with giant transmitter towers piercing the sky made driving into the parking lot impossible. In fact, it looked like the parking lot was totally full, before any students had even arrived. The big trucks plus countless vehicles driven by newspaper and magazine reporters were parked haphazardly throughout the lot. I had no idea how any of them would ever get out. But since they all stayed for the rest of the week, each more desperate than the next to have the final word on "An American Tragedy," I guess it didn't really matter.

Since people couldn't get into the parking lot, the traffic on the street quickly became a snarl. The arriving students resorted to parking their cars directly on the right of way. After ten or twenty minutes of sitting in absolutely still traffic, they would just give up, lock the car, and walk to school. Not even the cops could get through to direct traffic; there was nowhere to go.

Not really knowing what to do, I pushed my way through the mess and went to first period, just like I always did. At least, I tried. The moment I set foot on campus, I found myself surrounded by reporters, all asking variations of the same questions:

"Did you know your school is poisoned with lead?"

"Did you know Steve Williams?"

"Did you know he died from lead poisoning?"

"Do you plan to sue the school?"

I kind of shrugged and shook my head as I worked my way through the mob toward the school. But when I got near enough to see, it was obvious I had pushed through in vain. The police had returned, the doors were shut, the yellow police line tape was back up, and school was obviously canceled. Reporters were standing in front of the building, taping broadcasts at 20-foot increments from one another. I listened to a few of their reports, which uniformly went like this:

"Students at Fall Valley High School, one of the largest high schools in the country, were shocked this morning with the revelation that the school contains ten times the legally allowable amount of lead in paint, dust, and plumbing. It's a problem that has left at least one student, star athlete Steve Williams, dead. And this morning, concerned parents are calling for the dismissal of Principal Edward Patterson and the permanent closure of Fall Valley

High. Environmental groups are again raising the cry of lead awareness, a silent killer much like asbestos, which is often forgotten until it is too late."

As it turned out, the EPA had released its findings the previous night, well after midnight. The press had gotten wind of it, the story spread like wildfire while most of us slept, creating an instant catastrophe. Later, I read the report in full. Yes, Fall Valley had an ambient lead level ten times higher than the legal limit, largely confined to dust and two lead pipes discovered in the boy's locker room. But, the report clearly stated, the school should simply be cleaned, the paint stripped, and the pipes replaced. Closure was not a recommendation. The report also cast doubt on the possibility that ambient lead had been responsible for the death of a student, and that unless Steve had a special susceptibility to heavy metal poisoning, he had likely consumed lead from another source in order for it to be fatal.

I give the EPA a lot of credit for a very well thought-out and accurate report that, nonetheless, went utterly ignored in the media frenzy that followed.

And what a frenzy it was.

Hours passed on Wednesday morning as the student body buzzed around the campus, and it soon became clear that we weren't going to be having classes. When the excitement wore off, the students went home, anxious to avoid yet another day of school. But the madhouse surrounding FVH got worse.

Fall Valley High became a twenty-four-hour Mecca not only for the news media, but also for thousands of angry parents. As the mob scene outside the school grew, local authorities had to call in the National Guard to keep a full-fledged riot from breaking out. Broadcasters set up huge spotlights around the school, basking the building in permanent day. Rumor had it that the top officials, including the school board and the principal, had sequestered themselves inside the building while they decided what to do about the situation. They didn't come out all night.

By Thursday morning, you couldn't get within a mile of the school building by car. You just had to park on the side of the road and walk the rest of the way. Some people rode bicycles or motorcycles.

The bigger the crowds got, the more media attention the school earned, building even bigger crowds and even more media attention. It was a vicious cycle that wasn't going to end until, as the parents commonly pleaded, "somebody got hanged for this."

At about noon Thursday, that somebody was Principal Patterson, the scapegoat chosen by the school board as the one who was ultimately responsible for the physical well-being of the students, including the completion of all necessary inspections and maintaining a healthy school environment. I watched it on TV: The principal, looking beaten-down and haggard after a sleepless night, his hair mussed and his tie askew, was escorted out by a cadre of six armed officers. They took him straight to an armored car, pushing through a seething mob (some people actually spat on the man) and quickly driving away as parents screamed after the vehicle.

The media trial of Fall Valley High had been far swifter than any court. The facts were clear: FVH was a deathtrap. The judgment was simple: Fire everyone involved. Murder is bad, but in the eyes of the public, negligence is unconscionable. These were, after all, *our children's lives.*

After four days, the principal was released. He'd really done nothing wrong, after all: The inspections were found to be completely in order. Still, his arrest had pleased the mob. His release did not, however, and he was fired for "mismanaging the Steve Williams situation." After having no luck finding another job, eventually he moved to Mexico. Or so I heard.

No one ever called or said anything about the status of classes, so I just stayed at home, in my room, with the door locked. I thought about calling Travis to get his read on the situation, but I never did. My head was pounding, and it got worse every hour that went by without a knock at the door by the cops, ready to tell me that the jig was up.

Finally, on Thursday night, we received telephoned instructions to come to school on Friday to pick up our final exams. We would have the weekend to complete them, then we'd have to drop them off on Monday for grading. Apologies were offered for the situation, but our understanding was appreciated, said the voice (a volunteer of some kind) on the other end of the line.

Friday saw the biggest crowd at Fall Valley High in its history. 5,000 students, 300 faculty and administrators, 6,000 parents, 600 news media, 350 police officers, and 10,000 random spectators jammed the streets, the parking lots, nearby houses, everywhere. Anywhere grass had been was trodden to mud. There were no bathrooms, so people just went wherever.

Overhead, helicopters hovered, airing footage of the scene on CNN for about an hour that morning. Even *60 Minutes* arrived to shoot a segment called "School: Hazardous to Your Health?" They interviewed me as I stood in line to pick up my exams. (Question: "Do you think you'll come back to Fall Valley next year?" Answer: "What choice do I have?") My footage wasn't used when the show aired in early 1990. At the time, I could only think that I would have made for a much better *60 Minutes* interview had the truth of the situation been known.

Everywhere you looked: people. In the face of death, there was nothing but sweaty anger all around me. And all I could see were faces looking for someone to blame. The lynching of Principal Patterson would never be enough. "It's 1989! How could this happen!?" was a common refrain. If only they knew how easy it had been!

If I wasn't losing my mind, I could have done the same thing again and again and again.

❖ ❖ ❖

April 26, 2000

I barely remember those final exams. I do remember picking up the yellow envelope with six thick tests in it along with the admonishment that these were "closed book" and that I was not to seek outside assistance. I took the tests in my room, but mostly I recall staring out my window at the old, dead tree on the edge of our backyard. Every year it rotted away just a little bit more. By the time I left for college it was hollow and blackened inside, infested with termites. Eventually someone cut it down as an eyesore and public safety hazard, but it always fascinated me.

My mom delivered my exams for me on Monday. Some of them hadn't even been opened. My grades arrived in the mail two weeks later. By my calculation, I should have failed half my classes and made C's and D's in the others. Through some miracle, I earned straight C's. Apparently I wasn't the only student who had completely blown off his finals, what with the "tragedy" and all. Leniency was the new rule at FVH. No one wanted yet another outrage over poor grades, considering the mental state of half the school's students.

Summer arrived. People slowly started to forget about Steve Williams, along with the other sensations of that spring: the *Exxon Valdez,* which had caused a genuine EPA catastrophe, and Oliver North, who had been a real scandal-maker. An earthquake would kill sixty-two people in San Francisco. Washington mayor Marion Barry would get busted smoking crack in a seedy D.C. motel. And we were going to invade Panama. There was plenty in the news for people to get upset about.

Incidentally, I quit going to Dr. Carter about a month ago. I'd seen him for fourteen months straight, and I felt that we'd explored everything we could. I was never going to tell him what was really bothering me, and I don't think it's right to pay that much money for something that you're just going to lie about.

I guess that means I should quit writing in this journal, since it was his assignment that made me start it in the first place, but I think Dr. Carter was right. It really is good therapy. It's certainly better (and cheaper) than sitting on his couch for an hour every week.

And besides, there's still a bit more to the story.

❖   ❖   ❖

April 27, 2000

There was a long and awkward silence between us the next time I saw Travis. The summer was hot, like the gods were trying to boil away the damage that had been done. But the heat only made it fester. At least for me, there was no way to forget what had happened.

But the public did. As quickly as they arrived, the news crews departed, and the tragic story of a dead hero ceased to be news.

The summer was here, and Travis and I sat downstairs in his living room, getting the hammering of a lifetime before the rest of the gang—even including the now-ungrounded Tommy—showed up.

We were onto our fourth shot of tequila apiece when Travis asked, "You think you got away with it?"

"I guess so," I shrugged. The cops had never returned. And though Principal Patterson had been released, the case was closed. The authorities found the school district guilty of criminal negligence. The Williams family and about three dozen other gold-digging families were suing, claiming their children were sick due to the lead. They were going over the entire school with a thorough cleaning—stripping paint, removing flooring, and replacing all the plumbing. The retrofit took the entire summer and cost over $7 million, according to news reports.

I continued, "They talked to me for about five minutes then sent me packing. I never heard from the police again."

"Pretty stupid, I guess," said Travis.

"I dunno, I think they were on to something. They had some good questions, but nothing I wasn't expecting." I downed my shot. "Lazy is more like it."

Travis downed his shot, too. "I'm leaving for the summer," he said.

"What?"

"My parents are taking me to Colorado. We're going to be there until the end of August."

"Really? Why?"

"Camping and shit. They want to take a long vacation and they want me to experience the great outdoors. I don't think all the craziness around here helped any."

"No thanks to me, right?"

Travis laughed. "Yeah, no thanks to you."

James and Tommy showed up soon after that. We had a good time, a really good time, that night. It was just like the old days, with music and Truth or Truth, and nobody talked or asked about Steve Williams. And I thought back to the really old days, before I'd ever even met Steve Williams, when Travis and I would play video games all summer, forgetting there was a real world out there.

A week later, Travis left for Colorado. He knew better than to let his parents ask any of us to house-sit. They hired a professional to watch it.

I had to drink by myself, up in my room on the sly, hoping that my parents wouldn't come knocking on the door, leaving me scrambling to hide the booze.

But I had bigger problems to worry about than getting busted with a bottle of vodka. Nightly, the demons came: memories of Steve as a ghoulish monster, his head swollen and his skin a ghostly white. He sat at the foot of the bed while I slept, staring at me, asking how I could kill him in cold blood, pleading for his life. He had done bad things, he would admit, but he didn't deserve to die. Look at what I'd done to his family. Look at what I'd done to the community. My actions had caused effects far beyond his death. How could I live with myself?

Steve still talks to me when it's especially dark and quiet in my apartment. He still stares at me from the foot of the bed, and he still looks like he did in high school.

The dead, it seems, do not age.

April 29, 2000

I whiled away the summer in a menial, brainless job at Blockbuster Video. Rent out tapes to people, put tapes back on the shelves, explain that somebody owed $25 in late fees for *The Road to Zanzibar,* then have them go ballistic and insist on speaking to the manager, who would tell them exactly the same thing.

At least you got to see a lot of five minutes' worth of movies as they played on the TVs mounted throughout the store. That was as long as you could zone out on the job before somebody would start to miss you. Sit around for too long and you'd get a lecture, and there's nothing I hate more than a goddamn lecture.

The only other thing of interest that summer occurred when the school yearbook arrived in the mail in late July. I had forgotten about it altogether, but my mother always made me order it at the beginning of the school year, "because you will always want to cherish those memories forever." What I wanted to do more than anything was *forget.*

The freshly printed pages stuck together, and the book crackled as I opened it for the first time. There, on page one, was a full-page color photo of the face I would never scrub from my mind: Steve Williams, staring out at me with a wry smile and a rakish look in his eye.

The legend read simply, "In Memory of Steve Williams, 1971–1989."

The picture dated back to his junior year, when he was at the height of his athletic career and before the poison had consumed him. It was the rough-and-tumble Steve that everyone wanted to remember, not the sickly, dying Steve that everyone prayed to forget.

I was shocked to find pages two through seven devoted to Steve as well. His legacy was obviously sports. Pictures of him running on the football field, pictures of him pitching a baseball. Plus plenty of pictures of him posing for the camera, sitting in the stands, talking to girls, dancing at the prom, whatever. The book also printed his entire history of sports statistics: touchdowns, home runs, strike-outs—everything you could want to know about his life with a ball. I did note that all of his 1988–89 stats were marked with an asterisk, accompanied by a note at the bottom: "Partial season."

Throughout the photo memorial, no mention of the cause of Steve's death was given. Again, people probably wanted to remember Steve's greatness, not his ugly and pathetic death slumped against the side of a telephone booth.

I flipped through the pages, looking for myself. The funny thing is that I was nowhere to be found in the yearbook, nowhere at all. I had sat for the photo shoot; I remembered the plaid shirt my mother made me wear. But my name wasn't listed, and my picture didn't appear. Not even a "Photo Not Available" placeholder. I checked the other grades—senior, sophomore, and freshman—and I wasn't misplaced. So I just kept flipping and flipping through the book. I was nowhere, not even in the index.

In page after page, I was able to find out where people went for spring break (South Padre Island, Daytona Beach, Cancun), who our favorite TV stars were (Bruce Willis and Cybill Shepherd), our favorite musical group (Erasure—groan), our favorite TV show ("The Wonder Years"), and even our favorite restaurant (Burger King).

Finally I reached the last page. It was official: I didn't exist.

I put the yearbook back in the envelope in which it had arrived and buried it deep in the trash outside, just like I did with everything else that reminded me of Steve.

❖ ❖ ❖

May 2, 2000

I returned to Fall Valley High in September 1989 for my senior year. The school had been under heavy renovation all summer, and in a mere three months it had leaped ahead in time, décor-wise, some twenty years.

The lime green exterior had been repainted a sedate brown. New roofing had been laid. The parking lot had received a fresh coat of asphalt. The grounds, trampled into a barren wasteland during the media sensation, had been replanted and manicured to perfection for opening day. The centerpiece: a memorial garden, commemorating the life of Steve Williams. Naturally, the American flag flew at half mast that first day.

Inside, the changes were even more dramatic. The flooring, once a dull, gray linoleum, had been replaced with shiny faux marble. The walls had been stripped and repainted in various colors to clue you to which wing of the school you were in. We had also been told, in letters mailed to everyone in the community, that the entire plumbing system had been replaced with new, plastic and stainless steel pipes (even the toilets and urinals were new), and that the EPA had done three separate tests to ensure the entire school was lead-free.

The courtyard had also been refinished. They had poured new concrete, eliminating the ancient, weedy cracks. The grass and shrubs of the courtyard had been replaced and bloomed with a vibrant green color that didn't seem quite real. The gym had seen even bigger changes. In the locker room, all of the lockers had been removed and replaced by new ones. The concrete flooring was resealed throughout. The gym itself had had its wooden flooring totally torn out and replaced, refinished, and resealed. A brand-new Fall Valley High logo had been carefully painted in the center of the basketball court.

In first period, familiar faces found themselves in familiar seats: geeks up front, popular crew to one side, people like me skulking in the back. The ranks had thinned, as overly concerned parents had chosen to ignore the safety assurances and place their children in nearby or not-so-nearby public or private schools. The school district had been very accommodating to those who chose either option. My parents asked me if I wanted to move schools, but I had declined.

Soon, a new voice came over the loudspeaker: Principal Sharon Desantis, a former vice principal at FVH who had taken charge during the summer renovations following the ouster of Principal Patterson and proven herself worthy of promotion at summer's end.

Her voice was far too cheery for that early in the morning. "Welcome back, students of Fall Valley High! Many of you already know, but I'm your new principal, Ms. Desantis, and I'm looking forward to working with all of you on a new school year at the new Fall Valley!"

She paused. I figured she was waiting for the applause—of which, there was none—to die down. She went on, "We all have an exciting adventure ahead of us. As our upperclassmen have surely noticed, the school has been extensively remodeled, inside and out. We have a new freshman class, and we have a brand new challenge for all of the students. We have doubled our staff of counselors, so if anyone is feeling lonely, stressed out, or if you just need someone to talk to, please drop by the counseling office. It is open all day, and you don't need an appointment.

"So, Raiders of the class of 1990 and the rest of the student body, welcome to the best year of your life!"

The speakers squawked and cut off abruptly. That would be enough inspiration for one day.

May 4, 2000

I soon found that I had gotten exactly what I wished for in the death of Steve Williams.

There were no more beatings, no more bullying by anyone, period. Tensions ran so high at FVH that under Desantis's rule any hint of aggression was dealt with by the immediate suspension or expulsion of the offender. Anyone caught moping or spending too much time alone was immediately ordered to the counselors' office to head off suicidal tendencies. Vandalism, cheating, or anything even remotely close to inappropriate behavior was dealt with immediately. The Gestapo had descended on Fall Valley.

It felt a little strange not getting lunch for Steve. Most of his friends had graduated and left for college. Only Vogon, Dewie, and one other guy whose name I can't remember still attended FVH. They kept to themselves, and they never spoke to me. Out of fear, stupidity, or ambivalence I didn't know. And I didn't care.

I ate alone, mostly. Once in a while, I'd see somebody from the days of the party house, and they'd sit with me, but usually only long enough to ask when we were going to find another party house.

I stumbled through class without studying at all. In the afternoon, I watched TV. I rarely stayed up more than an hour after dinner. I coasted through, mostly drunk out of my mind. Alcohol makes an excellent sleep aid.

The tyranny had ended, and my life became much simpler. However, I found it had also lost the edge that had once defined it. For the last three years, I had lived in fear for my life on a daily basis. I had eliminated that fear, suddenly and completely.

If you beat a dog every day of its life, then suddenly stop the beatings, what happens to the dog?

❖ ❖ ❖

May 5, 2000

I took the SAT drunk. I wasn't hung over; I was drunk. I got up early, took a fifth of bourbon with me in my new car (a very used Nissan sedan my dad bought me for $2,000), and I got quietly hammered in the parking lot before the test. I scored an 1180, high enough to get me into Ohio State, the only college I applied to, but not high enough for a scholarship.

With Travis back from vacation, I tried to get back into the swing of our drunken weekends, but it wasn't the same. I think the summer had given him time to reflect on the last few months. Something had changed between the two of us, and I'd be foolish not to recognize the discomfort that having a cold-blooded murderer sitting in your living room can cause. The fact that he and James were accomplices only made it worse. We didn't "bond" over the death of Steve Williams. Quite the contrary: We didn't talk about it, and the silence was almost unbearable. But none of us could find the will to break it.

So we went through the motions of friendship awkwardly, listening to the same old records and telling the same old stories, drinking as much as possible to make the conversation seem less stilted. By Christmas, we were usually getting together one night a week, and not for very long. By spring break, it was only once a month.

Travis and James both got themselves girlfriends. Trav met a busty, blonde junior named Jennifer who, inexplicably, had a crush on him. James finally got his ROTC chick. I actually went out on a couple of first dates, but my heart wasn't in it, and I never called either of the girls back. I doubt they minded.

Against all expectations, I actually went to the senior prom. My date's name was Lori Langford, and all I remember about her is that she had short, black hair, and she didn't say anything the whole night. She was a fairly intelligent but deathly shy girl from my Chemistry 11 class. Apparently, her mother called my mother and suggested the arrangement. My parents were so thrilled that they sprung for a nice dinner at a fancy Italian place and even paid for a limousine. That was nice, because you can drink all you want in the back. Lori was a prude, though, and she didn't have one sip, which made things pretty boring.

Before I knew it, the school year was over and I was about to graduate, never to return to Fall Valley High. But Steve Williams wasn't completely dead. He made a visit to campus, in spirit anyway, on Friday, May 11, as FVH celebrated Steve Williams Day one day early due to the weekend. Again, the flag was lowered halfway and the principal made a big speech about how she remembered his heroism and some shit, and how we'd never forget him. God, was she right about that.

Then school was out. Seniors didn't have to take final exams if they were comfortable with their grades, and I was fine with the straight C's I had earned without cracking a book. I was right in the middle of the graduating class, 399 out of 851. My parents were thrilled nonetheless when I walked across the stage in that black graduation gown and ridiculous hat (with, as I've mentioned, a Wild Turkey label affixed to it) and collected my diploma from a teary-eyed Principal Desantis.

It was her first graduation ceremony. It was my last.

❖ ❖ ❖

May 6, 2000

The last time I saw Travis was late in the summer of 1990. We'd avoided one another fairly successfully for months, but Trav was getting ready to head to college at Southwest Texas State, and both of us felt it was time for one last reunion.

For some reason we decided to meet at a Bennigan's, the crappy chain restaurant that serves all-fried food and watered-down drinks. Over Monte Cristo sandwiches, Trav and I said our awkward goodbyes.

"It's going to be weird, being in San Marcos, being away from Fall Valley," he said.

"Yeah. Ohio is nothing like here. It actually snows there!"

"San Marcos is nothing like here, either. It's just closer."

"But you've been to San Marcos. I've never left Texas, not in the winter, anyway."

"Huh. You better take a coat."

"Yeah."

We mostly ate in silence, with a little chitchat here and there. And we splurged on dessert, hot fudge sundaes or something with a brownie in it, I can't remember.

Finally Travis said, "You going to be okay?"

Like anyone, my knee-jerk answer is always to say, "Sure, I'll be fine. Don't worry about me!" But something about the moment made me reflect for a moment before answering. I hadn't been "okay" for months. No, years. I hadn't been okay since the eighth grade.

"I don't know, Trav," I said. "I really don't know. I *want* to be okay. I really do."

"You regret what happened?"

"I guess so. But there's no sense in wishing I could undo it. Not anymore. I had that chance, and I went ahead with it. Regret only makes it worse. Fuck it. He was a bastard. He deserved it."

"Yeah. So you just gotta live with it now, right? For better or worse?"

"For worse," I said.

"For worse, right. Well, you're a tough guy, you know, psychologically. If you weren't, you never would have been able to do it in the first place. You'll come through just fine, I know it."

"Well, thanks. Of course, the same goes for you, Trav."

"For me? I didn't do anything. I just held a flashlight and drove a car."

"I guess so. But you know what happened. Doesn't it bother you?"

"No," he said, looking me dead in the eye. "I don't know *anything.*" The glare that followed made it clear that this would be our last encounter. Seeing me only reminded him of the past. Travis's plan was to forget everything that had happened, to erase it completely from his mind. He was peripheral enough to the murder to be able to do that.

But I had no such luxury. Steve Williams practically died in my arms.

Two days later, Travis left for Southwest. The day after that, I headed out to Ohio State. I drove by myself, despite protests from my parents that I needed a chaperone.

The occasional Christmas and Thanksgiving notwithstanding, I didn't return to Fall Valley for ten years.

❖   ❖   ❖

May 7, 2000

Ohio State was everything I had dreamed it would be. Loud, enormous, and completely oblivious to whether you were successful or not. Classes populated by hundreds of people. No roll call. Awful professors who spoke barely a word of English. Two exams to determine your grade. Total anonymity.

I put no more effort into my college career than I had in high school. I ended up with a 2.95 GPA and a degree in computer science, skipped most of the latter half of my coursework along with graduation, all of which qualified me to become a COBOL programmer for a Chicago company with a desperate need for mid-1990s computer talent and very low hiring standards.

I still work for this company, and my job is basically the same, only I get paid a little more. I still live in the one-bedroom apartment near Wrigley Field that I found when I moved here six years ago, and a few of my moving boxes are still unopened.

I started seeing Dr. Carter in January of 1999. I called in sick and just stayed home and watched TV all day, I don't really know why. Oprah was on and she had a bunch of therapists as guests. I watched the whole thing. I've never really watched an entire episode of that show in my life, except for the therapist one. What they said made a lot of sense, and I figured I ought to look into the miracle of therapy myself. Enter Dr. Carter.

Dr. Carter, of course, didn't have the flash and glam of an Oprah-class TV therapist. He was calm and sedate and probably got a 2.95 GPA at therapist school. For what I was paying, it seemed like a pretty good deal, and at first our chats in his cramped downtown office seemed beneficial, but soon it became obvious: He didn't know how to help me any more than I knew how to help myself.

Since I quit going to therapy, though, I can't say things have been going that well. I'm not sleeping again, and I'm drinking more than I used to, usually five or six vodkas a night, more on the weekends. I feel hung over all the time, and I smell a little funny, no matter how much I shower. They say the booze does that to you. I don't care that no one at work wants to talk to me, but I do wish I had some friends like Travis and James who I could at least drink with. It's just not as much fun drinking alone at home as it was back in high school.

Yesterday a card arrived in the mail: It was postmarked from Fall Valley, Texas, and it wasn't from my parents. I opened the envelope to find an invitation heralding the Ten Year Reunion of the Fall Valley High School Class of 1990. The reunion takes place in four months, and if you register by mail you can get a $10 discount on your tickets, and you can sign up for the FVH Golf Day for $45 per person, which promises "good times on the fairway with your old friends!"

I do not golf.

May 11, 2000

Still, I found myself buying a plane ticket to Texas on the Internet. I arrived last night.

I don't really know why I came to the reunion. Something compelled me to come back. Maybe I was grasping for the chance to close the book on Steve Williams forever. The chance to scrub him from my mind and get on with life. The chance to see that the world is indeed a better place now that he's no longer in it. The chance to find that some good has come from something heartless and evil.

I'm writing this from my old room in my parents' house, where they still live, and where nothing much has changed in a decade. The big reunion party was earlier this evening, and my mind is heavy with the sudden rush of information from an evening filled with old faces and new facts.

The flight from O'Hare was uneventful, and I rented a car and went straight to the event. Held in the ballroom of a third-rate hotel forty-five miles from Fall Valley, the reunion was more like a political fundraiser than a nostalgic homecoming.

After a speedy registration and mandatory photograph, a nametag with my senior-year picture (I *did* appear in the yearbook that year) was pinned to my chest. Inside the ballroom I found a nightmarish vision of balloons and crepe paper, a prom-like revival reminiscent of a Halloween party.

Looking around, I saw no familiar faces. So of course I headed for the refreshments table, disappointed to find that the only snacks to be found were cubed cheese and fresh melon, and the only beverage a murky red punch that after one whiff I knew was alcohol-free. What were these people thinking? No booze at a class reunion? Not very sporting, and definitely not worth $85 (after the $10 discount) plus airfare.

There weren't a lot of people there, even though I was an hour late. Maybe fifty people out of our class of 851. Pretty pathetic, I guess.

Everyone just looked lumpy and ugly, like they had let themselves go all to hell. It was not like high school at all. In fact, it was pretty sickening. And these people, like me, were only in their late twenties. Can you imagine what it will be like in ten more years?

I sat at one of the tables with the silly party favors and drank the murky punch, futilely wishing to get drunk despite the chemical impossibility of it. Surely, I thought, the hotel would have a bar, and I could just go there. But I didn't have money for hotel drinking, so I just slouched in the metal chair and sulked.

That is, until someone else approached the table and sat down. He was trying to catch my eye, obviously trying to figure out who I was. I looked up and did the same. The face was familiar, but years of sun damage, wrinkles, and a pair of eyeglasses made identification difficult. The nametags were printed in such small type and it was so dark inside the ballroom (the mirrored disco globe above notwithstanding), they were practically useless.

After a few moments he said, "Isn't your name Alex?"

The voice was on the tip of my tongue, but still I couldn't place him. "Yeah," I said.

"I'm Brett Vogon. Remember me?"

Vogon, of course! Finally I made out the fresh-cheeked jock, buried under the worn hide of a discontented yuppie. But why he wanted to talk to me was a mystery. Did he want to revive the years of torment after all this time? He had never struck me as *that* much of a sadist.

I said, "Yeah, Vogon. Sure." Not one for chitchat, I went with the usual, "Well, how have you been?"

"I'm okay. I'm pretty good. It's not like it was in high school, you know?"

"Sure. Yeah. So what are you up to these days?"

"I'm regional sales manager for Southwest Insurance Partners. How about you?"

"Computer programmer. I live in Chicago."

"Chicago, huh? I got up there a few years ago for a sales conference. Pretty cool place."

"Yeah, it's all right."

"Well, cool."

There was a minute of silence while we sipped our drinks. Finally, Vogon said something more. "You know anyone else here?"

"No. You?" I replied.

"Not a soul. I guess I should have tried to meet more people in high school."

"Yeah, I guess so."

"Have you kept up with anyone from Fall Valley?"

"Nope. Nobody."

"I see Dewie Stevenson now and again. He works in the city."

"Didn't go far from home, huh?"

"Nah, not many of us did. Except you!" Vogon thought this was particularly hilarious and he laughed out loud for a good ten seconds.

"What's the Valley like these days?" I asked, finally forcing myself to get to the real reason I was here at all.

"I don't know. The same. Nothing much has changed."

"Really? No one has gone on to do great things? Nothing extraordinary?"

"I heard Dave McCarthy almost got drafted as a tight end for the Cowboys. That's what he says, anyway."

I'd never even heard of Dave McCarthy and wasn't even sure he had attended FVH. I said, "Well, I'm not sure that really counts."

"Yeah, the guy's a pussy."

"No one's ever lived up to the legacy of Steve Williams, huh?"

"Steve. Yeah, the football guy that died. That was too bad."

The football guy that died. That was the most anyone had to say about Steve Williams that night. Few people at the reunion could remember Steve at all. Those who could remembered little more than the fact that he died. The media frenzy had made a much bigger impression on people, and a lot of people said they had the *60 Minutes* episode on tape.

Vogon and I talked for a few minutes more. He could barely remember any real details about Steve Williams, and Vogon was probably his closest friend in the world. He seemed to have utterly forgotten the years of ritualistic abuse he had put me through. I guess he had simply dismissed them as the antics of an overly enthusiastic youth, the kind of thing every teen goes through, at least in his mind. Unlike me, he had locked his childhood memories away for good, and he obviously had no problem living his boring suburban life.

Was I the only one carrying around Steve's memory? Everyone else seemed to have moved on with their lives, even if absolutely nothing was happening *in* them.

I changed the subject and Vogon clued me in to what had happened to several key players in this indulgent monologue. I also did a little more nosing around among some old faculty who attended the reunion and some random people who remembered me from the party house or from classes. Here's an update on the people whose lives have intersected mine, based completely on hearsay but condensed so you won't get too bored to read to the end:

Dewie Stevenson is a junior product manager with Philip Morris. He didn't make it on the football team at Texas A&M because he was too fat and too slow. Now he sells cigarettes wholesale to Stop N Go franchises.

My good friend Travis Pickford quit college at Southwest after one year, and spent the next nine years tending bar. He married that girl Jennifer in Las Vegas, and they have a five-year-old son.

James Johnston, our tall freak of a friend, dropped out of society after high school. Word has it he moved to the eastern seaboard somewhere and works in a vegetable cannery.

Tommy Steuart still lives at home and is still trying to "make it" as a rock musician. He could not afford to attend the reunion.

Marisa, the girl I comforted during her abortion, left Texas and moved to Florida, or so the rumor goes. No one is sure what she does now, but most stories have her working in an event-planning capacity on a Carnival cruise ship.

Principal Patterson, who had been fired and nearly lynched for endangering the lives of schoolchildren, did not move to Mexico. He got a job with the State of Texas Department of Education.

My parents are still married. We talk twice a year.

One of the teachers at the reunion knew a bit about the Williams family because Steve's little sister had gone to FVH and graduated a few years back. This was apparently something of a surprise, as she immediately moved to L.A. after graduation and embarked on a failed career in the adult film industry. Allegedly there are videos on the market today in which she stars, though I do not know her stage name.

Steve's parents divorced in 1995. His mother married a man ten years her junior, and they moved to a ranch in west Texas, leaving her ex with the kid. Steve's father raised his budding porn star all by his lonesome. Apparently he didn't do such a great job. When the Oilers moved to Tennessee in 1997, Major Williams stayed behind. No one really knows what he does now. Probably nothing.

That guy Tino moved to New York and became an unknown off-off-Broadway actor in such stage productions as *Grease* and *Sweet Charity*.

Gene Thomson, the kid who worked on the sign out in front of the school, was shot in the stomach in 1996 under suspicious circumstances in the course of a convenience store robbery. Newspaper reports later hinted that Gene owed a host of nefarious characters tens of thousands of dollars and the robbery was simply a front for his murder. The author of one of those pieces was a guy named Dan Fosbert, an FVH alumnus who was one year behind me.

He won some kind of award for the story.

What shocked me was not the endless variety in people's life stories. What shocked me was that no one seemed to have done anything in ten whole years. Like Vogon said, nothing much had changed. Hell, I had an excuse: *I killed a person.* What did all these other bright youths have to say for themselves? They were all just ordinary oxygen thieves on a dying planet, useless consumers padding the GNP.

Maybe, I thought, I killed the wrong guy. Everyone whose life I spared has turned out to be completely useless. Just like me.

❖   ❖   ❖

May 12, 2000

I was dead tired by the time I went home to my parents' house. I even felt drunk, despite the virgin punch.

When I got home, it was well past 2 a.m. and my parents were asleep. I didn't bother to wake them. Barely able to stand, I collapsed on my bed and immediately fell asleep.

I woke up around four in a sickly sweat—the kind that usually breaks out only when you're really, really sick. The knot in my stomach felt like acid was eating a hole straight through. Maybe I am really, really sick. I don't know.

Now I look at the date on my travel clock and all I can think is that it's Steve Williams Day once again. Every year it comes around and every year I feel like I'm being emotionally reset to zero. Coming back to Fall Valley has only made it worse. Far worse than I had ever imagined.

After crudely transcribing the details from last night, I decided to go through some of the things in my old room and sort the keepsakes from the trash, a task my mother bugs me about every time I come home for a holiday, but which I never do.

I had gone through stack after stack of school notes, comic books, and cassette tapes when I found them. Deep in the recesses of my closet was something I thought I'd never see again: a trio of lead miniatures, obviously spilled from the bag James had given me. I guess I wasn't as careful as I'd thought. Any cop doing a half-assed job would have found them during a search of my room.

The miniatures feel heavy in my hand. Looking at them, most people would see children's toys, but I see nothing but death. I see

216

it all the time, everywhere I look, and all too often I wish for it myself, especially on nights like this.

If I'm right, my dad has a metal file or two down in the garage. And I'm pretty sure I can get a good twenty or thirty grams of powder out of these little guys.

ABOUT THE AUTHOR

Christopher Null has been an entertainment and technology writer and editor for more than ten years. He founded the popular entertainment web site filmcritic.com in 1995 and has written for *Wired*, *Men's Journal*, *Yahoo! Internet Life*, and dozens of other publications.

He resides in San Francisco with his wife Ashley; together they expect their first child this fall.